Deadly Marriage

Book One of Series

"Nazis in the Americas"

By

W.R. Ziegler

W.R. Ziegler

Copyright 2012 by William Roy Ziegler Pending

All rights reserved. Except as permitted under the U.S. Copyright Act of 1976, no part of this publication may be reproduced, distributed or transmitted in any form or by any means, or stored in a database or retrieval system, without the prior written permission of the author.

Printed in the United States of America

ISBN 978-1475274547

First printed in 2012

Deadly Marriage

I would like to thank all those who helped with their patience, knowledge and encouragement. You know who you are!

I would also like to take this opportunity to thank all the members of the armed services, past and present, and the workers involved with the industrial complex that keeps the military functioning.

"Those who cannot remember the past are condemned to repeat it."
George Santayana, Philosopher 1863-1922

Prologue

The darkness was his world. No sound, no feeling and no sensations of any kind. The first time the light came, it came with mind crippling pain, short bursts of color and fear.

The thoughts were more like nightmares. He saw pictures of distorted faces, images of places that kept shifting, and feelings of his falling into a black endless abyss. He was experiencing random thoughts and feelings of fright, hatred and sorrow which intruded on his semi-conscious mind state.

Over an undetermined period of time the light came and went with the same sensations coming back time after time. Orange circles of bright light, which grew and subsided, but on this one occasion it was different. He could see shadows moving about over him, the pain was tolerable and he was able to put a few thoughts together.

The shadow bent over him and he tried to focus on the vague image. He tried with all his will to come back to life. He thought of giving up, but his mind (or was it his soul), wouldn't allow it. He could feel the shadow touching him, but he wasn't afraid, he knew these sensations, they were soothing and comforting. His mind finally let him rejoin the living.

The shadow was now a nurse and she was giving Jackson a sponge bath. She stopped the bath and came closer to his face, looking intently into his eyes.

"Hi Marine, welcome back to the land of the living." She was smiling as she ran to tell the doctor.

While he was alone he tried to feel his body, to determine what his condition was. He couldn't make his muscles function. He tried to move his hands, but could barely get his fingers to move. Then he tried to turn his head and almost blacked out from the intense pain.

The doctor came in, shown a light in Jackson's eyes, listened to his heart and took his pulse. Then a big smile formed on his face, which until just this instant had shown great concern.

"We were afraid you might never come back Sgt."

"You sustained a severe concussion and quite a few wounds, but the wounds are minor and are healing nicely. The concussion is still a problem. I don't want you to rush things; don't try to move but can you speak?"

Jackson hadn't thought to try. His mind still wasn't functioning normally. After a few moments of trying to move his tongue and jaw, he finally gave it a try.

"Hi Doc," said Jackson somewhat surprised. A smile now found his face.

"Those are the nicest words we've heard today, right Lieutenant Harsten?"

The beaming lieutenant agreed and introduced Jackson to Commander Lewis his physician.

"Don't try to force your mind to grasp all that's happened, try to relax. It will come back on its own, naturally, in its own time. I'll come back later to see how you're doing," said Lewis.

After he left, the lieutenant returned to completing Jackson's sponge bath. As she was finishing his legs she noticed a slight rise become evident in Jackson's hospital gown.

She laughed and said, "I think you're going to be just fine sergeant. Thanks for the salute."

Jackson just grinned, he had no control of the rise, but was happy in the thought that something still worked.

Chapter 1

In the first few months of 1939, Jackson's battalion had been sent to Nicaragua in support of the Somoza government. The Somoza dictatorship would survive, with US support and different family members in power, until 1979.

The first day after arrival in the country Jackson received an order to gather his noncoms and take them to battalion headquarters for a briefing at 0900. When he arrived at the large Quonset hut that served as company headquarters there were more officers than he expected or wanted. Four new shave tails (lieutenants) were seated behind Colonel Roberts, the battalion commander, and his normal assortment of field grade officers sitting on each side. This was trouble for Jackson and his noncoms.

"Hello Marines, I'm Colonel Roberts, your battalion commander," Roberts began.

He introduced his officers, including the new lieutenants and Jackson as senior noncom. Then he gave an outline of their task and the present situation in the volatile country of Nicaragua.

"Here are the basics. There are rebel forces forming in the mountainous region on the eastern edge of the country, near the border with El Salvador. We are tasked with helping government forces root out these rebels and eliminate them as a threat. We have been assigned a territory and you will be briefed by your company commanders and given maps as soon as they are available."

"We have a three hundred mile trip inland, mostly through jungle. You will be happy to hear we can make most of the trip by train and government trucks."

A cheer rang out from the experienced members of the company, including Jackson.

"Enjoy this evening we leave 0600 tomorrow morning."

Major Hardesty rose and dismissed the troops, except Jackson.

"Yes sir Major Hardesty," said Jackson.

Deadly Marriage

"The colonel wants to see you and your three most experienced noncoms back here at 1200." Jackson thought, "Oh shit, here it comes."

"Yes sir" was all he said.

Jackson walked back to where his men were camped. He walked from tent to tent until he found the three sergeants he wanted. He brought them to the shade of a tall palm tree. They all looked at Jackson expectantly.

"What's up Sarg?" asked Sergeant Goodner. Robert G., Sgt. Goodner, was a bit of a smartass, but a good marine.

"We have been ordered back to headquarters at 1200 to meet with Roberts. And we all know what that means."

"Yeah, we get our baby sitting orders," groused Goodner. The others grinned, but shook their heads.

"You all saw the green lieutenants at the briefing, so you're probably right Goodner, but no smartass remarks when we get there and all of you remember, they may be dumber than rocks, but they're still officers and gentlemen."

The noncoms gathered outside the headquarters building until precisely 1158, then entered the building.

Roberts and Hardesty were sitting on one side of a folding table and there were four chairs on the other.

The noncoms approached, stood at attention and saluted.

"Sgt. Jackson reporting as ordered, Sir."

Roberts and Hardesty returned the salute and Roberts waved them to the chairs.

"This is where I give you your tightrope walking orders. We have four new officers that need housebreaking, but we have to break them gently. You've all had the joy of this kind of assignment before, but let me remind you of a few things."

"Order one; try to keep them and your men alive."

"Order two; try to teach them how to be a marine officer."

"Order three; as much as you want to, don't shoot them."

"If you have issues bring it to the attention of Sgt. Jackson."

"Sgt. Jackson, if you cannot handle the issue, see me or Major Hardesty."

"Are we clear men?"

"Yes Sir," said the noncoms in unison.

"As you leave, Sgt. Jackson, ask the new lieutenants to come in."

"Yes Sir, Colonel." Jackson had been dismissed.

Jackson's squad leader was 2nd Lieutenant Stiles, Gary W. a fresh graduate of the Naval Academy and, as it turned out a good guy, thought Jackson.

The lieutenant had taken the Colonel's words to heart. He had been told, "Your noncom will keep you alive and from making any grievous errors if you let him."

On the 163rd day of his battalion's deployment, Jackson's squad was on patrol in the rain forest to the east side of the central highlands near Ocotal, close to the El Salvadorian border. They were in pursuit of a band of rebels, which had attacked a government outpost the previous day near the town of Somoto.

His patrol had just finished climbing down a steep canyon wall and had reached the stream, which had carved the canyon over thousands of years. The jungle they had been moving through blocked out the sky with creeping vines, giant plants and huge trees with canopies forming a ceiling as thick as any building.

The opening to the sky above the stream was letting in beautiful rays of sunlight and caused steam to float up from the jungle floor. Stiles stopped his squad short of the stream.

He held up his right hand palm forward as a signal for all to stop. Using hand signals Jackson called his point man, Jerry Kim and Lieutenant Stiles, over so they could whisper.

Kim was an American of Korean descent who had proven to be the best jungle fighter, tracker and point man in the squad. The squad counted on his ability to reconnoiter an area without being seen or heard. His was a very valuable skill when chasing bad guys through the jungle.

Lieutenant Stiles whispered "Jerry, what do you think, about 20 yards across the stream?"

"It looks about that, Lieutenant."

Deadly Marriage

"I hate to send him out in the open like this, but I don't see another option. Do you see another option Sgt.?"

"No, I agree Sir. Good call."

"Okay, I don't like it, but it's our job. Jerry, when you make it across look around and wave us in if it's clear."

"No problem Sir, we're all just doing our jobs. See you in a little while," said Kim as he slowly crept down the stream bank. The stream was littered with large boulders. Kim made his way slowly from the shade of one boulder to the next, stopping each time to visually search the area for any sign of movement or anything that didn't look natural. He wouldn't move until he was satisfied nothing was out of place and that the jungle sounds seemed normal. It took Kim over a half hour to cover the 20 yards to the opposite bank. He then silently scooted up the bank and disappeared into the jungle.

While Kim was making his way across the stream, Jackson had set a perimeter and had let the men rest quietly. Some ate C-rations, some slept and some just tried to release the tension that had built up trudging through the jungle in pursuit of a force that wanted nothing better than to kill them.

Kim finally waved Jackson and his men forward. Jackson signaled for them to form up on him. He would lead them across with the lieutenant right behind him.

Jackson made his way down the bank followed by his men. He had reached the midpoint in the stream when he heard the swoosh of an incoming mortar round.

"Incoming!" he yelled, but he was too late. The mortar round hit the water about eight feet in front of him. If it had hit a rock directly Jackson, Stiles and probably two or three others would have been killed. As it was, the force of the blast picked him up and threw him backward. He bounced off Lieutenant Stiles, then his head hit a boulder and his world went black.

******

10 September 1939
Danzig Germany (Poland Free City Prior to German/Russian Invasion on 01 September 1939)

W.R. Ziegler

1100 Local

Obergruppenfuhrer (Lieutenant General) Meinhard Egon von Richter returned to his newly confiscated headquarters in the Bank of London building on Rycerska overlooking the Motlawa River. He had just left Obergruppenfuhrer (Major General) Walter Heitz's headquarters in the capital building.

Obergruppenfuhrer Heitz was the Commandant of Danzig and, as such, was in overall command of Westpremisen section of German occupied Poland. Heitz had ordered von Richter to take charge of gathering and transporting the spoils of war to Germany. It hadn't been worded quite that plainly, but von Richter knew what his assignment was. The actual written order covered four pages.

"Standartenfuhrer (Sr. Colonel) Zimmerman, would you please come in?" said von Richter through the open door. Standartenfuhrer Franz Zimmerman had been working for two days to set up a functioning headquarters prior to von Richter's arrival.

"Yes Sir."

"When can we expect our office staff?"

Zimmerman flipped a few pages on his clip board until he found what he was looking for.

"They are scheduled to arrive by train at 8:45 am on the 14th Sir."

"And have you found suitable housing for our staff Standartenfuhrer?"

"Yes Sir. I was able to find a small hotel within walking distance and I believe our staff will be comfortable there until they can find their own housing."

"I'm sorry, Zimmerman, please get your sergeant to get us some coffee and take a seat. We need to discuss our new assignment."

"Thank you, Sir." Zimmerman stuck his head out the office and asked for coffee.

"Why don't you look at these orders while we wait?"

Deadly Marriage

Zimmerman read through all four pages in detail trying to ferret out any hidden meanings. The Sergeant brought a formal coffee service and Danish pastries and left.

"What do you think, Franz?"

Zimmerman was shocked. Obergruppenfuhrer von Richter had never used his first name before. Zimmerman thought von Richter was an aristocratic arrogant bastard that thought himself better than a common German.

After a few moments thought he said, "I believe you have been given a great responsibility and honor Sir."

"Yes, yes, but what do you really think?"

"I think you have been given the responsibility to plunder Poland and send all things valuable home to Germany," said Zimmerman.

"Obergruppenfuhrer Heitz waltzed me around for half an hour, but that is what I make of the orders also." He let that simmer for a second then started giving orders.

"We need a system to document and track every item we confiscate. We need to contact all commands and make them aware of our orders. At the same time they need to be made to feel we are watching them. Thievery will not be tolerated in any form by anyone." As he gave this particular order he watched Zimmerman closely for any sign of agreement or disagreement, but saw none.

"Please start to formulate a plan with staffing requirements based upon these orders, Zimmerman, and have a preliminary plan for my review before our staff arrives."

Zimmerman got up to leave and said, "Yes, Sir, I will start immediately."

"One more thing, as soon as telephone service is available I want to talk to SS Major Felix von Krieg-Rupold in Berlin."

It was another 36 hours before Obergruppenfuhrer Meinhard Egon von Richter's call to Sturmbannfuhrer (Major) Felix von Krieg-Rupold was put through.

"Hello Felix, how is Berlin?"

"Berlin is overjoyed with the news from Poland, Obergruppenfuhrer."

"I should think so. I have an assignment for you my friend. I would like you to meet me here as soon as possible. It is a delicate matter that should not be discussed over the phone. Zimmerman will make the arrangements and contact you."

"I am at your orders, Obergruppenfuhrer."

******

15 October 1939
Jacksonville Naval Hospital
Jacksonville Florida, USA
1145 Local Time

Colonel Roberts, Alvin T., came to see how Sergeant Jackson was recovering, if he needed anything and to offer him a new assignment. Jackson was sitting in the sun on the lawn behind the east wing of the Jacksonville Naval Hospital beside a single large palm tree reading about the invasion of Poland in the newspaper and enjoying the sun.

He was waiting for a fellow Texan. This Texan was a blond, blue-eyed and very sexy, Lieutenant Victoria Harsten from Dallas. Jackson was thankful Vicki thought the regulation regarding officers taking up with enlisted personnel was silly. They had become close soon after Jackson's arrival and his being put under her care.

When the Colonel walked up, Jackson sprang to attention and saluted.

The Colonel eyed him suspiciously and said, "That didn't look like you're any the worse for wear, Sergeant? You move pretty well for an invalid."

"Yes Sir, I'm ship shape and ready for duty, Sir" said Jackson, still standing rigidly at attention.

"As you were, Sergeant," ordered Colonel Roberts.

Jackson relaxed and asked, "Sir, how are my men? Did they all make it out?"

"Your men are fine. Jerry even got the mortar crew before he crossed back over the stream. And Stiles is turning out to be as good an officer as you suspected."

Deadly Marriage

"He's a good man, Sir."

Roberts wiped his brow with a handkerchief. The sun was warm.

"Would the Colonel care to sit in the shade, Sir?" said Jackson.

Roberts nodded and they moved out of the sun and into the shade of the palm tree. As they sat down at a small table on a pair of matching lounge chairs, a female voice, with a very sexy Texas drawl, called out "Where's my favorite patient?" as she came around the corner of the Jacksonville Naval Hospital East Wing.

Jackson looked at his commanding officer, flushed and called out too loudly, "Lieutenant Harsten, I was just telling Colonel Roberts here, that I'm fit to go back on active duty. Would you care to join us Ma'am?"

Both Jackson and Roberts got to their feet.

Lieutenant Harsten saluted Colonel Roberts and said, "Nice to meet you Colonel."

"The pleasure is mine Lieutenant. So, how is this 'goldbrick' really doing?"

"His doctor, just this morning during rounds, said this 'goldbrick' would need another month at a minimum, unless the Corps could find some really soft duty for him. The Doc said he wasn't ready to send him back to the jungle yet. I believe he was referring to a chance of any jarring of his little brain in his big head."

"I can call Commander Lewis, his doctor, if you would like to talk to him, Sir?" asked Lieutenant Harsten.

Roberts acted like he was giving some thought to calling the doctor, but by the way the two young people were avoiding eye contact and blushing, he thought he knew what was going on.

"I don't think that will be necessary, Lieutenant. I think you've given me what I needed to know. Now, if you would be so kind, I need to speak with the Sergeant, in private, for a few minutes. Then he's all yours," said Colonel Roberts grinning.

This caused Jackson and Harsten to blush again. Lieutenant Harsten stammered, "Of course, Colonel, I'll be at the nurse's station if you need anything else, Sir," and took off, walking quickly, for the safety of the Hospital.

"Well Steve, I see you've suffered mightily, while we were lounging in the Nicaragua's version of a tropical paradise." After a pause, he said "Be that as it may, our battalion has been pulled out and ordered stateside to teach what we learned in the jungle to a new batch of recruits. I hear from the grapevine that the Military Brass thinks that we are going to get in this war within the next year or so and they're staffing up accordingly. Our outfit is scheduled to be in San Diego by Monday and I'm told we will be there for training and being trained for 6 months."

"Actually I talked with Commander Lewis yesterday, before coming down here. I got basically the same assessment of your condition as from the Lieutenant."

I need you to teach 'hand to hand' combat Steven, there are very few in the Corps with your kind of expertise."

"Sir, I'm ready to go now," interrupted Jackson.

"Not without a doctor's release you're not. Listen Steve, I don't want to lose you, so I started to look for a temporary duty post after talking to Lewis. The only 'soft' temporary duty posting I could find was for a Marine instructor at Portsmouth Naval Yard in Maine. They're outfitting and staffing a new batch of subs and needed a Marine to teach sub security. If you take this assignment, the Doc agreed to let you go. So, if you're a good boy and spend the next eight weeks without getting in too much trouble, I'm confident I can get you back. How about it Jackson, you ready for some cold weather duty?" asked Colonel Roberts.

"Sir, if you can set this up, I'll do my best. And Sir, I appreciate your looking out for me" said Jackson.

Colonel Roberts said, "You did a great job in Nicaragua Jackson and you made the battalion look good, too. There are quite a few young Marines alive because of your skills and leadership. You at least deserve a little consideration."

"Thank you, Sir."

Deadly Marriage

"I figured you might accept and I am really sorry to pull you away from Miss Texas, but I got you a seat on a C47 flight tomorrow morning at 0900. Can you make it?" asked Roberts.

"Yes Sir, no problem," said Jackson.

Chapter 2

23 November 1939
Near Portsmouth Naval Shipyard
Kittery, Maine USA
0900 Local Time

The "Chief," Bronski, Willard R., was retired Navy COB (Chief of the Boat on a submarine).

This cold clear morning the Chief looked like a large Santa Clause, complete with a red and white floppy hat. His wife of 35 years, Lihua (meaning: beautiful and elegant) was sitting beside him in their 1933 Ford, looked more like a China doll cocooned in blankets. She was 13 years younger than the Chief, but looked twenty years younger, she was still very attractive, but seemed not to know it. She had waist length shiny black hair, very few wrinkles and a slim lithe figure. This very different couple still acted like teenagers deeply in love.

They had met while Bronski served on the river boat, Panyang, during the Boxer Rebellion in Shandong China in 1900. The boat was tasked with bringing out Christian missionaries who were under attack by rebel Boxer troops. Bronski was part of a squad sent to retrieve the American missionaries at Qui Shi. Lihua had been raised by the missionaries and was working as an assistant teacher when the Rebellion started. Bronski noticed the slight beautiful Lihua immediately. The missionaries wanted to bring Lihua and some of the other children out of the country, because the Boxers were known to take out their hostilities on converted Chinese Christians. When the Captain allowed Lihua and five others to come aboard, Bronski was well pleased. The thought of spending time with Lihua gave Bronski hope of ingratiating himself to her.

There had been an immediate, if somewhat subdued, attraction between Bronski and Lihua. The problems were enormous; but this didn't stop Bronski from campaigning for Lihua's affections during the two week race down river to the coast. He had to overcome the fact she was only fifteen years

Deadly Marriage

old, a practicing Christian and was controlled closely by the Missionaries.

Lihua (Li) settled with the missionaries in Seattle, Washington, while Bronski was stationed at Portsmouth Naval Shipyard, Kittery, Maine between deployments. For three years they exchanged letters at least weekly and Bronski traveled to Seattle at every opportunity. When Lihua turned 18, she petitioned the Church to allow her to marry Bronski. Reluctantly they agreed and the wedding occurred on one of the few sunny days in Seattle that year, on March 2, 1904.

She had moved to Kittery and set up housekeeping with the Chief in a rented duplex near the water front.

Li was good for Bronski. She made him save a little money each month and soon had enough saved for a down payment on a small beach house. It would be better called a cottage. It was located at the end of a long winding gravel road, through sand dunes covered with brush and stunted trees. The cottage was very private and looked out on the Atlantic. Over the years the cottage was enlarged as their family grew. They had raised five children there and even though all the children had moved away they still lived there. They were very happy, life had treated them well.

The Chief was driving slowly. He knew the ice on the downhill section of Walker Street was treacherous. He had driven this same route for the last two years. The business they owned was located on the corner of Dame and Walker Streets. He was a large solid man with a growing beer belly, a white "Santa Claus" beard, a sarcastic grin and humorous eyes. The Chief always had a good joke, mostly at the expense of the Navy Brass, and a welcoming smile for his customers at the "Ship's Bell". Li worked the kitchen and when they were really busy, acted as hostess. The Chief worked the bar.

They had bought the "Ship's Bell Bar and Grill" after his retirement from the Navy. He and Li made a comfortable living serving workers, sailors and marines from the Portsmouth Naval Ship Yard. They shared a joyous holiday feeling as they pulled up to the "Bell" this morning.

The interior of the "Bell" was festooned with nautical gear. Fishermen's nets, brass dive helmets and portholes, sharks teeth, mounted sport fish, Japanese glass floats, old spear guns and a complete helm from a scrapped destroyer. This time of year they added a Christmas tree and lights around the ceiling.

The Chief and Li both smiled. They were comfortable and content with their life at the "Bell."

They had arrived at 9:00, so they would be ready to open at 11:00. The process was the same each day Monday through Saturday; they were always closed on Sunday. It began by checking the night cleaning crew's work, firing up the kitchen, checking the food and beverage stocks, doing the bookkeeping for the previous day and putting the change fund into the cash register. At 11 Li yelled, "Hey old man, unlock the door!"

The "Bell" served a wonderful menu at lunch and dinner and was usually crowded from 11 to 7 with diners. Today was no exception.

Around 6:30 a regular customer came in. He could have been taken directly from a recruiting poster. He was just less than 6 feet tall, with a dark "high and tight" haircut, dark brown eyes and dressed in an immaculate, everyday Marine Corps utilities uniform and carried his cover under his arm. He had strong features and a jutting jaw. He wore the Chevrons of a First Sergeant and the bearing of a man who had seen much and could handle himself. First Sergeant Steve Jackson was enduring his eight weeks of "soft duty."

He had made it his practice to have dinner most nights after work at the "Bell". Navy chow beat Marine chow, but not Li's cooking. Li came out of the kitchen, walked behind the bar to where Jackson had taken up residence. Li was in her cook's outfit - a white apron and tall white chef's hat with her long hair crammed up in it.

"Hey good lookin," said Jackson in greeting.

"How they hangin', Jackson?" asked Li. Living with the Chief all those years had made her vocabulary much more colorful than the missionaries would have allowed.

"What do you want for dinner?"

"I think I'll have some of your delicious fried scallops and French fries." He continued as she wrote down his order.

Where's the Chief?"

"Probably sleeping in the office," she said, then yelled "Hey you, old man, Jackson is here!"

The Chief came out carrying a case of beer bottles.

"I swear you get louder every day, old woman," said the Chief smiling.

"And you love it, old man," Li said as she passed the Chief, headed back for the kitchen. She patted his butt as she passed.

"And you do love it, you lucky old fart," said Jackson.

"She has her moments. How you doing, Jackson? Having any luck teaching those pups how to get on and off a sub without cracking their heads or breaking anything?" asked the Chief, handing Jackson a beer.

"The young recruits I have the honor to train are barely housebroken true, but they are eager and appear to be trainable. Another couple of weeks and they'll know what's expected of a Submarine Security Marine," said Jackson.

"Well, I better get to work. I'll talk to you later," said the Chief.

Jackson enjoyed his meal and then, later, talking with the Chief.

After a few beers and the required "head calls" Jackson was feeling pretty good.

His mood changed when Lieutenant Decker, Edward R. entered the "Bell" with two other young officers, both Lieutenants, unknown to Jackson. They settled at a table near the door and ordered a bottle of Scotch and three glasses.

Jackson had reported to Decker when he had arrived at Portsmouth. They had developed a mutual contempt of each other over the ensuing five weeks. Jackson was "short" and Decker had his first command assignment. Jackson just wanted it over and to be able to join his company, while Decker wanted everything to be perfect and by "the book." Decker believed the Navy actually ran just like he was taught at the Naval Academy at Annapolis, Maryland. Jackson had eleven years of real world military experience, been in combat and led men in battle. Jackson had patiently tried to impart his wisdom to the new Lieutenant. This was neither well received nor appreciated by Decker.

"Well Chief, I don't want to speak poorly of a naval officer, but that lieutenant there sitting in the middle is really a pain in the ass. He's fresh out of Annapolis, thinks he knows everything and believes that Marine First Sergeants should be seen and not heard."

"You've been in the Corps long enough to know that just ain't so. Besides, aren't you going back to your unit after this class is over?" asked the Chief.

"Yeah you're right, Chief. I've only got three more weeks of his shit before I head out to Pendleton and get to play commando. Besides, a real Marine can live through anything for three weeks, right?" After a few seconds he grinned and asked, "How about another beer, Chief?

Jackson sat on his bar stool, leaning against the far wall, watching the people come and go for a couple of hours. The officers must have been celebrating their Scottish heritage for they were getting very drunk on very old Scotch whisky and showed no signs of stopping or leaving.

Jackson had made up his mind it would be best for all concerned if he left for the evening and let the officers enjoy themselves, then Decker walked up to where Jackson sat.

"Hey Jackson don't you salute officers in Corps?" slurred Decker.

Jackson decided it was easier to salute than try to explain Corps procedures to an inebriated naval officer. So he said, "Yes Sir," and saluted.

"Will there be anything else, Sir?" asked Jackson.

"Stay the fuck away from me, you stupid fuck!" slurred the Lieutenant.

"Yes Sir, it would be my pleasure, Sir," said Jackson sarcastically and turned back to his beer.

"What the fuck did you mean by that remark, Sergeant? Where do you get off talking to a superior officer that way?" asked Decker.

"Sir, with all due respect, I was just complying with the Lieutenant's orders," said Jackson with as little respect as possible.

Then Decker turned purple with rage and stepped to within 12 inches of Jackson's face and started yelling, stuttering and spitting.

"You fucking cretin, who do you think you're talking to?" asked Decker.

"Sir, I think you've had a little too much to drink. I'm going to leave now, if you have anything further to discuss with me, we can discuss it tomorrow in front of the Colonel," said Jackson and started for the door.

Decker grabbed Jackson's arm, spun him around and tried to hit him in the face. Jackson stepped aside and tripped him to the floor. The other two officers came charging down the length of the bar.

"Sir, please don't try that again!" Jackson asked calmly.

"Fuck you Jackson!" yelled Decker, as he came up from the floor with a haymaker swing aimed at Jackson's chin. Jackson hit him with a short right hand to the chest, to knock the wind out of him, but Decker went down like he was struck with an ax. Then the two other officers reached Jackson.

One tried to tackle Jackson and Jackson tripped him and pushed him to the floor. The other Lieutenant tried to punch Jackson, but Jackson pulled him close to his body by grabbing and pulling on the punching arm and came up with an elbow to the Lieutenant's chin, which sent him to the floor out cold.

By this time the Chief heard the commotion and had come around the bar. He got between the remaining conscious officer and Jackson. The Chief grabbed the Lieutenant in a bear hug and said, "That's enough son."

The Lieutenant calmed himself and said, "Let go of me Old Man, I'm okay now."

Jackson was kneeling to check on Decker when the Chief let go. All Jackson saw was the Lieutenant running out the front door of the "Bell" yelling at the top of his lungs for the police, then the SPs (Shore Patrol) and finally the MPs (Military Police).

"You're fucked, if he's dead," said the Chief.

Jackson knew that the little punch should not have killed Decker. "I was just trying to knock the wind out of him, so I could make it to the door."

"It doesn't matter what you were trying to do, you have to get out of here. That young pup will scream until he finds a cop and then swear you started everything. It will be your word against the word of two officers. The officers on the JAG tribunal won't believe one of their own was being such an asshole and started this. With your skills you will at least get manslaughter charges levied against you, if not murder."

The Chief took some twenties from the cash register, stuffed them in Jackson's pocket and said, "Get out the fucking backdoor. Find a ship, jump a train or something, just get the fuck away from here!" shouted the Chief.

Jackson's mind was spinning, showing flashes of pictures of what happened, what was going to happen and what he thought he should do. None of the pictures were very pretty.

He looked at the Chief and said, "I don't know how to thank you Chief."

"Thank me by getting the fuck lost." He handed him a matchbook and said, "Send me a post card some time."

With the Chief's words filling his head, he trotted out the backdoor and headed down to the harbor. As he ran down alleys and back streets, ignoring the bums who called out to him, he began questioning how he should have handled Decker and realized there was nothing he could have done. He cursed aloud, "That drunken asshole son of a bitch is dead and my career is over. I can't even stay in the country!"

His country and his career meant everything to Jackson. He had joined the Corps just before the Great Depression crippled the country. He had joined up for somewhat unpatriotic reasons. It was either enlist or go to jail.

But, for Jackson the Corps had meant food, shelter and a little money, when most of the country was losing everything they had. After receiving a "Dear John" letter the Corps became his family. He had liked the discipline, camaraderie and sense of being part of something special and important.

Jackson needed to think. He saw an all-night diner and sat in a booth in the back. A waitress with a name badge that read Judy came over and asked if he wanted a menu.

Judy was pretty in kind of a hard way. She was probably younger than Jackson, but appeared to be older. She was a well-built woman, but the roots of her dyed blond hair were showing and she wore too much makeup.

When Jackson just looked at her she said, "Sorry doll, but it's late and I'm tired, so if you want something just shout."

Jackson came alive and apologized for his zombielike state. He asked for a menu and a cup of coffee.

She handed him the menu, smiled and went to get the coffee.

Jackson couldn't explain why he just sat there, she wouldn't understand anyway. He gazed at the menu and decided he had better eat, no telling what the future held in store for him. It might be a long time before he ate again.

She came back with the coffee and newspaper.

"Someone left the paper if you would like something to read. What can I get for you doll?" she asked.

"I think I'll have a 'Chili size' with cheese and onions, Judy. Oh yeah you better keep the coffee coming, I may have had a little too much to drink tonight," said Jackson.

She smiled at his use of her name and said, "A lot of my late night customers may have had 'a little' too much to drink, but they aren't smart enough to know it. You're the exception, not the rule. I'll get your order right up for you."

Jackson's mind was spinning again. He stared at the pages of the newspaper, but really didn't see anything.

Judy brought his meal, smiled and said to let her know if he needed anything else.

The size was perfect and he realized he was surprisingly hungry. It had been five hours since he had eaten Li's scallops. When he was finished he felt much better and tried to get his thoughts focused on what needed to be done. He had a thought; didn't newspapers have a list of all the ships leaving port? Now he scanned the paper more seriously.

The list showed mostly ships heading to England with supplies for their war effort. Jackson felt the British authorities would probably turn him in and ship him back to the U.S., so those ships were out. He kept moving down the list. He decided on a tramp freighter leaving berth E-7 with the first high tide in the morning for South America, the *John's II*.

Jackson got up to leave and met Judy at the cash register.

He gave her one of the twenties the Chief had given him and said, "Keep the change."

"Thanks for taking care of me tonight, Judy," Jackson said smiling, and he meant it!

Judy said, "You know that is more than all the tips I've gotten this week, thanks. Sure you can't stick around until I get off? I'd like that!"

"I'd like that too, but sorry I've got a boat to catch," he said smiling and walked outside into his new reality.

Once out of the diner, his smile quickly faded. He felt depressed and overwhelmed. He knew he had to find the *John's II* and somehow get aboard. It was too late to try to sign on and if he had signed on then his name would be on the records, which would not be a good idea anyway. He needed to stow away until the *Johns II* was out of U.S. waters.

The berths were laid out in a row by letter, but the harbor was enormous. He moved from shadow to shadow making his way to row E. The long dock was filled with ships from all over the world loading and unloading cargos. The flood lights that allowed loading and unloading to continue all-night made the trip down the docks like a long walk at midday.

Deadly Marriage

    Jackson needed new clothes. A Marine uniform would stand out in the light of the flood lamps. There was some kind of service building that ran the length of the dock. Jackson moved down the side of the building, trying to stay in the shadows, until he reached a "man door." The door wasn't locked and he stepped inside. He stood with his back against the door until his eyes adjusted to dim lighting after being on the dock.
    There were two rows of offices with a center aisle. Each office had glass making up the top half of the walls and was open to the ceiling. He was relieved to see that the offices all appeared to be empty. He made his way slowly past the offices. He was thinking "at least I'm heading in the right direction; maybe I can make it to berth 7 inside and out of the damned lights."
    After about 100 ft. the offices ended and a solid wall with two doors blocked his way. Jackson tried the door closest to the berths and it was locked tight. He walked to the far door and tried the handle. He then heard something or someone moving in the office adjacent to the door.
    He stood perfectly still; it was a skill he'd perfected in combat. You either learned to be still no matter what bugs were biting you or how badly you needed to cough, piss or sneeze, because if you didn't someone, probably yourself, would die. He hadn't learned to not sweat from the adrenalin coursing through his body though. He waited and sweated for what he thought was sixty seconds and heard nothing more from the office. He slowly and quietly opened the door to the office. He could see nothing moving inside the office. He thought he was losing it and hearing things, but as he closed the door a huge rat ran out of the office. The rat startled Jackson to the point he could feel his heart pounding in his chest. He realized he needed to calm down, he wasn't thinking clearly. After taking a few minutes to calm himself, he decided there was nothing else to do but look at the last door.
    The door was locked, but looked as if someone had broken in before and the door handle was loose. Jackson tried to break it open with his shoulder, but it didn't give way. He stood back

and started to search for something to use to pry it open. He moved back down the aisle between the offices and he found an emergency fire/first aid box that he had missed the first time by. He took the fire ax and moved back to the door. So far he had seen no one, but he wondered how long his luck would hold.

It only needed one swing of the ax to knock the door knob off and the door came open. With the racket from the dock out side he wasn't too worried about noise, unless there was someone on the other side of the door. It opened on a row of lockers, like in high school gym class or the Marine Corps barracks. He found a coat rack and borrowed a coat that fit. He thought he might get away with his utility pants, if his blouse was covered by the coat, but his very shiny boots would give him away. He had to find some shoes at least.

He had to break off nine locks to find clothes and shoes that fit and would make him look like any other stevedore on the dock. He changed, put his uniform, boots and the ax in a large trash bin. Then he covered them with trash. Then he realized his "high and tight" would also look out of place on the dock. He found a watch cap and pulled it down over his ears to complete his disguise.

He found a door leading out onto the dock at the end of the locker room. Now the rough part begins, Jackson thought. As he was standing in front of the door going over in his mind all the things that could go wrong, he heard another noise. This time it was definitely bigger than a rat. This forced Jackson to take the first step out onto the dock. He closed the door quietly and hoped to God that his luck held out.

Jackson tried to appear as if he belonged on the dock. He walked purposely from berth 3 to berth 7. He now could see the rusted old freighter and was very glad she wasn't going to cross the Atlantic. The red copper anti fouling paint looked fairly new and the machinery looked serviceable, but this was not a luxury liner by anyone's standards.

He decided to walk her length and beyond to try and find a way aboard. He had just made the main loading gangway when someone called out.

"Hey you there!" yelled a tough looking giant of a man. He looked to be 6'5" or so and maybe weighed somewhere between 250 to 300 lbs.

Jackson looked around to see who he was yelling at and realized he was yelling at him.

"Yeah you, how about giving us a hand?" the giant bellowed with an English accent.

Jackson thought oh shit, now what, but managed to say "Sure."

They had a terrible time rolling a cart filled with packing crates up the ramp. Jackson was sweating again, but this time it was from hard work.

While the crates were being lowered into the hold, the giant came to Jackson and said, "Thanks. One of our regular crew must have got a better offer or got thrown in jail. Now we're a man short. You a stevedore or heading back to your ship?"

Jackson was stunned. He had no idea what to say. In his life Jackson had decided that when all else fails tell the truth.

"Well the truth is I ran into a little problem earlier tonight and am trying to stay out of jail myself," stated Jackson blushing slightly.

"Have you ever been in jail before?" The giant asked.

"No and tonight wasn't my fault either. I've been in the Marines since I was 17. I didn't have much of a chance to get in trouble," replied Jackson.

"I'll have to clear it with the captain, but if you're willing to work hard and obey orders, I think we could use a seaman's helper. Doesn't pay much, but we don't ask many questions either. Besides, if you fuck up you have to deal with me, and since you're not on our crew list, I can throw your ass overboard." The giant wasn't grinning like that was a joke. He looked mean and serious.

Jackson replied, "If I can stay on board and out of sight until we leave U.S. waters, I'll be the hardest working son of a bitch you have aboard."

The giant looked at him for a moment then chuckled and said, "Welcome aboard. My names Kingsley and the captain's name is Stoneheath. You may have guessed, but we're both loyal British subjects. They call me Mr. Kingsley, because I'm first mate of this here freighter. I don't take shit, I give shit and if you keep that in mind Yank we'll get along. If not, it's a long swim or a beating as my mood goes."

Jackson wasn't concerned about a beating, but the long swim didn't make him feel warm and fuzzy.

"And remember," continued Kingsley, "if you get caught on our ship, you're a stowaway and me and the captain won't know a thing about your being aboard." After a few moments to let his words sink in he asked, "What do you want to be called Yank?"

"If it works for you, Mr. Kingsley, you can call me Yank?" asked Jackson,

"Well Yank, go down in the hold and help tie down the cargo. We leave in a half hour. So move sharply. I'll find you when we're out of the harbor and get you settled in."

Jackson said "Yes Sir" and headed below.

Kingsley was good to his word, after the harbor was astern; he found Jackson and led him to the crew's quarters. There was a total of ten crew, six were Filipinos, three were Indonesian and the cook was Chinese. All spoke very little English and they seemed to stick with those they understood. Jackson didn't feel like making lasting friendships anyway.

His bunk was above the cook's bunk. It was canvas draped between two pipe rails, with a little light and shelf against the bulk head. Jackson had lived in worse.

Mr. Kingsley said, "Come with me to the locker Yank. I think we might find you some clothes that fit. Cookie only does laundry once a week so you'll get pretty ripe between washings without another set."

Deadly Marriage

When he returned to the crew's quarters the Filipinos were sitting at the only table drinking. The Indonesian crew appeared to be out about the ship working. Jackson didn't want to guess what they were drinking. He looked around and took in the table bolted to the floor, personal lockers and coat racks for jackets and foul weather gear. He really just wanted to get in his bunk and get some much needed sleep. It had been a very long day.

As he slept the noise from the drinkers got louder and louder, until it woke him from his coma like sleep. Jackson could not understand anything they said, but it sounded like they were getting excited and building up to something.

When they realized that Jackson was awake, two of them came over to his bunk.

"Who you?" one of them asked in broken English.

"Yank," Jackson said simply.

"You think you better than Filipinos Yank?" asked the larger of the two.

"No," said Jackson, he really was not in any mood for harassment. He started thinking, I better not hurt these guys too bad or I'll have to deal with Kingsley.

The closest one grabbed Jackson's right arm to pull him out of his bunk. Jackson used the man's grip and weight to roll on his right side and break the man's nose with the palm of his left hand. The other man jumped back, but wasn't fast enough. Jackson swung out and down from his bunk, again using the first man's weight, still gripping his right arm to kick the second man in the head before he hit the deck.

The first man was bleeding, cursing and holding his nose. The other was out cold. Jackson started for the remaining four when Mr. Kinsley came into the cabin.

"What the fuck's going on in here?" asked Kingsley.

All six shied away from Kingsley as if they had felt his wrath before and didn't much like it.

"Nobody talking huh, how about you, Yank? Did these little fucks get drunk and try to tell you who's boss of the cabin?" questioned Kingsley.

Jackson thought about being on a long voyage with the "little fucks" and decided he had better just try to get along.

"I'm not sure, Sir. I just woke up. I assumed they were practicing martial arts or something and it got out of hand," said Jackson.

"You're full of shit, Yank, but if that's the way you want to play it, Okay," said Kingsley and left the cabin.

Jackson sat on Cookies bunk, while waiting to see how this would play out.

There was much shouting and arm waving from the men at the table, mostly from the man with the broken nose. Finally, what looked to be the oldest and the man that had been unconscious came slowly toward Jackson.

The older one appeared to be about 50. His hair had streaks of grey and his shaggy beard would be called salt and pepper. His weather worn face broke into a wide toothless grin and he reached out his hand.

"I'm Di, Yank," said the man.

Jackson stood up and shook the offered hand.

"Nice to meet you, Di," said Jackson.

The younger one offered Jackson a cup of whatever it was they were drinking. Jackson thought, I sure don't want this shit, but I better try it. This may be the only peace offering I get.

Jackson accepted the glass and swallowed a large mouth full. It tasted like straight alcohol, looked like dirty dishwater and burned all the way down.

Jackson couldn't keep from choking and sputtering. After a second he lifted his head up, smiled and voiced a long drawn out, "Smooooooth!"

This got them all laughing, even Jackson. They all came over to shake hands. The man with the busted nose shook Jackson's hand then grabbed Jack's other arm and looked at the palm of his left hand. He walked back to the table shaking his head and grinning. He'd had his nose broken before, but not by the palm of a hand.

******

Deadly Marriage

30 November 1939
Private Residence of Obergruppenfuhrer von Richter
Danzig Germany (Poland)
2400 Local

Sturmbannfuhrer Felix von Krieg-Rupold was from an aristocratic family like his mentor Obergruppenfuhrer Meinhard Egon von Richter. Although too young to have served in the First World War as von Richter had, the two officers had much in common. They both were born into highly thought of German families who had lost most of their possessions and money with the armistice ending WWI and both wanted their wealth and position back.

Felix arrived in Danzig by train at 2030 in the evening. It was a rainy and miserable night. He caught a taxi and went to the Hotel Dwor Oliwski as he had been ordered and checked in. As he was signing the register the desk clerk handed him a message.

It read, "Felix please call soonest, Meinhard." It also had a strange telephone number listed.

Felix had called the number as soon as he got in his room and got the private residence of Obergruppenfuhrer Meinhard Egon von Richter. A woman answered and got von Richter on the line.

"Hello, Felix, how was the trip?" asked von Richter.

"It was fine, Obergruppenfuhrer, thank you for asking."

"If you are not too tired I'll send a car for you? I'd like to see you as soon as possible."

"That would be fine, Sir."

Fifteen minutes later a staff car arrived at his hotel. The driver, a SS-Oberschutze (Private), held the door and said, "Good evening Sturmbannfuhrer."

"Good evening Oberschutze."

They drove in silence until they reached a neighborhood of expansive villas.

The Oberschutze turned into a gate in the rock wall surrounding a rock constructed villa of three stories. The rock walls were covered in ivy and the effect was beautiful and rich looking. The Oberschutze stopped the car at the door of the mansion, on the circular drive and opened the door for Felix.

An attractive woman of perhaps 40 with light brown hair, a slim figure and bright green eyes greeted him and introduced herself as Anna Schmidt, von Richter's personal secretary.

Felix followed Anna Schmidt up the winding stairway to the second floor. He noticed how sensuously Anna Schmidt walked. She opened a set of double doors and led him in the Obergruppenfuhrer's study.

"Welcome Felix. I see you've met Anna. Won't you sit down?"

"Thank you Obergruppenfuhrer."

"Would you care for some refreshment gentlemen?" asked Anna.

"I think a Cognac for me, dear, what would you like, Felix?"

"Cognac would be fine, Sir."

While Anna was making their drinks von Richter gave Felix a copy of his orders.

Felix read the orders and came to the conclusion that they were a license to steal.

Anna served their drinks and surprised Felix by sitting next to von Richter on a small couch. Felix sat opposite in an armchair.

"How do you like my quarters?"

"They are very impressive, Sir."

"Until two days ago they were owned by a Jewish banker. Do you remember when our families lived like this Felix?"

"Yes, Sir, until the Armistice our home in Stuttgart was much like this one."

"Mine, in Düsseldorf, was also the same until the Armistice. Do you wish to live this way again?"

"Yes Sir, hopefully someday soon."

"Felix, you read my orders. What do you think of them?"

"With all due respect they seem to be a license to steal for the Reich."

Deadly Marriage

"That's exactly what they are. I already have started receiving valuables from all over Poland."

"Are you willing to take a risk to live like this again, Felix? I am."

For a few minutes Felix was deep in thought. Felix never would have believed what he was hearing from von Richter. But he admitted to himself he wanted wealth again.

"Yes Sir, I am also."

"I was hoping that would be your answer, Felix. What I have in mind is to ship a number of valuable paintings to Argentina along with adequate funds and gold for you to buy an Estancia on the Pampas on which to hide the paintings until after the war. After the war ends, you will have your Estancia and 25% of what we can sell the paintings for. Felix, we will both be rich and comfortable in Argentina."

"Thank you for trusting me Obergruppenfuhrer; I will not fail your trust."

"You've earned my trust, Felix." After a pause he continued "You are a smart fellow Felix, so you probably figured that Anna is more than my secretary." Anna put her hand on von Richter's hand and smiled. "I hope we will spend the rest of our lives together, God willing."

******

02 December 1939
Marine Corps Training Center
San Diego, California

Colonel Roberts was in his office at the training center at Camp Pendleton when Sgt. Rucker, Phillip W. his aide knocked and stood in the doorway.

"Colonel, I just received a call from a friend of mine at Portsmouth. The way he hears it Sgt. Jackson got in a fight with three officers, one died and Jackson ran away. I thought you might like to have me check on Jackson, Sir?"

"Good thought Rucker. If you verify the story, let me know immediately. That doesn't sound like Jackson's style."

It took Rucker less than 15 minutes to verify the story with the Shore Patrol officer of the day. He rushed to the colonel's office knocked again and waited to be acknowledged.

"Sorry Sir. The Shore Patrol officer of the day confirmed the basic story I was told. He's sending us a copy of the report, Sir."

"Please get me the Judge Advocate's Office in Washington on the phone Sgt."

Just a few minutes later Rucker poked his head in Robert's office again and announced, "The JAG office is on the line, Sir."

"This is Colonel Roberts USMC. I have a question, but don't know who to ask."

"Hello Colonel, this is Lieutenant Murphy and I will try to answer your question or direct you to someone who can, Sir," said a young boyish voice.

"Thank you, Lieutenant. I was just informed that one of my men, First Sgt. Jackson, Stephen N., was involved in an altercation with three naval officers. First, I would like to confirm that the JAG is investigating, if so second, I would like to talk with the person handling this investigation; third, what can I do to help Sgt. Jackson?"

"Sir, where did the alleged altercation take place?"

"Maine, Kittery I believe."

Colonel Roberts could hear paper shuffling in the background.

"Yes Sir, here it is. It was filed early this morning and assigned to Lt. Commander Lawson. The Commander is in meeting at the moment, can I have him call you when he's available, Sir? He should be able to answer all your questions."

"Thank you, Lieutenant, you have been very helpful," said Roberts, left his number and hung up the phone without waiting for a response.

Sgt. Rucker reached Commander Lawson the next day and put Colonel Roberts on the line.

"Good morning. Colonel, what can JAG do for you?"

Deadly Marriage

"Hello Commander. I was trying to get an understanding of the charges against one of my men, a First Sergeant Jackson, Steven N.?"

"I was just given the case yesterday, Colonel. It appears to be a pretty simple case on the surface. I understand the Sergeant ran after the altercation which doesn't look good. Is there something I should know about Jackson, Colonel?"

"Please look at his file, Commander. As you'll see he is one hell of a Marine. This altercation doesn't sound like Jackson. I would ask that you investigate the incident and not think of it as simple, Commander."

This angered Commander Lawson and he said so.

"Colonel, we investigate every case, this one is no different. If you will excuse me I have to go to court." He then hung up the phone.

******

04 December 1939
Off the Atlantic Coast of the USA

The voyage of the costal freighter *John's II* was scheduled to be a milk run from New England to the Falkland Islands (Islas Malvinas in Spanish) and back to the USA. The trip would run the full length of North and South America.

From Portsmouth the freighter sailed for New York City, where it loaded machine and communication equipment for delivery to South American companies in Rio de Janeiro, Brazil, Montevideo, Uruguay and Buenos Aires, Argentina. She first sailed to Savannah, Georgia where she loaded cotton and peanuts. Then continued on to Trinidad, where she off-loaded the peanuts and took on a large consignment of rum. She then moved on to Rio de Janeiro, where she off-loaded the cotton, most of the rum and equipment. At this point, Jackson thought one case of rum would not be missed and it was sure better than the Lambanog the Filipinos drank, so he snatched one.

They then continued down the east coast of the South American continent to Montevideo, Uruguay. There they delivered some of the machine equipment and the rest of the rum, except for Jackson's stash naturally.

The *John's II* then sailed across the Rio de la Plata to Buenos Aires and off-loaded the rest of the cargo. They then loaded oil in barrels, food stuffs and supplies for the remote Falklands. Finally they set sail for their last stop, the isolated sparsely populated Falkland Islands.

Jackson awoke from a fitful sleep and noticed how bad the cabin smelled. Diesel fumes, sweat and mold made a disgusting mixture that Jackson never became accustomed to. Climbing up the passage way from the crew quarters to the cargo deck, he was standing near the rail enjoying the early morning, the sweet ocean air and the faint smell of land nearby. They had entered the channel that separates the East and West islands that make up most of the landmass of the Falkland Islands.

Mr. Kingsley came charging down from the bridge yelling for Jackson to wake the crew and prepare for landfall. Jackson scurried back down the passage way and started yelling to wake everyone up. For this kind and helpful service he was cursed and hit with an array of projectiles thrown by his fellow crew members.

They made landfall at Stanley on 17th day of December 1939 at 10 am. Captain Stoneheath was in a hurry to unload and depart before 2 pm, so that they could make it through the Falkland Channel with the tide. The rushing put the first mate, Mr. Kingsley, in a foul mood, he didn't like to rush. Though Jackson had gotten along fine with Mr. Kingsley, on this morning he was the object of much of the mate's dissatisfaction, he was running the crane used to offload/load cargo. The crane was old, rusted and in bad repair. It slowed down their loading and offloading progress, but that didn't seem to matter to the mate, it was Jackson's fault.

"Hey Yank, get a move on you worthless piece of shit!" cried Mr. Kingsley.

Deadly Marriage

Jackson was prepared to answer with the customary, "aye aye sir," when the captain's stern voice shook the rigging.

"Belay that cursing Mr. Kingsley; we'll be having ladies aboard shortly."

This came as a surprise to all the crew including the first mate. He whispered under his breath, "That's what I need, damn women aboard!"

"What was that, Mr. Kingsley?" asked the captain in a barely controlled voice.

Covering his ass Mr. Kingsley replied, "I was just thinking out loud, Sir, that we should make the passenger cabins ship shape for the ladies, Sir."

"Good thought, Mr. Kingsley, make it so," ordered the captain.

By noon they had off-loaded their cargo and taken on two large crates wrapped in canvas. Each crate was tied to the open deck. One was unusually heavy and one was unusually light for its bulk thought Jackson. Both were marked *Printing Press* and were to be delivered to Buenos Aires. Along with crates came two German women looking to be in their thirties, well dressed and obviously wealthy.

Jackson was intrigued. One crate may have contained a printing press, but the other held something else, it was much too light. He wondered why two German ladies would travel by freighter and why were they traveling with the crates? Jackson knew many Germans were going home because of the German war effort, but why these ladies? Jackson felt the U.S. would soon be involved, but that didn't affect him the way it would have three months ago. He was at loose ends on what he should do and where he should go. He couldn't hide onboard the *John's II* forever.

That night Jackson had pulled the watch duty while they transited the Channel. He was bundled up in long johns, a sweater, jacket and foul weather gear against the cold. He also stowed a bottle of rum under his coat for medicinal reasons. He was high above the deck ensconced in what served as the

John's II's crow's nest. He had powerful binoculars and a talking tube to the bridge.

It was a cloudy cold night and the *John's II* was making her top speed of 10 knots. The movements of the ship made it feel much colder than the air temperature of 48F and Jackson was shivering.

There was a full moon, but it wasn't visible due to the overcast sky. Jackson took his responsibility seriously. If they ran aground all loss of life or cargo would be his fault.

At the beginning of the third hour of his watch he spotted something sitting on the water ahead displaying no lights. He notified the bridge and was told to keep visual contact. The bridge being 30 feet lower than the crow's nest could not see the ship or whatever he was seeing. Jackson decided it must be a ship in trouble because it was still in the water. Jackson kept looking at the mystery vessel and reporting its lack of movement, until the clouds parted for a brief moment. Then he knew what he was seeing was a submarine. He called down to the bridge and told them what he saw. Mr. Kingsley asked, "What you drinking up there, Yank? All the U-boats are up North sinking our merchant marines and I don't think any of these banana republics down here have any subs."

Jackson said into the tube, "I understand that, Sir, but I really think we ran up on somebody's sub recharging their batteries."

Before anything else was said Jackson saw a flash of light and he knew what it was. The submarine had fired its deck gun and they had found the bow of the *John's II*. Jackson was shedding garments, so he could get down from his perch. Before he could leave the crow's nest the *John's II* was hit amidships and rolled to starboard with the impact. Jackson was thrown out of the crow's nest into the ice cold water. The *John's II* was between Jackson and the sub. Another shell hit the engine room and again the *John's II* rolled toward Jackson. The two crates tied to the deck broke free and slid off and into the water. The heavy one went down like a stone, but the light one floated.

Deadly Marriage

Jackson swam to the floating crate and made his way onto the top. He was floating away from the *John's II* as she took more hits and started to sink. He watched as she went under and was surprised to see the life boat filled with the crew and the two passengers. The sub now had a spot light on the life boats and was heading towards them. Jackson thought the sub was picking up survivors and started to yell.

When the sub got within 50 yards of the life boat it opened up with its machine gun ripping the life boats and their passengers to shreds.

Jackson shut up, flopped down on the crate and watched. He was beyond shocked. The cold blooded killings didn't make any sense to him. He had only killed because he had too. Not for sport. The sub shut down its engines and it appeared they were trying to hear if anyone was still alive. After a few minutes he heard orders being given in German. The sub closed all hatches and sank beneath the calm sea.

Jackson was alone floating on a crate twenty five miles from the closest land, without food, water or method of propulsion. He thought his luck had finally run out! He drank his bottle of rum.

Chapter 3

18 December 1939
Marine Corps Training Center
Office of the Commanding Officer
San Diego, California

"General, Colonel Roberts is here, Sir," said General Dawkin's secretary, a Marine private clerk typist.

"Send him in, Private."

"Hello Roberts, what's the problem?"

"Sir, you remember Sgt. Jackson?"

"Sure. As I remember he was wounded in Nicaragua."

"That is correct, Sir. It seems he got in a fight with three officers while recovering on soft duty at Portsmouth. The report doesn't sound like Jackson, Sir. He doesn't lose control. The JAG officer seems to think it's a simple case and Jackson is presumed guilty because he ran. I don't know how much investigating will be done."

"I assume we don't know why he ran or where he is, right Roberts?"

"No we don't Sir. What I wanted is your opinion of this letter I wrote to the JAG."

Dawkins read the letter and thought for a moment before commenting.

"Colonel, I don't know if your letter will do any good, but if you'll add my name, I'll put my signature to it."

******

18 December 1939
South Atlantic Ocean
Off Argentine Coast

His first night floating on the sea was a nightmare of cold and thoughts of sharks. The rum was the only thing that kept him partially warm. He must have dozed off, because when he opened his eyes he could see the sun rising in the East. He

Deadly Marriage

was cold, hungry, hung over and mostly thirsty. He surveyed the sea around him. The only thing he could see was a few strands of seagrass floating towards the West. Then he saw the large grey shapes crossing under his floating crate. They must have been drawn by the bodies of his crewmates. The rest of his problems faded as the sharks took control of his mind. Would the crate float long enough for the sharks to lose interest? Would they just tag along until he fell off? What would if feel like to torn apart by razor sharp teeth?

He lashed himself onto the crate with the broken lines that had held it to the deck. Thinking he had done all he could he settled down and had a chance to think.

Then it hit him, the seagrass was being taken to the West. That's where land was, to the West. Argentina lay to the West. Jackson started believing he might have a chance to make to land alive. He watched the sharks for the rest of the day.

When the sun started to sink in the West, Jackson thought he could see a dark line on the horizon. But he wasn't sure and gave in to thinking it was just wishful thinking. Then the dark, with its own horrors overtook him, colder than Jackson could remember ever being, but at least on this day he was dry and he hadn't seen any sharks for hours.

The morning brought a fog that blocked out everything. His little floating home was wet with dew. Jackson quickly licked all the dew he could from the canvas cover. It was a little salty, but made him feel he was doing something to survive. Jackson knew he wouldn't last for more than another day or two. He didn't want to end his life this way. He had dreams that would never be fulfilled. He would never have a wife and family. He would never grow old and have grandchildren.

After the sun broke through and he was warm again his thoughts roamed from the events at the "Ships Bell", to his life in the Corps, to his growing up in Rio Pecos, Texas, to his first and only real girlfriend and lover, Juanita Maria Garcia.

Jackson's parents had not approved of Juanita. Her father and uncle were farmers and worked hard every day to support their families. They lived down by the river, where all of the small town's kids used to swim and play. They were just kids, black, brown or white, it meant nothing to them.

Juanita had been just one of the kids, one of young Steve Jackson's playmates, until she reached about thirteen years old and started developing into a beautiful young woman and not a kid anymore. She had long black hair, down well past her waist, dark brown expressive eyes and all the signs of a beautiful budding body.

Steve enjoyed being around Juanita and spending summer days talking and flirting. Neither Steve nor Juanita knew much about sexual games. Neither wanted to ruin what was so special between them by being the first to make an overt romantic move.

When summer was over, Steve started going to Pecos High School and Juanita had two more years at Hamilton Junior High. The first few months of his high school career were proving to be hectic. After school he began playing football and working odd jobs when he could find them. His time for playing seemed to be over. But, he missed talking with Juanita and being around her. She never really left his mind at peace.

Near the beginning of December, Steve was out buying Christmas presents. He saw a St. Christopher's medal on a delicate silver chain and thought of Juanita. How the medal would lie between her breasts. Steve thought this was a great excuse to go see her and tell her he missed her.

On a clear, cold Texas morning, Steve walked down to Juanita's house by the river. He was worried what she might think of his gift and if her parents might object.

He knocked softly on the screen door. Juanita's father opened the door and said, "Hello Steve, long time no see."

"I've been kind of busy lately, with high school, football and I work when I can."

"Could I speak to Juanita, Mr. Garcia?" Steve asked shyly.

"I guess that's how life goes when you grow up. I'd say sure you could see her, if she was here. I think she's walking down by the river, but I'm not sure. That girl gets more moody every day," said Mr. Garcia.

Deadly Marriage

"I'll go see if I can find her. I have a little present for her, if you don't object?" said Steve.

"No objection, Steve. I think she misses your being around and it would make her happy to see you. Good luck finding her and Merry Christmas to you and your family," said Mr. Garcia.

"Merry Christmas to you and your family too, Mr. Garcia. I hope to see you again soon," said Steve.

Steve knew where Juanita would be. They had found a special spot down the river about a mile, where three large boulders formed a shelter from the West Texas wind and rain. It had a rock overhang, about five feet deep, that would protect you, but you could still see the river and be out of the wind.

Juanita and Steve had spent their hot summer days in the shade of their special spot, Juanita teaching Steve Spanish and talking of all the things important to teenagers: families, friends, school and dreams. Juanita wanted to be a nurse, but Steve hadn't decided what he wanted to do with his life. He just knew he needed to get away from his parents.

Steve's father was the Reeves County Sheriff and his mother kept active with the First Baptist Church of Rio Pecos, Texas. They were about as conservative as anyone in an already very conservative community.

Steve's parents had been happy when Steve got so busy that he didn't have time to spend time with Juanita and had told him so. They thought she was lower class and that Steve could do much better for himself than a "Mexican's farmer's daughter". They wanted him to go to college in Austin, which they believed would put more distance between Steve and Juanita. They had visions of him becoming a lawyer. Steve wasn't sure what he wanted, but he knew he didn't want to be controlled by his parents and their bigoted beliefs.

As Steve walked down the trail he began to smell smoke. As he rounded the last bend before he could see their spot, he could see that the smoke was from a fire in amongst the rocks.

He came in from the river side so Juanita could see him and not be startled. He walked up to the fire and smiled. Juanita glared back at him.

"What brings the Gringo down to the river in this cold?" asked Juanita.

"I thought you might like to see me?" questioned Steve.

"It's been three months since you've come to see me. No call, no visits. I didn't think your parents would allow you see me anymore. I assumed you'd taken up with some nice respectable white-bread girl named Barbara Ann," said Juanita.

So that was it, Steve thought, she misses me too!

"My parents still say I can't see you anymore, but that doesn't matter to me. No white-bread girl named Barbara Ann either," replied Steve.

"I'm sorry I haven't been to see you. I've really missed you! I won't let my parents get in our way anymore. Please forgive me?" asked Steve.

Juanita started crying and when Steve tried to put an arm around her to comfort her, she pushed him away and hit him on the shoulder.

"Don't think because you finally made an appearance and say nice things, Gringo, that I'll get all mushy and forget how you deserted me!" yelled Juanita.

Obviously she had been stewing for some time, thought Steve. He wasn't sure of what to say or do. Finally he just told the truth.

"Juanita, I love you and I'll never let anything keep us apart again. Please forgive me?"

Juanita stared directly into Steve's eyes, as if to see if he was telling the truth. She then stared at the fire for a few moments, then said, "I love you too Steve, but it hurt so much when I thought you didn't care and had deserted me. I'm scared."

Steve was at a loss for words. He finally held out the present to her.

He said, "Your father said it was okay for me to give you a gift, I hope you like it."

Juanita stared at the small box and then took it. She opened the box and looked at the medal.

"Does this mean anything special to you, Steve," Juanita asked.

Steve thought the truth worked last time, don't be scared.

"Yes, it means I love you and want you to wear that medal until I can replace it with a ring," answered Steve.

"Hold me Steve and don't let go," sighed Juanita.

After that cold December day, Steve and Juanita were an item all through high school. They had explored sex together and found they were very compatible, if only amateurs. This led to Juanita's pregnancy, at the end of Steve's senior year. This started a string of events which would shape both their lives.

Mr. Garcia was hurt, embarrassed and angry. He wanted Steve to marry Juanita and be a father to his first grandchild. Anything else would be a disgrace to the family. Steve agreed with him.

Steve's parents wanted Steve to disown the child and Juanita. They wanted him to leave for college upon graduation.

Steve wanted to marry Juanita and take care of her and his child. When he told his parents of his plan he was shocked at their reactions. His mother yelled at Steve, "You are ruining your life, what are you thinking? Papa you have to put an end to this, now!"

Steve's father took another sip from his third cocktail of the evening and said, "Son, you're not thinking clearly. Take a few days and think it over. Don't do anything you'll regret for the rest of your life."

Steve yelled back, "I know what I'm doing and I know what I feel. You're not going to change my mind. I love Juanita and want to marry her and be a family. A few days aren't going to change my mind. Don't try to stop me. I'm going to Juanita's house to set this straight."

Steve's mother cried and Steve's father looked angry, but said nothing.

The road down to the river went through town and the 30 mph speed was posted every thousand feet. Steve hit the road at 60 mph and hadn't gone half way through town when he saw the flashing lights in the rear view mirror. Jackson pulled over to the curb.

Deputy Franklin Burrell walked up to the car and flashed his flashlight in Steve's face.

"Howdy Steve, where are you going in such a hurry?" asked Deputy Burrell.

"Hi Franklin, I just had it out with the folks about Juanita and me. I was heading down to Juanita's to settle things and plan a wedding," replied Steve.

"Sorry Steve, but your old man just called me on the radio and said to take you in. I have to follow his orders. He'll fire me if I don't and I need this job," said the Deputy.

"I don't know what he's up to, but I don't want to get you in trouble Franklin, so I'll follow you in," said Steve.

"He wants me to take you to the station in my car and leave yours here. So how about hoping in the back seat and let's get this done?" asked the Deputy.

Steve stomped on the gas and roared away from the flashing lights and a stunned deputy.

He fishtailed down Main Street, past the bank and Tasty Freeze heading for the South side of town.

Deputy Franklin Burrell called the sheriff and told him what had happened. The Sheriff said, "Don't fret, just take your time and head down to the Mexican's place. I'll meet you there."

Steve was sitting outside on the porch with Mr. Garcia. He had asked for Juanita's hand in marriage and had received her father's approval. Mr. Garcia knew how much they meant to each other and believed they could have a good life if left alone. Now they were talking about all problems they would incur caused by Steve's angry parents, the bigoted locals and society in general.

Two police cars pulled into the yard. Deputy Burrell got out of the first car and, Steve's father got out of the other. The Sheriff told Deputy Burrell to do his duty.

"Steve, you are under arrest for speeding, reckless driving and evading arrest. Please turn around so I can put on the cuffs," said Franklin.

Deadly Marriage

"This is bullshit, Dad. You can't do this, I'm only trying to make things right," said Steve.

"We can talk about this at the station, now do as the Deputy says," replied his father.

Mr. Garcia told Steve, "Do as he says or you'll just cause more problems for everyone. I'll get you a lawyer tomorrow and bring Juanita down to see you."

Steve went along with the Deputy.

Steve was brought before Judge Jubal Rachine, a poker pal of his father's, first thing the next morning. He was given a choice - five years in the State Penitentiary at hard labor or take the opportunity to enlist in the service of his choice for a minimum of five years.

Juanita and Mr. Garcia brought the only lawyer interested in Steve's case. After hearing what Steve had to say and reading the transcripts of the hearing, he stated that there wasn't very much he could do. He could appeal, but they all knew that would be a waste of time and Steve would still be in jail. They jointly discussed his options and came to the conclusion that the service was the lesser of two evils. Juanita and Steve thought after his training, they could be together and be a family, long before the baby was due.

Steve stood before Judge Jubal Rachine and said he would enlist in the Marine Corps as directed.

The Marines were happy to have a bright young man enlist, no matter how the enlistment came about. They tested Steve physically, mentally and morally. The Corps decided he would make a proud Marine and be a benefit to the Corps.

Steve was shipped out the next week for Camp Legune, Louisiana for training. As soon as Steve boarded the bus for Louisiana, Steve's father started making inquiries about how to get the Garcia family run out of town or deported. It only took two weeks to force them off their rented farm and send them back to Mexico.

Steve kept sending letters to Juanita, but none were delivered. Finally, he received a letter from Juanita. She told him about what his father had done and how much she hated his father. She told him that she had miscarried on the rough drive back to Mexico and said it was probably for the best. Her grandmother had agreed to pay for her nursing education in Guadalajara and she had signed up for classes. She told him that she still loved him, but would not bring more shame and misery to her family.

She didn't want to ever see him again and hoped he would respect her wishes.

She closed saying, "There is nothing more to say. I hope you have a good life and someday be happy and I'll try to get on with my life too."

Steve realized he was crying. "Some tough Marine," he said out loud, crying like a fucking baby. "You maudlin ass, shape up, start thinking like a Marine!" Steve shouted out loud and to no one.

Jackson calmed himself, started looking around his little world and began to take inventory. He had about forty feet of rope, the canvas crate cover and the wood frame of the crate. He also had whatever was in the crate.

It had been ingrained in his being by the Marine Corps, always carry a knife. Now it was his only tool to save his life. It was the Marine Combat Knife, the predecessor of the K-Bar used throughout WWII. The knife had an eight inch blade, four inches of which was serrated on top. He studied the canvas, deciding the best way to cut it open. He started by cutting a two foot straight line in the center of the crate length wise, with two one foot lines perpendicular to it on the ends. This would make an opening large enough to work through and hopefully to fit through.

When the cutting was done, he found another layer beneath. This was something like oil cloth, but different. (He would later find out it was plastic sheeting and the reason his crate was still afloat.)

Thinking this layer might be used to catch rain and dew, he cut an oval about the same dimensions as his cut in the canvas. His Marine survival training at work!

Deadly Marriage

Now he could see the wooden slates that made up the shell of the crate. They were made of 6x1 inch pine boards. The boards were soft enough to be cut by the serrated edge of this knife. It was slow going, digging a hole big enough to insert the blade. He worked on the boards until late afternoon, when he finally was able to remove the first board.

He reached into the crate and found Nazi propaganda handouts written in Spanish. The women that had brought the crates aboard were Nazi sympathizers at best, but most likely spies, thought Jackson. He threw a few of the pamphlets on the water and watched them float away, toward the setting sun. He was still being drawn towards land.

The nighttime sky in the Southern Hemisphere is bright with a million stars. Steve decided to work all-night, if need be, cutting the boards. At least he would keep himself a little warmer from the physical exertion. Just before dawn he completed his task. He laid the boards under the canvas, reached in and dug down into the stacks of handouts. He found nothing that would help his situation. He started throwing the handouts over the side, trying to make room for him to enter the crate. Jackson reasoned that the inside of the crate would offer some relief from the elements and be much more comfortable.

He waited until the sun was up, so he could see what he was getting into, when he dropped into the crate. He found nothing but handouts, but knew something heavier was in the bottom of the crate to keep it upright. The wind, salt spray and sun had taken their toll on Jackson's hands, lips, ears and face. He was cracked and bloody in spots. Just being out of the constant Patagonian winds was a wonderful improvement. Jackson threw out more handouts until he could lie down flat and covered himself with more pamphlets. He quickly fell asleep, a dreamless exhausted sleep.

When he awoke it took a few minutes for Jackson to figure out where he was. He poked his head out of the crate to see the sun setting on the sea, no land in site.

Three days (or was it four) without food was starting to hurt. He was losing energy along with his minimal fat deposits. He was hoping for a squall to replenish his fluid levels and now he needed to eat.

He lowered himself back into the crate, settled in his "bed" and covered himself with pamphlets. He was soon asleep again, but this was a restless sleep filled with nightmares about sharks and other ways to die at sea.

Something hit the crate hard, waking Jackson. He laid there and listened intently for another noise. Another slap against the side of his crate made him move to see what was changing in his little world. He grabbed his knife and carefully stuck his head out of the crate. He saw nothing that would have caused the noise. With his head sticking out of his crate, looking at the stars, he saw something silver flashing in the water next to the crate. Jackson crawled over to the edge of the crate, careful to not tip the crate over.

He could now see it was a flying fish which had hit the crate. It wasn't dead, but stunned. Jackson knew the meal from the sea would only be there a few minutes, so he tied a rope around his waist and stretched down to grab the fish, but couldn't quite reach. His arms were six inches too short. He kept trying as the fish came back to life. Then, when Jackson had given up hope and sat up, he was struck in the back by another flying fish. This one he quickly grabbed decapitated with his knife and started to eat raw. While he sat there eating for the first time in days, picking the meat off the bones, he noticed more flashes in the star light. The sea was filled with flying fish.

He finished half of the small fish and saved the rest for later. Waiting for another fish to hit him, he sat up for the rest of the night. None did.

At dawn a fog had set in dropping moisture on the surfaces of the crate. Jackson had made a crude catch basin from the inner layer of the crate. The water wasn't salty and tasted wonderful. He drained the water into the empty rum bottle. With the small meal and fresh water, Jackson felt better than he had since the sinking of the *John's II*. But his energy supplies had run out, he was exhausted. He slid back into his "bed" and was soon asleep.

Jackson woke with a start. His crate had been hit by another flying fish, he thought. He took his knife and stood up through the opening in the crate, eager for another meal. He didn't see any fish and the fog was still thick, but after turning around, found he was staring into the weathered face of an old fisherman in his boat. The fisherman was between 70 and one hundred years old, with wrinkles running everywhere, thick white hair and eye brows, beady dark eyes and yellow teeth. Jackson wasn't good at determining age, but this man was really old. The old man wore a colorful striped wool coat, an old red skull cap pulled down over his ears and on his feet shoes that looked like Indian moccasins with rope soles. Jackson realized the old man was rowing with the crate tied to his boat. He must have come upon his crate and thought he had found a treasure chest.

Jackson thought that land must be close if this old man was out in a row boat.

"Buenos Dias, Mi Amigo," shouted Jackson.

The old man just stared at Jackson like he was a demon rising from the dead. A look of dread, fear and acceptance was on the old man's face.

Jackson thought he would give it another try. "My name is Jackson, what's yours?" said Jackson in halting Spanish.

The old man moved very slowly to the stern of his little boat; and, to Jackson's surprise, drew a long knife from behind his back and cut the rope attaching his boat to the crate. He shuffled back to the oars and started rowing as if the devil himself was after him. He was almost out of sight when he raised a small sail and vanished.

Jackson had pulled himself up on top of the crate and watched as the man disappeared. He was now filled with conflicting emotions. Jackson was elated that he was close to land, but worried that the old man would tell the authorities. There was nothing he could do about either situation.

W.R. Ziegler

******

30 November 1939
Private Residence of Obergruppenfuhrer von Richter
Danzig Germany (Poland)

Sturmbannfuhrer Felix von Krieg-Rupold's journey began on a train back to Berlin. By the time he reached his quarters a package containing his orders, travel itinerary and travel funds was waiting. The package had been sent by the ever efficient Zimmerman, von Richter's aide personally.

He and his aide were to be on the Condor flight to Buenos Aires the following night. He called his aide SS-Obersturmfuhrer Christian Quinn.

"Good evening Obersturmfuhrer. I hope I'm not disturbing you?"

"No Sir, I was just reading"

"Quinn, we have been ordered to Argentina on somewhat of an intelligence mission. I'm sorry there wasn't more notice, but we leave tomorrow night on the Condor for Buenos Aires. I hope that does not pose a problem for you?"

"No problems, Sir."

"Good. Meet me at the Officer's Mess at 0700, we can have breakfast and discuss our new assignment."

SS Sturmbannfuhrer Felix von Krieg-Rupold and SS-Obersturmfuhrer Christian Quinn arrived in Buenos Aires two days after leaving Berlin. They were allowed a day to rest and then took a German Embassy plane for the flight to Rio Gallegos, near the tip of South America.

They made note of the town's layout as they came in on final approach to the small military airport. Rio Gallegos was situated on the mouth of the river of the same name and was dominated by its harbor. Everything was built around it.

They checked in, under fictitious names, to a small hotel near the harbor. After he had unpacked and cleaned up Felix called Quinn's room.

"Quinn, after all our traveling, how does a walk around the town sound to you? We could get something to eat while we're out?"

"Sir, my legs would appreciate a walk and my stomach would be happy with something to eat."

"Good, I'll meet you in the lobby in fifteen minutes."

******

Atlantic Ocean off Rio Gallegos, Argentina
24 December 1939

The next morning Jackson woke to sunshine, not fog. He crawled out of the crate, disappointed that he had caught no water in his catch basin. He was thinking of the old man when he saw a small motor boat approaching from the West. Jackson thought the old man had brought the police or military to take him in.

When the boat got closer Jackson could see that a tall thin man was standing in the bow of the motor boat waving at Jackson. The old man was at the stern seated by another fisherman. As they drew nearer, Jackson was surprised to see the thin man wore denim trousers and wool shirt under a leather overcoat with a fur collar.

As they approached, the thin man shouted, "Good Morning, Friend," in English with maybe a Scottish accent.

Jackson was shocked. He hadn't expected this kind of greeting, especially in English.

"That's the nicest greeting I've ever heard. I didn't think I would live to hear English spoken again. Good morning to you," shouted Jackson.

The fisherman at the helm knew how to handle his boat. Jackson couldn't feel anything as he pulled up to the crate.

The thin middle-aged man said, "My name's Mac Arthur, I own a sheep ranch; we call it Estancia Mac Arthur. The local fishermen think I'm something special because I own a lot of sheep and a lot of land. So, when something unusual comes along I get to check it out and your craft is truly unusual."

"My name is Jackson and I have a long story to tell, but this is my only possession and for some reason is very important to me. Would it be too much to ask to have her towed ashore? I'll come on board your boat and tell you my whole sorted story, if getting her ashore is possible? Jackson asked.

"Mr. Jackson, we'll be happy to tie her on and pull her in for you. I look forward, with the greatest interest, to hearing your story. Please climb aboard," said Mac Arthur.

Jackson started to climb down the side of the crate, but realized his muscles didn't want to do what he wanted them to do. His entire body hurt to move and he almost slipped into the water. Mac Arthur grabbed him by his jacket and pulled him aboard. He sat down hard on the middle bench seat, facing Mac Arthur.

"I didn't realize how weak I have become. Thanks for keeping me dry!" Jackson said.

"No problem, son," said Mac Arthur while removing a flask from under his overcoat. He handed it to Jackson.

"Looks like you could use a nip, friend." He rattled off a string of orders in Spanish, much too fast for Jackson to understand, but the fishermen did. They gave Jackson a wool blanket, a ceramic jug of water and something that looked like a tortilla filled with some kind of meat mixture (*empanadas* in Spanish).

Jackson thanked them in formal Spanish and smiled. This got him kind smiles in return. He thanked Mac Arthur, took a belt from the flask and drank from the water jug. It became very quiet as Jackson ate the first real food he'd had in days.

"Feel better now mate? Do you feel up to telling me your story?"

While Jack ate, he had been thinking of what to tell. The Scot seemed to be a good man, but Jackson had noted he was used to being obeyed. Maybe he was a military man or had been at one time. Jackson needed to be cautious.

Argentina was filled with Nazi sympathizers and its government. Though not a member of the Axis, Argentina supported the Axis war effort, providing wool, mutton, beef, leather, raw materials and, most importantly, oil. Germany had

Deadly Marriage

very small oil reserves at the beginning of its war of conquest and quickly depleted its domestic supply. This shortage of oil would eventually cause the war in North Africa and, finally, Russia.

Jackson looked into the thin man's eyes, trying to determine what his motives were. He was unable to gauge anything from the eyes. After a few moments he said "Here goes! I was a crewman on the coastal freighter *John's II*. We were just leaving Stanley in the Falkland's, coming out of the channel. We had picked up two female passengers and two crates in Stanley. The one we're towing now and another just like it, marked "Printing Equipment". I helped load them and noticed one was extremely heavy and this one was very light in comparison. I didn't take much notice at the time.

I was ordered aloft as a lookout, the old ship had no modern navigational equipment. Just after we had reached the open sea, I saw a vessel without lights sitting in the water. Then I saw flashes. They looked like mussel flashes, but I didn't believe it. We were being shelled by an unseen vessel. I was alone in the crow's nest, so I don't know if a radio signal was sent or what the Captain was doing to save his ship. I called down the tube that I couldn't see where the shelling was coming from. From that point on I just watched."

"The *John's II* was hit amidships and rocked violently. I was tossed into the sea. She righted herself, just to be hit again. This time the crates broke free and dropped into the water. Our ship was sinking and sinking fast. I climbed on the crate you see here and hung on. The other crate, the heavy one, sank like a stone."

"The mystery vessel now had search lights on the *John's II*, watching her sink. I was floating in the darkness. They hadn't seen me or the crate, because I was on the other side of the ship and floating away. After the *John's II* was low enough in the water, I was able to see the life boat, with what appeared to be all hands aboard."

"After our ship had sunk completely, the vessel followed the life boats with its lights and opened fire with what sounded like a heavy machine gun. They massacred all hands, the women included, and the bastards kept shooting until there was nothing left of the life boat. Like it was target practice, with human targets."

"Once they had finished their target practice she dowsed the lights and I could see that the mystery vessel was a German U boat. I couldn't read the whole number, but it started U-5," Jackson watched the thin man's eyes again, looking for some clue as to his feelings about the German attack. The man's eyes still revealed nothing.

Jackson continued, "I tied myself to the top of the crate and floated until the sun came up. I cut through the canvas and into the crate. I found what looks to be Nazi propaganda pamphlets. I threw enough out to make room for me inside and that's how you found me."

"That's quite a story, Mr. Jackson," said Mac Arthur.

Jackson thought he should give a fake name just in case his new friend had a way to check out his story.

"By the way, my given name is Jackson Stevens, Mr. Mac Arthur, please call me Jack," said.

"Right-O, please call me Graham. I was wondering, Jack, why does this crate mean so much to you?" Mac Arthur asked.

"I've been thinking about that too. I lost what little I owned when our ship sank and this crate saved my life. It seems to be my only possession in the world and my good luck charm. I don't think I can explain it any better than that," said Jack.

"I think I understand." He thought for a moment, and then said, "If you will do me the honor of spending Christmas with me and my family at our Estancia, I'd be happy to take you and your crate to my ranch?" asked Mac Arthur .

"What day of the month is it? I guess I lost track of the days floating around," asked Jackson.

"Why, it's Christmas Eve, Jack," said Mac Arthur.

Jackson had lost track of time. He had been on the sea for six days, but it seemed much longer.

"Won't your family feel that I am imposing on a family holiday?" asked Jack.

"Not in the least. We usually have a big dinner for our workers and what locals are in need. One more mouth to feed wouldn't hurt a thing," answered Mac Arthur.

"Then I accept your gracious hospitality and it would be my honor sir," said Jack.

Chapter 4

Rio Gallegos, Argentina
24 December 1939

The two German officers walked for over an hour and saw most of the waterfront area. They had chosen a restaurant by the number of automobiles in the parking lot.

Quinn ordered for them and they settled in for a relaxing dinner and conversation.

"I think we will need an automobile for traveling around Argentina, Quinn."

"I agree, Sir. Argentina is larger than most of Europe combined."

"A truck would be preferable, but someone might ask why we needed it. I think maybe a large car, something comfortable for long trips. Once we receive our cargo we have much traveling to do."

"Yes Sir. Would it be inappropriate to ask about our cargo, Sir?"

Felix had expected Quinn to be curious and ask this question. He had created a logical answer/lie while flying across the Atlantic on the Condor.

"I believe you are entitled and can be trusted to know the details now, Quinn, but remember that everything you hear is classified, top secret and there is no one on this continent authorized to know except you and I. Is that understood?"

"Yes, Sturmbannfuhrer, I understand."

"We are to receive valuable Reich assets from newly occupied territories. The plan worked out by Himmler is to have us store and protect these assets in Argentina to alleviate political fallout from occurring. He believes if we take the assets directly to Germany, claims will be made by the League of Nations that we are stealing national treasures for the benefit of the Reich."

"I now understand the need for secrecy Sturmbannfuhrer. Thank you for explaining our mission, Sir."

"This is why I was so vague at the Embassy with Krantz. He has no need to know our mission. Speaking of Krantz, he did provide an interesting contact here."

"While I was at lunch with Krantz he suggested that I contact a FBI man stationed down here. It seems he is fond of our money. Krantz said he has used him in the past for gathering information. He may be of some use to us."

Quinn nodded.

Felix laughed, "He has an office called 'US Agricultural Attaché.' Isn't his title laughable?"

"Yes Sir," smiled Quinn.

"Tomorrow I will visit the "US Agricultural Attaché."

******

As they motored westward Graham explained that they were headed for the small town of Río Gallegos, in the Province of Santa Cruz, Argentina. Rio Gallegos was situated on the river Gallegos and was a processing port for cattle, leather, wool and mutton. It also had a natural harbor, a naval base and was the capital of Santa Cruz.

When they approached the harbor's landing the fisherman handling the boat, again, barely touched the dock. The grizzled old man was a master of handling his craft. The Scot stepped ashore and offered a hand to Jack.

Jack took the hand this time and stepped up onto the dock. He was surprised to find he was barely able to stand, let alone walk. His legs were weak and he still felt as if he was at sea, rocking in the swells.

Jack leaned against a light pole and looked at the port. There were large docks for the loading of sheep and wool. Fairly large industrial buildings, Jack thought, were probably used for processing and smaller official looking customs type buildings. Dock workers had begun crowding around the unusual crate boat sitting tied to the dock.

Graham gave orders in rapid fire Spanish and the dock workers went about their business. Soon a small, rotund man in an official appearing uniform came strolling down the dock with an important air.

Graham introduced the chubby bureaucrat as Port Captain Sanchez. Sanchez clicked his heals like a German count and welcomed Jackson to Argentina. He asked if Jackson had anything to declare, to which Jackson said, "Just the crate there".

"May I inquire as to what is in the crate?" asked Sanchez.

"It is full of German pamphlets written in Spanish. You see, I was accidentally thrown off my ship when it was sunk and have been floating around since. The crate saved my life," said Jackson. This was basically true, but left out many facts Jackson did not want to share with a representative of the Argentinian government.

"I must make an inspection, you understand?" said Sanchez, as if it was the most important thing done in the harbor that day.

Jackson would have liked to see the pompous little man fall in the water, but instead said, "No problem, Captain, there is a whole cut in the top, but be careful she rocks quite a bit." Jackson still thought of her as his vessel.

Sanchez lightly reached out and put a foot on the top of the crate. The crate sank some six inches and Sanchez jumped back. He stood there thinking about how he could get out of climbing aboard; the thought of soiling his beautiful uniform or looking like a clumsy fool and losing face would not be acceptable. Then Jackson, still on wobbly legs, stepped on the crate, reached in and pulled out a handful of pamphlets.

Sanchez thanked Jackson and pulled out a pair of old fashioned wire frame reading glasses. He read the pamphlet from cover to cover and pronounced them beautifully done and they were very welcome in Argentina. He then pulled a printed orange tag from this coat pocket, signed it and handed it to Jackson. The crate and its contents were now welcome in Argentina, but Jackson wasn't so sure he was. He didn't have a passport for one thing; he had no money or means of support for another.

Deadly Marriage

"Please, sign the bottom of the tag for my records, please," said Sanchez.

Mac Arthur discreetly watched as Jackson signed the bureaucrat's paper work, which Jackson thought he pulled off rather well. He didn't flinch when he signed his new name, Jackson Stevens, for the first time in his life.

An impressive Mercedes two and a half ton truck, with Estancia Mac Arthur painted on the door, came down the dock towards them.

"If you'll allow me, I'll take the customs tag; we can get the crate loaded and then we can head to the Estancia when you are finished with Senor Sanchez. Ada and Sally will be waiting," said Mac Arthur.

Jackson handed the tag to Mac Arthur, who went to get the loading equipment to pull the crate from the water. When they were alone, Sanchez asked Jackson to come to his office.

Jackson thought now the real problems begin, but was totally surprised when they entered the office and Sanchez said, "Welcome, Herr Stevens."

Jackson stood there and looked hard at the little man, stalling, not really knowing what to say. He decided to go along with the charade.

"After my unusual arrival, you have been too kind, Senor Sanchez," said Jackson.

"I assume you have no papers or passport, Herr Stevens?" said Sanchez.

"Regrettably, all was lost in the sinking, Mi Capitan," said Jackson.

"Since we are both doing our part for the German cause, I think I can help, but I will need some funds to make bribes and such. I believe perhaps 2000 pesos, equivalent to 20 German marks, will do," said Sanchez. Jackson knew the bribes were for Sanchez, but he had no choice.

Thinking quickly Jackson said, "My people should be contacting me within the week and I will obtain the necessary funds and bring them to you," replied Jackson.

"How will they know of your situation, Herr Stevens?" asked Sanchez.

Playing his part to the hilt, Jackson said, "We know everything that goes on in your port."

"I see, I should not have been surprised, The Germans are very thorough," said Sanchez.

"Now back to business at hand. You will need to stop at the photographers on Angel Banciella on your way out of town for the passport photos. I will retrieve them from the photographer; he is also a friend of the Axis. Let us agree on your vital statistics. You were born in Puerto Deseado in the Province of Santa Cruz on March 1, 1910. You are the son of a fisherman and his wife. You are an Argentine citizen by birth. No visas or other documents are required that way," said Sanchez.

"It is the Port Capitan who is very thorough," said Jackson.

"You are very kind, Herr Stevens. May I ask you to be very careful not to be confronted by an overzealous policeman before you receive your passport? I would not be able to help. It may take an extra day or two to obtain the passport, so would it be convenient for you to return in ten days, rather than a week?" asked Sanchez.

"That would be splendid. May I ask who is my benefactor is? Mr. Mac Arthur, he seems to have a lot of influence that I was not aware of," asked Jackson.

"Surely, Herr Stevens, Mr. Mac Arthur owns the largest estancia, employs the most workers and spends the most money in our town, other than the naval base of course. He also supports all the local charitable organizations. His charity extends to all the local workers. For example, if one of the fishermen or dockworkers is injured or killed, he helps their families with jobs, food and sometimes money. He sells his beef, leather and wool to both the Axis and the Allied countries and is very prosperous, but I believe he politically aligns himself with the Allies. That's just an opinion," said Capitan Sanchez.

"You have been very kind and provided a wealth of assistance to me, Captain. It will not be forgotten and will be reported to Berlin," smiled Jackson.

"Thank you, Herr Stevens, it has been my pleasure. Now, if you require nothing further, I should attend to my duties," beamed Sanchez.

Jackson said, "I will see you again in ten days' time, Mi Capitan," and walked out of the office.

Jackson was shaking his head and laughing when Mac Arthur opened the door of the Mercedes truck for him.

"You found something amusing in dealing with that little horse's ass?" asked Mac Arthur.

Jackson thought for a moment, then asked, "How long a trip do we have this afternoon?"

"A couple of hours, why?" asked Mac Arthur with a smile on this face.

"It may take that long to stop laughing. Do you know where the photographer's place is on Angel Banciella? I need to stop there for a passport photo," said Jackson.

"Sure, it's on the way out of town. If you're able to get a passport after being in this country for less than an hour, I really would like to know how. That has to be an interesting story, Jack," said Mac Arthur.

"More like unbelievable, Graham," stated Jack.

Mac Arthur stopped in front of a small photography studio, located in an old downtown commercial building made of bricks. The street frontage of each individual business was painted a different bright pastel color. The photograph studio was yellow. He entered the central aisle of the building; Jackson noticed a bronze plaque inlaid in the brick, stating the building had been built in 1874.

Jackson had two photos taken, mentioned that the Port Captain would be along to pick them up, to which he received a knowing nod and left. The process took less than ten minutes.

Jackson wanted to believe the Capitan was right, that Mac Arthur was an Allied sympathizer and might help get Jackson back home.

During the long, somewhat monotonous ride through the grass plains to the Estancia, Jackson told his story as it had occurred. He tried to remember all the innuendos, posturing and lies just as they had happened.

Mac Arthur, in turn, smiled, laughed and sat quietly listening and thinking. When Jackson had completed his story, the Scot drove on in silence, for what seemed to Jackson to be a half hour, before deciding to comment.

"As you've discovered, there are many Nazi supporters in Argentina. Some are more open about it than others, but their percentage of the population is very high and reaches to the top levels of government," said Mac Arthur.

"Was Sanchez correct in thinking you are not an admirer of the Third Reich?" asked Jackson.

"I'll deny it if you repeat it, but the Captain is correct. How do you stand on politics, Jack?' asked Mac Arthur.

"As you say, I'll deny it if you repeat it, but I'm firmly behind the Allies. I'm a United States Marine or ex-Marine. I believe the US will be in the war sooner rather than later. I'd like to go home to be of service to my country, but that's out of the question now," stated Jackson.

"Thanks for sharing your story, Jack. I thought it might be something like that. I had you pegged as a military man right after we landed at Río Gallegos. How you described the attack without hyperbole, how you had managed to stay alive on the crate, how you utilized your knife to survive and your handling of the Port Captain, all indicated you were trained in survival of all kinds," said Mac Arthur."

Jackson just shrugged.

"We are almost to the outer gate, then just another half an hour and we will be at the house. Let me tell you about the Estancia and how it came into being? We will talk politics later, okay?" asked Mac Arthur.

Jackson didn't reply. He was deep in thought about what this meant to his future.

Graham began, not waiting for a reply, "I was the second son, so I would have lived a life working, first, for my father and, then, my older brother. It was customary for my father's holdings to go to the oldest son. It was just how it was always done.

"Our family owned sheep, dairy cows and horses. We weren't a large operation, by Scottish standards, but we were profitable. Our farm would have provided for all our families.

"I began to feel that war was inevitable and really didn't want any part of being in the British Military. It seemed to me, at the time, that it was just another round of fighting between old enemies. The old colonial powers were going to war again, not Scottish farmers.

"I had read an article in the newspaper about Argentina. At the time they were granting Patagonian land to European farmers. It painted a picture of endless grasslands, blue skies and bright futures for all those possessing of farming skills that were sorely needed in Argentina.

"I pondered my situation in Scotland and what it would be like in Argentina for months. At Christmas time in 1912, Ada, my wife told me I was to be a father. I had expected this, but it was still quite a reality shock. This blessing changed everything. If I stayed in Scotland I would never leave and my family would never be truly free. I tried to talk with my father about Argentina, but he wouldn't hear of my leaving. He said I was being foolish and reckless putting my family in danger. I gave up seeking his approval.

"I had spent hours wondering how Ada would respond. I worked on my 'selling her the idea', but it wasn't needed. I just shared my thoughts about our future in Scotland and Argentina with Ada and with her usual calm she said 'Whatever you think is best for our family, Graham, I'll support any decision you make. But Argentina sounds very exciting.'

"W.J. Mc Alistair was the agent handling the transport and land grants for the Argentine government. I contacted him and made arrangements for my family and two hundred sheep to begin a new life in Argentina.

"We sailed on, March 13, 1913, my four month pregnant wife, myself and two hundred sheep. The sheep were the only support I would receive from my family. I think my mother shamed my father and older brother into giving me the sheep; I'm sure against their better judgment. I think she understood why I needed to leave, but wouldn't say so in front of my father. It was a very patriarchal society at that time.

"The seven week crossing was very difficult for Ada and the sheep. She had 'Mal de mere' or maybe it was morning sickness every day, but she kept a positive attitude and never complained. We lost 29 sheep to various causes during the trip.

"We landed in Buenos Aires and were transferred to a coastal freighter. It took another week to finally reach our destination of Rio Gallegos.

"We spent another week arranging supplies, horses and wagons. It was almost three days before we were actually on our initial 2000 hectare farm.

"Our first son was born in one of those wagons. The house would not be completed for another two months. I wanted a 'respectable' house for my Ada, not a squatter's shack.

"Well, it seems I timed the telling of that tale pretty well. See the tall trees there on the horizon? That's the wind break around our compound. We're almost there."

"That was some story, Graham. You should be very proud of what you've built," said Jackson.

Graham just smiled and grunted.

He brought the truck to a stop in front of a wrought iron gate in a six foot high wall that surrounded the compound. Jackson jumped out, opened the gate, then closed it when Graham pulled through.

Graham pulled up to a row of small mud brick buildings, which backed up to the trees and faced the interior of the compound. There was a wind mill and water tower at the end of the row. They stopped in front of the last building and Graham motioned for Jack to get out.

Jack was confused. He could see the "big house" and he had been given the idea that he would be staying there. Was this some kind of trick to get him and his crate out to the middle of nowhere, and for what reason?

Deadly Marriage

Graham climbed down, left the door open and walked around the front of the big Mercedes truck. When he saw Jackson's confusion written on his face he started to laugh.

"Sorry, Jack, but I can't be taking you into Miss Ada's house smelling like you do. You're pretty pungent you know and, in fact, let's let the truck air out while you get cleaned up. The cab of the truck smells worse than the sheep pens," said Graham, still chuckling.

Graham was having such a good time, that he got Jack to laughing at himself. Jack realized he had had much more pressing issues to think about than how he smelled, up until that very minute in any case.

A short, round, stern looking older woman, probably an Indian Jack thought, came out of the little house.

Graham introduced Jack to the old woman, with the beautiful name of Carmen. She greeted Graham with what appeared to be a smirk, but was probably a smile. "Buenos Dias, Senor Mac," she scowled at Jackson.

"He stinks worse than sheep dip," said Carmen.

Jackson didn't understand what she had said, but Graham was having trouble catching his breath, he was laughing so hard. It took him a few minutes to regain his composure.

Jack understood a few words as "Senor Mac" told Carmen what was needed.

"Senor Mac, I like it, but I'm not sure about you. What was so funny?" asked Jackson.

"She thought you smelled worse than sheep dip," said Graham.

"What's sheep dip?" asked Jack.

"You'll find out soon enough, but for now, believe me it stinks. I'd love to stay and watch this, but I better get up to the big house and check in," said Graham.

Jack found out what Carmen's function at the compound was. She did laundry and supervised the bathing of the children, while the parents were working.

She, then, turned and started to enter the little house. Jackson started to follow, only to have Carmen put up both hands, in a definite sign to stop. She, then, led Jackson around back to a row of five pipes with shower heads dropping from a larger pipe. Each had a back splash towards the row of houses, a shower head and a chain.

Carmen, standing at least six feet from Jackson, illustrated with hand movements that he should take off his clothes and start bathing.

Jackson looked around the splash board of the first "shower" and found rough yellow soap, brushes and towels. Jackson did as he was told.

The water was cold, not like the Atlantic, but cold. The homemade soap didn't suds well, but accomplished its purpose. He realized he felt much better with the salt, dirt and grime washed from his body. He used a rough brush on his finger nails, feet and hair. His hair hadn't been this long in eleven years.

Jackson dried himself with the prickly towel and then wrapped it around his waist. He stepped around the splash board to find Carmen, with her sadistic grin. She had arranged a small table with a straight razor, soap cup, scissors, hand mirror and a chair. Carmen motioned for him to sit in the chair. Jackson reached for the mirror and got his hand slapped like a naughty child.

Jackson sat down as he was ordered, hoping there wouldn't be any blood spilling. Carmen took his head in both her small calloused hands and turned it to get a better look. This got Jackson to thinking.

He hadn't had the opportunity to grow a beard or mustache since he began shaving in the Corps. Before he joined the Corps he was in school and wasn't allowed any facial hair either. His parents would have had a fit, in any case. Maybe a beard would help as a disguise.

He motioned to his upper lip and around his chin trying to explain that he wanted it left on. She nodded her understanding and approval. "Muy bien, Senor," she said and gave Jackson the first and last real smile he would see.

Deadly Marriage

Carmen was an expert with the straight razor and surprisingly gentle, now that she had agreed on how to "clean up" Jackson. In less time than it took Jackson to shave with a safety razor, she had trimmed his beard, mustache and cut his hair. She handed him the mirror.

The face staring back didn't look like Jackson. His skin was burned, his lips cracked and his eyes looked sunken in his skull. The "high and tight" was now the same length as the rest of his hair. The first time facial hair was neat and showed promise. All in all, it was the best that could be expected. He had suffered on the sea.

Chapter 5

Jackson formally thanked Carmen, but she waved it off, as if it was nothing. When he asked for his clothes she turned and entered the house. She came back with a set of new clothes, his knife, everything from his pockets and his boots, which were now cleaned and shined. He thanked her again, but asked about his clothes.

She pointed to the other end of the row of houses where smoke was emanating from a black fire pit. His clothes were no more. His new clothes consisted of an undergarment cut off at the thigh with short sleeves, a white shirt with puffy sleeves, black puffy legged pants, Jackson thought of as Gaucho pants, his own Sam Brown belt, which he thought she had burned. Carmen held up each article of clothing for Jackson to put on, made sure it fit correctly and made no sign she was embarrassed by Jackson's nudity. Somehow it didn't bother Jackson either.

As Jackson was lacing up his boots, Carmen brought out a little boy about 5 and told him to take Jackson to the "Casa Grande."

Impulsively Jackson kissed the top of Carmen's head. This started Carmen squawking and waving her arms as if to swat a swarm of bees. The boy grabbed Jackson's hand and pulled him away, laughing.

As he walked, Jackson took in the details of what he now thought of as the compound. Besides the row of worker houses, there was what looked like an eight car garage at least twelve feet high, stables and several other unidentifiable buildings, all this surrounded by the block wall and protected by the 50' trees. There was a formal circular driveway leading to the entry of the "Casa Grande." All along the front were flower beds with roses of many colors and other flowers Jackson couldn't name and tall palm trees that gave the appearance of columns he had seen on Southern Plantations. The effect was beautiful.

Deadly Marriage

The "Casa Grande" had two stories, with large verandas on all sides, red tile roofs and colorful polished ceramic tile walkways. The construction was made of some kind of blocks covered with a type of plaster patch and rocks. The rocks were used as decoration thought Jackson. There were benches and comfortable looking armchairs made of cowhide and some kind of light colored wood spaced out on the verandas. All the windows had heavy storm shutters that seemed out of place. He guessed the house to be one hundred feet wide, but couldn't tell how deep. Compared to the homes he knew in Rio Pecos, Texas, this was a mansion.

As he mounted the entry steps, he heard a growl coming from the shadows. The little boy stopped and didn't move. Jackson did likewise.

Soon the front door was opened by a beautiful young lady. Jackson thought she could be somewhere between 17 and 20, Jack hadn't gotten any better at guessing ages. She was tall, about 5'7", with long blond hair parted down the middle, bright blue eyes and dressed much as Jackson himself was dressed. She spoke into the shadows until a very large furry dog came regally walking out.

"You would be Mr. Stevens?" she questioned in charming faintly Scottish tainted English.

"Yes, I am Jack Stevens," said Jackson.

"Well, Mr. Stevens, you had better make friends with the Queen."

She spoke to the dog first, "your highness" this is our new friend Jack Stevens. He is from America and has had a hard journey. Do you think you could find pity for this poor traveler in your kind and generous heart?"

For the dog's part, it came over to Jackson, sniffed at his hand and wagged her tail. Jackson rubbed its ears and thanked the Queen for her generous hospitality.

"Now I will finish the introductions, I'm Sally Mac Arthur. It's nice to meet you, Mr. Stevens"

"It's very nice to meet you Sally, please call me Jack and thanks for saving me from the Queen. What kind of dog is she?" said Jackson.

"She's a Scottish deerhound and the whole introduction is just a game she likes to play, it's the only time I hear her growl. She loves people. If someone wasn't home to play the game with her, she would have come out to meet you, barking and wanting to play. She's not much of a watchdog. I think little Juan here was having fun at your expense too, making like he was afraid of the Queen. Won't you please come in, Jack?" said Sally.

Jackson frowned at Juan and shook his fist at him, which sent little Juan running away laughing and then followed Sally into the "Casa Grande."

The Queen led the way, she was obviously a house dog, a very large house dog, but a house dog none the less, thought Jackson.

The entry was paved in colorful ceramic tiles, and was the size of the Jackson family's living room. On the right was the staircase to the second story. It was made of dark wood steps covered with green carpet and had a solid block rail support, with the same kind of dark wood rail. Before he could further survey his surroundings he was led through double doors immediately to the right of the entry door.

This was a room approximately 30x40 feet, with bookshelves covering the far end wall, full of leather bound books. A very large, hand carved desk made of what looked like mahogany sat regally in front of the bookshelves. On the desk was a green blotter with leather corners, two matching lamps made of bull horns and two telephones. There was a large table in the center of the room with large heavy ornate coaches, armchairs and wrought iron standing lamps with colorful woven shades surrounding it. The walls were covered with paintings of the Patagonian landscape.

"This is my father's study. He runs all our businesses from here. He asked me to make you comfortable until he returns.

Deadly Marriage

Please have a seat, could I get you something to eat or drink, Jack?" asked Sally.

Jackson was awestruck. What did her statement about businesses, plural, mean? Why had this very wealthy man brought him into his home? So he didn't come across like an idiot zombie, again, he asked for a whiskey.

Sally laughed and asked, "Scotch, Irish, Bourbon or Rye or if you prefer we make a wonderful local cognac, Jack."

Jack found her laugh to be charming and sensual.

"I'm not used to drinking cognac, so I better stick to Scotch, thank you," said Jack.

Sally walked behind the desk; put her hand under the edge. Within thirty seconds an older lady who Jackson thought could be Carmen's twin came through a door from the interior of the house.

Sally ordered two Scotches and beef sandwiches in rapid fire Spanish. Jackson understood about every other word.

"I've never been in a room like this, it's wonderful," said Jackson honestly.

"It wasn't always this nice. It was originally the entire house. Father kept adding on over the years, as the family and income grew, to what we have now," said Sally.

"Argentina has been good to your family."

"Argentina is all we children have ever known. All of us were born in this house, except my oldest brother, who was born in a wagon out front by the gate. It's our home!"

The old woman brought the drinks and huge sandwiches on thick dark bread and a bottle of red wine.

After Sally had thanked her and she had left the room Jackson asked, "Is that Carmen's sister?"

This brought about a laughing fit from Sally. When she had controlled her laughing she said, "That's not her sister, Amelia is Carmen's daughter. If you had said that to Amelia, she would have hated you forever and if you said that to Carmen you might have actually gotten on her good side. We don't see Carmen's good side too often, as you might have noticed," said Sally.

"Yeah, so I found out. I'm totally charmed and you're much prettier than your father, but I feel I should thank him for all he's done for me. When do think he will return?" asked Jackson.

"He will return when Asa fulfills her duty. Asa is one of our Arabian mares, who at the moment is dropping her first foal. It's in the hands of the horse god. If you're really as charmed as you say, you won't mind keeping me company a little while longer?" smiled Sally.

Jackson blushed and realized that this beautiful young lady was toying with him and he was enjoying it immensely.

"Then, if I must, I'll just relax and be the lecherous old man I am. Tell me about your life here on the Estancia," said Jackson.

Now it was Sally's turn to blush, which caused Jackson to laugh out loud.

"Touché, I guess I deserved that, but I don't believe you're as nice as my father thinks you are," and laughed.

"I never claimed to be nice, but I really would like to know about your life on the Estancia."

Sally looked into his eyes. "I think I might believe you, but before I forget; have Carmen shave your beard. You look like a pirate. The mustache is very macho though, I like it."

"Yes, Ma'am, I'll see that Carmen fulfills your wishes at the earliest opportunity. Now, about your life story," said Jack.

"Only if you promise to tell me about yourself when I'm done," countered Sally.

"You'll be bored, but anything to please my lady," said Jackson gallantly.

"I guess you know how my mother and father came to Argentina?"

Jack nodded his concurrence.

"I was born in the upstairs bedroom in 1920. I was told that at the time, there was just this room and a newly completed bedroom on the second floor. My first memories were of my fifth birthday. My father gave me a pony and Umberto, the Estancia's foreman, gave me a tiny black sheep to take care of. My mother gave me dresses and dolls, but I never wore the

Deadly Marriage

dresses and I didn't play with the dolls. I learned English in the house and Spanish from the kids I played with.

"They started calling me a 'tomboy' and I guess I was. I loved the Estancia, the animals and the land.

"My two brothers and my sister, just wanted to get away and move to the city. Alfred and Cecil, my brothers, are both attending classes at Cambridge. My sister, Danielle, is just three years older than me. She went to Buenos Aires to college, found a husband and hasn't been back in two years."

She paused as if she was finished.

"You must have left the Estancia sometimes, to school, dances, something? What about boys chasing you around the pampas?"

"I stayed in Rio Gallegos during high school, in a dormitory and hated it. The other girls seemed silly to me. All they thought about was boys, football and partying. As far as boys go, I met a boy and we became semi-serious, but he was of German ancestry and kept pushing the Nazis on me, so I stopped seeing him. It seems I'm only happy here on the Estancia. Now, how about you Jack?"

For some reason, Jack felt he should tell the whole sordid story, with the exception of Lieutenant Decker. He told Sally about his parents, his life in Rio Pecos, about Juanita and about how he got shanghaied into the Marine Corps. How he received his "Dear John" letter and how it affected him. He explained how he had gotten wounded and eluded to his being released from the Corps because of it. That led to a version of why he was working on the *John's II*. The tale of his escape and rescue finished his tale.

Sally sat in the armchair facing Jack, just staring at him. Finally, she shook her head and said, "That was quite a story, Jack. I'm sorry life has been so hard. I feel like I haven't experienced anything after hearing your tale."

Jack just shrugged.

"Would you like another Scotch, Jack? I think I could use one," said Sally.

"That sounds great to me. Talking makes me thirsty," said Jack.

Sally left the room this time. She came back with the Scotch bottle, an ice bucket and a soda bottle.

As Sally was fixing their drinks, little Juan came running in.

"Miss Sally, Senor Mac says that Asa is being stubborn, but he'll be back as soon as possible."

"Tell him we are fine and not to worry, I'll keep Mr. Stevens entertained." Sally smiled at Jack and winked again.

Juan ran back out of the room and Jack could hear a door slam in the rear of the "Casa Grande".

It was beginning to get dark. At the end of the year Argentina has its longest days. It was after ten when Sally started turning on a few of the lamps.

They sat up until after 1:00 talking, adding more details to their life stories and drinking Scotch. Sally told him about her life in detail and Jack did the same. He told her things he hadn't shared with anyone, ever.

Finally, Sally said, "I'm sorry, Jack, I can't remember when I've enjoyed an evening more, but I get up early and I'm exhausted. I think I better show you to your room, so we can both get some sleep."

"No, I should be the one to apologize. I was just enjoying our talk so much I didn't pay attention to the time."

"Let's do this again Jack, okay?" said Sally.

"I look forward to it, Sally," answered Jack.

Sally led Jack up the stairs and to the end of a hall that ran parallel to the front of the house. She opened the door and said "You should be comfortable here. I'll see you in the morning. Thanks for the great evening," she, then, reached up on her toes and kissed Jack on the cheek. She, then, turned quickly and walked down the hall.

Jack was left with the feeling of her kiss on his cheek, the sweet smell of her hair and feeling of her body stretched out against his. It took Jack a long time to get to sleep.

When he awoke he surveyed his new surroundings. The room was large, with large heavy wooden furniture and drapes that blocked out the sun. Jack opened the drapes and let in the bright sun light. Now he could see the walls had been painted a sand color and all the trim was in dark brown. The floor was covered with a wool rug in a bright red, yellow and orange pattern. There was a chest of drawers with a wash basin and pitcher.

Jackson washed up, dressed and went in search of the head. He found the bathroom two doors down from his room. He availed himself of the facilities and headed downstairs.

He ran into a pretty, middle-aged blond woman in an apron starting up the stairs, an image of Sally at middle age.

"Hello, Mr. Stevens, I'm Ada Mac Arthur. Merry Christmas and welcome to our home," she said as she offered him her hand.

Jack shook her hand and said, "It's a pleasure to meet you, Mrs. Mac Arthur and thank you for your hospitality."

"It's our pleasure. Would you please join us in the Living?" she asked. She showed him across the entry and through another set of double doors.

The Living, Argentineans dropped the word room as was the practice of the time in Europe, was exactly like the study, but more comfortable and decorated for the season. Graham Mac Arthur, in pajamas, housecoat and slippers, was sitting in large armchair with his feet on an ottoman and eggnog in his hand.

"Have a seat, Jack. Sorry I missed you last night, but Asa didn't drop her foal until two this morning. We're trying to establish an Arabian breeding program and Asa is our first successful breeding attempt. I hope Sally didn't bore you too much," he said.

Mrs. Mac Arthur interrupted asking Jack if he cared for eggnog.

Jack shook his head and said, "Thank you, but no thanks. I think I drank enough Scotch last night to keep me pickled for a month."

"If you change your mind or would like something to eat, just let Amelia know. I need to excuse myself and check to see how the preparations are coming along," said Mrs. Mac Arthur as she left.

"Graham, I wasn't bored for a second. On the contrary, she's a very entertaining young lady. I suggest that I probably learned more about your family in one evening with Sally than I could talking to you for a month, besides she's much prettier than you are," Jack said smiling.

Graham laughed, "That she is Jack, that she is. You noticed she takes after her mother."

"And thank God for small favors," said Jack chuckling.

"You must feel better, you're getting pretty feisty, Jack?" said Graham trying to make a face like he was insulted, but it was obvious he was enjoying the banter.

"Thanks to you and Sally, I am."

"You 'am' what Jack?" asked Sally from the door. She stood in the door wearing an off the shoulder peasant blouse, which showed off her smooth tanned shoulders, and a matching flowing skirt of finely embroidered white cotton and her blond hair braided down her back. Jack tried not to stare.

Finally, Jack got his tongue back and said, "That I am feeling better, even a little feisty, if you believe your father."

"I always believe my father," she said as she walked over and kissed the top of his head.

"I must get back to the mausoleum. We will start the festivities in about a half hour. I just wanted to say hi and see if you had a hangover this morning?"

"Please call it what it is, a solarium not a mausoleum, Sally."

"Sorry Daddy. Now, answer my question, Jack." said Sally.

"I'm much better than I deserve to be, but as I remember you refilled your glass as often as you refilled mine. How do you feel?" asked Jack.

"I feel great. I was just worried since you're so much older and you've just been through such a harrowing experience, you might not be feeling too well," she said.

Then, Graham and Sally broke out laughing. Jack threw up his hands and said, "I give, you win, I surrender!"

Deadly Marriage

"Oh, poor Jack, did I hurt your feelings? You know it's said 'you only hurt the one you love,' Jack," she said as she moved to the side of Jack's chair, leaned over and kissed the top of his head, then scampered out of the room laughing.

Graham noticed Jack blushing and said, "Very interesting" under his breath.

Wanting to break the spell Sally's kiss had left on the room, Graham said, "We better get dressed, Jack. Amelia laid out an appropriate outfit for you to wear. It should be in your room by now. I'll meet you here in twenty minutes and we'll sneak a drink. I think you will need one, at least I always find it helpful."

Jack had no idea what time it was. The Living had no clock; it was a room for relaxing and family conversations, not worrying about time. When he got to his room he noticed a small alarm clock next to his bed. The hands weren't turning; it had run down at some point.

Amelia had done as Graham suggested. His "dress" outfit was laid out on the bed. It consisted of dark brown bombachas (pants), a white billowy sleeved shirt, alpargatas (canvas shoes with rope soles) and a faja (brightly colored waist band). As he was dressing he thought how he had no control of his life. He dressed as he was told, went where he was told. He questioned why this didn't disturb him.

Sally was her own person, not just a beautiful woman. She knew what made her happy and was going to have it. She had awakened dormant thoughts of a having a future, a future he thought had died with Juanita's "Dear John" letter.

He found a safety razor and soap on the dresser next to the wash basin. He proceeded to shave off his new beard as Sally had directed. He didn't know where his life was taking him, but it didn't matter, he was happy this Christmas morning.

Graham was standing in the Living pouring Scotch into two crystal glasses; he added ice and a splash of soda to each. He handed one to Jack and said, "To your good health, Jack."

"And to yours, Graham." replied Jack.

They looked at each other, both wondering what was happening between them. Jack didn't understand Graham's generosity and concern. Graham didn't understand Jack's motivations towards Sally, himself and his new country. There was much to discuss, but first there was the Christmas celebrations to attend to.

Jackson hadn't realized how large the "Casa Grande" really was. They walked down the hall that split the house into two separate wings. He guessed the house to be about 100 feet by 100 feet, 10,000 sq. ft. on each floor.

When they reached the back of the house they stepped out onto the veranda. There was a large canvas sunshade covering rows and rows of tables and benches. The tables were filled with happy laughing people.

As Graham stood on the edge of the veranda shouts of "Patron!" were heard from the crowd.

Graham stood there and waved, while Jack eased back into the shadows. When the crowd had settled down and become quiet, Graham welcomed all his guests, thanked them for joining his family for this year's Christmas celebration, then introduced Father McDona and asked the good Father to lead them in prayer.

Father McDona began by thanking all those who had been able to attend Midnight Mass the previous evening. He turned his head slightly and glared at Graham. Graham shrugged and smiled. He, then, blessed all the attendees, the Patron and his family.

He, then, said a prayer in Latin that most of the crowd, including Jackson, could not understand. Then it seemed the priest repeated it in Spanish. Jackson just understood when all those assembled said amen.

Graham followed the priest down the middle aisle between the rows of tables to the head table. Jackson, who was still standing in the shadows, noticed Sally getting up and heading his way down the side aisle. She saw him looking and waved to him wanting him to follow her back to the head table.

Jackson was uncomfortable with the entire ceremony and was not happy to be sitting at the head table with the priest, the

Deadly Marriage

Patron and the family. He was not a religious man and had only been enlightened to the ways of Southern Baptists.

He felt some relief when Sally indicated for him to sit by her in the last seat on the family side of the large table. The family sat on the right half of the head table and the priest, Umberto and his family on the left half.

A team of waiters brought trays of side dishes to the end of each row of tables. From the side aisles the dishes were passed from one person to the next down the length of the tables. People started laughing and talking again. When this had been completed large ceramic pitchers of wine were passed down. With this act the volume of chatter got much louder.

The crowd went quiet when Graham rose and asked the Father to rise. As soon as they had risen, two large portable barbeques, on full-sized automobile tires, were rolled in front of the head table. One came from each side until they met in the middle.

To Jackson it seemed like the one from the left held what a complete steer on a spit being turned by two young men. The other held four huge birds (rheas) that looked like ostriches.

The father blessed the food and drink, somewhat quickly, thought Jackson. Then el Patron told everyone to eat and enjoy, which caused applause and cheering to break out.

Sally leaned over and said, "You made it through the hard part, now we can relax and enjoy our dinner and the rest of the celebration."

Jackson tried to help by trying to pour wine for everyone, but only made it to Sally's glass before she stopped him.

"Handing the food and drink the length of the table is family tradition. I'm told it started well before I was born, so just sit there, relax and enjoy," said Sally.

"Yes Ma'am. This is really overwhelming, Sally. I'm just a poor small town boy. I pictured maybe 10-20 people when your father first described this get together. There must be 200 people here," said Jackson.

"Actually there are 213, including our special guest, let's see, that would be you! So please relax! Our family wants you here and I especially want you right here," said Sally laying her hand on Jackson's hand.

Jackson looked at Sally's hand and then looked up smiling. Miss Ada saw him smiling and grinned. Jackson blushed, again, and moved his hand away.

Things were happening too fast thought Jackson. I think I'm falling for Sally and she seems to feel the same, but I don't know what my future holds or if I even have a future.

After the feast was consumed to everyone's satisfaction, a Chamamé band started playing and more wine was dispensed from a barrel on a hand truck. The priest made his exit to allow the more pious among the revelers to enjoy themselves and let go.

Sally tried to teach Jackson the native country folk dances, with other than complete success and much laughter.

People started to leave in large numbers as the sun set. Graham dismissed the band shortly thereafter. The Graham Mac Arthur family, the Umberto Gonzalez family and Jackson went into the house and entered the Living.

Sally hung back by the door and grabbed Jackson's arm. She whispered, "Another ritual begins. Father will give Umberto his yearly bonus and Umberto will argue that it is too much and that Father is being too generous. Father, then, will explain Umberto's accomplishments for the year and how grateful we all are for his efforts. Then Umberto will humbly accept the bonus and he and his family will leave. This takes place the same way every year," said Sally.

It took about five minutes, but Sally was right. Umberto went through all the procedure she had described, finally accepted his bonus, thanked each family member, shook Jackson's hand, gathered his family and left.

"Well, that's done for another year. Would anyone care to join me for an after dinner cognac?" asked Graham.

Deadly Marriage

"Just a small one for me, then you and I are going to bed and leave the young people alone. It's been a long day," said Miss Ada.

Graham grinned while he was pouring the cognac, looked at Jack and Sally then said, "I'm not sure I trust Mr. Stevens with our Sally." Jackson blushed again.

"I'm not sure I trust our Sally with Mr. Stevens!" said Miss Ada giggling. Sally turned bright red at her mother's remark and everyone laughed.

Graham and Miss Ada said good night and went upstairs. They were both smiling and holding hands.

Sally said she would be right back and went to the study. She returned with a rectangular box about 15 inches long and two inches wide, wrapped in bright red Christmas paper.

She came and sat on the arm of Jack's chair. She handed him the package and said, "I hope you like our gift, it's from our whole family?" she said.

Jack opened the package and opened the box. The contents were wrapped in a white velvet draw string bag. Jack opened the bag and found an obviously old knife in a heavy leather sheath. The handle was made of dark brown wood and was worn and polished from use. When he drew it from the sheath he found it had a blade made of the fine steel and was razor sharp.

"It's beautiful, Sally, but you shouldn't have. I assume there's a story to go along with this fine knife?" questioned Jack.

"Actually, I was surprised when I asked Father for something we could give you for a Christmas present that he suggested this Facon. It means a lot to him.

"The story goes that Umberto and Father were camping out while checking for stray cattle and sheep. Sometime in the early morning Father's first Scottish deerhound, King started growling waking them both up.

"Four bandits attacked from four different directions. The King caught the nearest bandit and locked onto his arm with his teeth. After being warned, Father and Umberto were able to shoot the other bandits, without being harmed. When they turned to the bandit King had caught he was lying on his back, unable to move with King still clamped to his arm. He had killed the King with that very Facon and was waving it at Father. Father shot him on the spot. You must remember the Pampas was a very wild country in those days.

"They buried the bandits the next day and Father gave Umberto all their gear except that Facon. He said it reminded him that without the King, he and Umberto would probably be dead and rotting in the grass. It has been locked in his desk since he brought it home" said Sally.

"I can't accept this, it means too much to your father," stated Jack.

"Jack, I'm not sure why he was willing to part with the Facon, but it was his idea and I think he would be offended if you refused his gift."

"I'll talk to him about it, I need to talk of many things with him," said Jack.

"Jack, I don't want my mother wondering what we're doing. Would you mind if we called it a night?" asked Sally.

"That is probably a very good idea, I do mind, but it is still what we should do," said Jack.

When they had reached Jack's room Sally came into his arms, pressed her body against his and kissed him passionately. Jack, after a few moments, finally broke the kiss and said, "I don't think we should have done that."

"Maybe not, but I wanted to and so did you," she said as she turned laughing and started down the hall to her room.

She called out over her shoulder, "Pleasant dreams, Jack."

Again, Jack would have a hard time going to sleep.

Chapter 6

30 November 1939
Office of Obergruppenfuhrer von Richter
Danzig Germany (Poland)

Obergruppenfuhrer (Major General) Meinhard Egon von Richter sat at his ornate oak highly polished desk, deep in thought. This troublesome day he didn't notice the beautiful view of Danzig and the river his office afforded.

Reichfuhrer SS Himmler had called him from his office in Berlin to personally reemphasize that von Richter's assignment was crucial to the war effort and was being scrutinized by Hitler himself.

This had not been a usual occurrence in von Richter's career. Himmler was either conveying a concern or a warning, he didn't know which.

He went home that evening and called his wife in Düsseldorf.

"Hello, Letta, how are you?" asked von Richter.

"Meinhard darling, I'm fine, it is good of you to call."

He hadn't called as often as he should have. He had his responsibilities to the Reich and his personal covert mission. Anna also kept him happy and glad he wasn't home.

"How are the children?" He thought to himself, they aren't really children anymore. All were either away at school or had lives of their own. There were none left at home.

"As far as I know they're all fine. I don't hear from them regularly any more than you do," replied Letta somewhat sarcastically.

"Meinhard, is everything okay? You sound distant and distracted."

"I'm just busy, Letta. I should get back to my duties. Take care of yourself. I'll talk to you soon."

"You do the same, goodbye." Letta wanted to ask how Anna was, but didn't think it would help anything, just add more hostility.

W.R. Ziegler

******

Estancia Mac Arthur
Rio Gallegos, Argentina

Jack was jarred from a deep sleep when someone knocked on this door. He heard Graham say, "Sorry for waking you, Jack."

Jack opened the door and said, "No problem, Graham, what's up?"

"Umberto and I have to fly out to the vineyard, a small emergency. Sorry, but we will be gone most of the day and I wanted to get a chance to talk to you before I left, but it is something I have to do. How about breaking away from Sally long enough for us to talk after dinner tonight?"

"That sounds like a good idea, we have a lot to discuss, Graham," said Jack.

Graham looked at Jack seriously, not sure just what Jack was alluding to.

Then, changing the subject, Graham said, "You might want to spend the time finding what's in your crate. It's been put in the garage, Sally can show you. I'm probably as curious about its contents as you are, Jack."

Jack dressed and went downstairs. He found Amelia in the kitchen with the cook. Amelia asked if Jack wanted breakfast.

Jack answered slowly in his broken Spanish, "Thank you, but not right now, Amelia. Could you please direct me to the garage, it would be appreciated?"

Smiling, Amelia walked him to the backdoor and pointed to the building Jack had guessed would be garages when he first got to the compound.

The doors to the garages were not locked. Inside he found an old heavy duty Ford four wheel drive pickup truck, an older Mercedes Benz four door sedan and a new Ford wood sided station wagon. At the far end sat his crate, just as it had been pulled out of the water.

Jackson walked around his crate trying to figure out the best way to examine the interior.

Deadly Marriage

He decided to cut away the canvas and the underlying cover to see if the crate could be easily disassembled. After removing both layers, the crate looked very sturdily built and without finding some tools, it was easier to just enter from the top, as he had done on his voyage. For some reason Jack wasn't comfortable with tearing the crate apart in any case.

He climbed up the side of the crate, noting that something weighed enough in the bottom that it didn't tip with Jack's weight pulling on one side. He knew it wasn't just filled with pamphlets.

Jack dropped into the crate. He noticed now how bad it smelled. Erie thoughts and feelings surrounded Jack. He had to fight to stay inside.

The pamphlets fluttered to the ground as Jack started emptying the crate's contents. He thought he was just over half way empty, when Sally said, "You're sure making a mess, Jack. Wouldn't you rather just burn this Nazi trash?"

"Why, Miss Sally dear, how are you this fine morning?'

"If you must know, Mr. Stevens, I couldn't get to sleep right away last night, so I slept late this morning."

"I must have a clear conscious. I went right to sleep."

"You're a liar, Jack Stevens," she said laughing. She continued, "Seriously, should I get a fire barrel brought in to burn this propaganda?"

"Yes Ma'am. I still have at least a foot of propaganda to throw out."

Sally said, "Don't call me Ma'am, it makes feel as old as you are," and ran from the garages, when Jack made like he was getting out of the crate to come after her.

She came back a few minutes later with a 55 gal drum carried by two teenage boys. They set the barrel just outside of the open garage door so the smoke wouldn't get caught inside. As it turned out the drum would burn for hours.

Sally started the fire as the boys picked up the pamphlets. As they dropped them in the drum the flames could be seen over the drum edge.

Jack got down to boards that made up a false bottom for the crate. He asked Sally for a crowbar or a claw hammer. She, in turn, asked one of the boys to bring the tools and he took off at a trot.

He returned with both a crowbar and claw hammer. Jackson thanked him in his best formal Spanish. Jack thought of cutting into the crate while at sea with his knife. It was a long and arduous job he would remember for the rest of his life.

With the proper tools, it took Jack just a few minutes to remove the false bottom. Jack removed the inner liner and stopped. He was elated, confused and scared all at the same time.

"So, what did you find?" asked Sally.

Jack stayed in the crate for some minutes, thinking, before poking his head out and answering.

"I'm not sure, Sally. I am sure that I need to talk to your father as soon as possible. "

"What is it, Jack, you're scaring me?"

"Sally, I'm going to ask you to please trust me, at least until I can talk with Graham. You know I care for you and don't want you to be harmed in any way, believe me it may be dangerous for you to know what's left in here."

"Now I know I'm scared. I do trust you, why I don't know, but I do. I'll go call Father on the radio and ask him to come home as soon as possible."

When Sally returned, carrying a large canvas bag, she said, "Father says he is just about finished at the vineyard and should be back in about an hour. You looked like you wanted to stay in the crate, so I brought you some leftovers from yesterday and some wine, which you can have, only if you share it with me."

"Have I told you how wonderful you are today?'

"You've never told me 'how wonderful I am', any day, but thanks for noticing."

When they had finished they sat on the ground and made small talk, passing the time until Graham returned.

Deadly Marriage

Graham came in and asked Sally to let him talk to Jack in private. She reluctantly walked to the house and went inside.

"Jack, I believe I know what you found in the crate and thank you for not sharing your news with Sally."

"How could you know, Graham?"

"I can't say right now, but after dinner I'll answer all you questions. Sally said you asked her to trust you and now I'm asking you to trust me."

"I don't think it wise to leave the crate unguarded, Graham. You must agree if you really know what's inside."

"Jack, your crate has been under constant guard since we unloaded it off the truck. There have been two of my men on the roof of this garage, watching for anyone coming near it. They will stay there as long as you and I agree they should be."

"To quote your beautiful daughter 'I do trust you, why I don't know, but I do', at least until after dinner anyway."

Everyone except Miss Ada was quiet and reserved at dinner. They all had thoughts of their own.

Sally was thinking she had finally found someone she was really interested in and now he had secrets. She had only really kissed him once and known him for a couple of days, why was she so concerned?

Graham was thinking about how to handle Jack, what he thought about Sally and Jack and how much to tell Jack.

Jack didn't know what to think. He knew Graham had an agenda, but couldn't figure out what it was. He wanted to trust Sally and his feelings for Sally, but couldn't trust that she wasn't part of Graham's plans. He was in the habit of taking people at face value, but had learned that was naïve.

When they had finished dinner, Graham asked Jack if he would like to see the rest of the compound. This didn't make sense to Miss Ada, but she knew not to ask the obvious, Graham how are you going to show him anything in the dark? Both she and Sally said nothing when the men left taking a bottle of Scotch and two glasses with them.

They walked in silence out back, through an ornate wrought iron gate and then on through the wind break. To the left was what looked like an aircraft hangar and to the right what sounded like a power generating facility? There was also a single table, from the festivities of yesterday, set out in the open, twenty feet from the trees. Graham motioned for Jack to take a seat.

Graham poured them both a drink and then began.

"Jack, you found counterfeit printing plates for U.S. currency, didn't you?"

"Among other things, I thought you wanted me to trust you, Graham?"

"I do, Jack. What's the problem now?"

"You can tell Umberto to come out and join us or go home. I can smell his stinky ass cigars from a hundred yards."

Graham laughed, "I should have known. Umberto, thank you, but your services will not be needed tonight."

Umberto walked out of the shadows from the trees. He lit his stinky ass cigar, grinned at Jackson, extended the middle finger of his left hand in a universal sign of affection and walked off towards his house.

"Maybe I should share some of our history together, Jack. Umberto has been with me since I arrived in Argentina. I hired Umberto as a temporary guide, translator and business assistant. He had just returned from Buenos Aires where he had just completed his second enlistment in the Army. Under his tough, reckless Gaucho façade he is an intelligent and resourceful businessman. We didn't plan to become companions and partners, it just worked out that way. His "bonus" is the same every year: an amount equivalent to one percent of the profits of the Estancia. He is, as I'm sure you've noticed, very protective of me and my family. He is a good man and an even better friend."

"I have never heard him speak English, I would have never known, but I think I understand. I might have said something interesting in English, thinking he wouldn't understand, right?"

Graham gave Jack his now usual shrug. Jack was beginning to know Graham.

"Every officer needs his aide de camp. Tell me Graham, what force are you an officer of?"

"Jack, I'd much rather tell you my story my way, if that's acceptable?"

"Please, Graham, tell away."

"Jack, we live in very troubled times. My country is controlled by President Ortiz., who is controlled by Vice President Castillo, as I'm sure you are aware. Though they claim neutral status, they lean heavily towards the Nazi cause. Many members of the military and business class would rather see them removed from office and a pro-Argentina administration in power. These powerful individuals have started to organize and will take action if it becomes necessary. They call themselves the Grupo de Oficiales Unidos or G.O.U. I am proud to say that I am the head of this organization in our province."

Jack interrupted, "Graham, that really puts you and your family at risk, doesn't it?"

Graham smiled, "I'm happy to see I haven't misjudged you, Jack. Your first thought was for the safety of my family. Thank you, but to continue. I have been contacted by your Federal Bureau of Investigation. They are very interested in you and your crate. They have paid agents watching the harbor. They knew when I brought you in and every move you made until we entered the Estancia. I have told them I don't know anything about you, but I did tell them about the sinking of your ship. I was informed of what they thought was in your crate and that it should be protected. I don't really know what else is inside and you can tell me if you wish, but it's not necessary."

Jack absorbed all this and tried to make sense of all that he had been told and all that had happened to him since the sinking. Nothing was what it seemed.

It appeared Graham had said enough, they sat there sipping their Scotch in silence.

Jack said seriously, "Graham thanks for everything you've done for me, regardless of your motivations. I don't know how I fit into your plans or what you want from me, but I want you to know what I found in the crate, it might be important."

"There were the printing plates you mentioned, along with an assortment of South American currency and twenty gold bars weighing about twenty pounds each, stamped with German words and a Swastika."

Graham sat deep in thought for some time before saying, "Twenty German gold bars, huh Jack? That makes you a very wealthy young man. The FBI just knew about the printing plates, nothing else. In my opinion, the gold and money are yours to keep."

Graham pulled a pen from his shirt pocket and a slip of paper from his wallet and made some calculations.

"If my arithmetic is correct, your gold is worth almost 4,000,000 pesos or about 300,000 US Dollars!"

Jack was shocked. He just sat and stared at Graham.

Graham brought him out of his stupor when he said, "Jack, you asked what I wanted from you. At first, I just wanted to know if the crate you were riding on was the same crate the FBI was looking for. Then, after we talked and I understood a little about your background, I began to wonder if you might be convinced to help our cause and through it your country.

"All I can ask is that you think about it, Jack. Talk to Sally, she knows what problems our country faces with Ortiz and Castillo in power and is also concerned about Argentina's future. She acts like a school girl around you, but she really is an intelligent person and is aware of the position Argentina holds in the world situation."

"That brings up other problems I have, Graham. I don't know where I fit in the world right now. I don't know what to do with my feelings for Sally. If, as you say, it is really mine, I don't have a clue what to do with the loot from the crate. I don't even know if it's safe for the FBI to know I'm here."

"Well, Jack, as far as your feelings for Sally, that's between you two. No one can help you with that one. If you ever figure out what to do about the weaker sex, you'll be the first, my friend.

"I hate to think of my baby girl as an adult, but that's what she is. She will make her own decisions and I have confidence they will be good ones. I would just ask you to do your best not to hurt her.

"As far as your 'loot' goes, I can help with that, if you trust me?" Bringing that much wealth into the country is very illegal, but with the help of my bankers there are ways around that issue.

"Jack, as far as I know, all the FBI is aware of is your name and physical description. I'll make sure that it stays that way as best I can. If I hear anything else I'll let you know."

Jack leaned back and stretched his arms over his head and gazed at the stars. This is just too much to take in, he thought.

"Graham, I think my mind is overloaded. Can we talk again tomorrow, after I digest everything we've talked about tonight? I'll probably have a million questions for you by then."

"That is a wise suggestion, my friend. One more thing, Jack, my wife and my daughter don't know what I'm involved with and I would appreciate you not telling them, for their safety."

"Not that I totally understand what you're involved with, Graham, but they won't hear a word of it from me."

Jackson went upstairs to his room without joining the Mac Arthur family in the Living. He needed time to himself to think. He hadn't had much alone time since he arrived. Sally was a distraction that consumed his conscious mind and didn't let him think of much else. He locked the door for the first time.

He had removed what he thought of as his "Gaucho outfit" and gone to bed. He had gone to bed to think not sleep.

This is insane. I've only been on dry land for three days. I'm just now feeling healthy and able to walk without a seaman's gait. Now I think I'm in love, I may be wealthy, but I'm not sure yet and I'm skirting the edges of a revolt in a foreign country. I'm still a wanted man in the U.S. I'm no longer a Marine. Soon I'll be an Argentine citizen.

Come on, Jackson, think logically. What can't you do anything about? You can't change the fact you can't go home, either to the U.S.A or to the Corps, so put it out of your mind. Having said that in his mind shocked Jackson. He hadn't thought that through before, at least he hadn't come to a definite conclusion.

He felt a sense of loss and of being alone. He wasn't really afraid of starting a new life, that wasn't it. It was just sad how his life, as he had known it, could end so quickly and permanently. Jackson would have a hard time getting to sleep again.

Chapter 7

When Jackson awoke it was after ten. He got dressed quickly and went downstairs in search of the Mac Arthurs. That wasn't quite true; actually he wanted to see Sally. He finally found a live person in the kitchen, the cook.

"Good morning, how are you today?" said Jackson in his best Spanish.

"Very well, thank you," she replied.

"Where are all the Mac Arthurs?" asked Jackson.

"The Senora and Amelia went to town, I don't know what for. Mr. Mac Arthur and Umberto flew somewhere, but if you really want to know where Miss Sally went, she went riding early this morning," she said grinning.

Jackson thanked her and walked out thinking that the gossip mill in the compound must be working overtime.

Jackson walked out to the stables. He found one of the stable hands, Jasper, a young man with a slim build, red hair and freckles. Jackson asked for a saddle horse. Jasper asked if Jackson was a horseman to which Jackson replied, "I was riding by the time I was five in my home state of Texas, I ride pretty well." Jasper grinned and walked into the adjacent barn. Jackson wondered why, there were over twenty head wandering the open corral.

Jasper brought out a large sorrel gelding named Rico, with a white face and four white socks. The gelding was beautiful and acted proud. Jackson walked around the horse, examining both the animal and the tack Jasper had mounted on the gelding. The horse was fitted with two saddle blankets and a small leather saddle without a horn, but with a sheepskin pad.

Jackson swung up on the geldings back. The horse started turning in circles. Jackson got the horse under control and smiled at Jasper.

Jasper smiled back and said, "You will find Miss Sally down by the river. Follow that trail," and pointed to a trail that ran off to the north through the thigh high grass. Jackson wondered if

Sally had left a clue to where she might be found or if Jasper was privy to the compound gossip mill also.

Jackson let the horse have its head. Rico was full of energy and wanted to run. After fifteen minutes of hard exertion Rico slowed to a walk. When Jackson first saw the river he road Rico into the shallows and let him drink and cool down.

Jackson rode on slowly for an hour, thinking furiously about what he should do, until he spotted Sally's horse. The horse was tied to a tree near a wide spot in the river. The river, at this point, was filled with large boulders which formed a quiet soothing pool.

Jackson approached the water's edge watching large schools of small fish moving amongst the boulders. He then noticed Sally's reflection. She was sitting on a large boulder five or six feet above Jackson's head. She had obviously been getting some sun, she wasn't wearing anything.

Jack had wondered how she had gotten so tan, when she appeared in her 'off the shoulder' blouse at the Christmas ceremony. Without looking directly at her, just staring at her reflection in the smooth water, Jackson asked, "Would you please put something on, I need to talk to you?"

She laughed and said, "So I need to be dressed for this talk huh, sounds serious?"

He was still watching her reflection in the water; as she did a reverse strip tease, laughing all the while.

Jackson was still standing when a fully dressed Sally walked around the boulder and came up behind him. She didn't appear so amused now, maybe worried.

"Okay Jack, you followed me way out here to just talk, so talk!"

Jack turned toward her and stared intently into her beautiful blue eyes. After a moment he took her in his arms and held on like she might run away. Sally could feel the tension coursing through him. She put her arms around him and held on tightly. Jack seemed to be unable to talk or move, so Sally led him to a rock they could both sit on in the shade. They sat side by side holding hands, Jack looking at the ground and Sally looking at Jack. After a few minutes Sally couldn't wait any longer.

"Jack, what was said last night that got you so upset? Did my father say anything that I need to hate him for? Is there something I should hate you for?"

"No one needs to hate anyone; it's just the state of the world, at least the state of my world. I'll try to explain what I'm feeling and experiencing," but then didn't continue.

Sally moved back slightly as if to get a better look at Jack. Concern was now etched on her face. "This sounds pretty ominous Jack, would you share some wine with me while we talk? It sounds as if I might need it."

"Wine sounds like a great idea."

She left Jack sitting on the rock staring at the ground again. She went to her horse, reached into the saddle bags and came out with a bottle of wine, a single small wooden cup and a blanket. She spread the blanket on a bedding of grass in the shade and put the wine and cup on it. She then went back, put her arm under Jack's and led him to the blanket.

They sat cross legged facing each other, holding hands. Sally reached across and knocked on his forehead as if it was a door.

"Damn you, Jack, if you don't start explaining what's going on I'm going to explode!"

Jack had put a lot of thought into preparing for this conversation, but everything seemed confused and jumbled in his head. He decided to fill in his history, adding the details he had omitted, to what he had shared with Sally before.

"Sally, when we shared our life histories, I left out something, I think you should know. The reason I was on the freighter. An officer was harassing me in a bar. He took a couple of swings at me and I hit him once. He was with two other officers who then came after me. When it was over I found out the first drunk officer was dead. I ran because I didn't trust the military to give me a fair trial or court-martial."

"Sounds like you just defended yourself to me," said Sally.

"I gave that a lot of thought, Sally. I could have just fended of his blows until he got tired. I was in control of the situation and just tried to make him stop by knocking the breath out of him. Maybe I hit him too hard. That doubt made running seem like the best of my bad available options.

"Also, I was friends with the bar owners and if they stood up for me against the Navy officers, it could have cost them their business. They were good people who would have done just that, no matter what it cost them. I couldn't let that happen."

"Well, you're safe here. In another week you'll be a counterfeit Argentine, passport, history and all. You just have to play Herr Stevens again, but I suppose America is still your country no matter where you are."

"America will always be home, but other than the Corps I don't have too many good memories. My parents, Juanita and the Corps are all closed to me now. That's why I'm so confused about where my life is going. Your father told me I have lots of options now."

Sally sat there saying nothing, waiting impatiently.

"I better tell you the contents of the crate. First, there were counterfeit engraved printing plates for making phony U.S. bills. The FBI knew of them somehow and wants them. Your father is looking into getting the plates to them.

"There was also eight bags of different South American currency and the real big deal, twenty bars of Nazi gold. Your father thinks that since the FBI only knows about the plates, that the rest is mine to keep!"

Jackson's announcement silenced both of them. Now Sally was staring at her hands and Jackson had stretched out on his back on the blanket. An old leg wound was hurting.

"I'm having trouble putting this all together. Let me see, you tell me you are a bandito from America, but you're soon to be Argentine. You didn't even have a change of clothes when you got here, but now you're wealthy. You have something the FBI wants, but since you're a bandito my father is now involved. Is that about right so far?"

Deadly Marriage

"I can't elaborate, but your father had contact with the FBI before I came here."

Sally said softly more to herself than to Jack "I knew he was up to something, but didn't know what. You are aware of an underground movement of business and military leaders looking to overthrow the Ortiz/Castillo government, aren't you, Jack?"

"I wasn't until I talked with your father last night. He explained how the intent of the movement is to keep Argentina neutral and not to become a puppet state of the Nazi's. He also wants my help. I'm not sure what for, but he thinks I can be of service to Argentina and America at the same time."

"Jack, why are you telling me all this?"

Jack didn't hesitate for a change, he just blurted out, "Because I'm falling in love with you! But how can I ask you to be a part of a world I don't even understand?"

"Calm yourself, Jack; you're over the hard part, saying you love me. Since I'm silly crazy in love with you, we can now work together trying to understand what to do about *our* new world."

Jack closed his eyes. Sally saw moisture leaking from the corners of his eyes. Her first thought was to make a joke about tough Marines crying, but then thought better of it. She just kissed his cheek and laid her head on his shoulder and held him.

An emotional dam had burst for both of them. With its release, both were exhausted and soon fell asleep.

They were awakened by noise caused by restless horses. Jackson jumped up, drew his Facon and ran to where the horses were tied. Sally arrived seconds later and drew a 12 gauge double barrel saddle gun from its scabbard. They stood back to back, one looking back down the path, the other watching for anyone coming from above.

A few minutes later Jackson thought he heard whistling. He pointed to his ear, asking Sally to listen. Soon she smiled and said, "It's Jasper, he is embarrassed and is trying to be polite."

"Jasper we're over here!" she called out.

Jasper reined in on Rico's twin. They looked exactly alike except Jasper's had only two front white socks.

"I'm sorry, Miss Sally, for intruding, but Senor Mac would like to talk to both Mr. Stevens and yourself as soon as possible."

"No problem, Jasper. Please tell Senor Mac we will be along shortly."

"Have I told you how wonderful you are today?" asked Jackson.

"You don't really know how wonderful I can be, but you will shortly." She then added, "This is a great place, but we don't have the time," She giggled and started folding the blanket.

"Save the wine and blanket. I think I could get used to taking rides with you," said Jackson and they both laughed.

They walked in to Graham's study and found him in conversation with a small dark man with sharp features that were being dulled by the signs of a life of drinking excessively. He wore a brown, poorly cut suit and an unhappy expression on his face.

Sally and Jack turned to go when Graham waved them in, seconds later Amelia came into the room.

"Amelia, please take Senor Birchall into the kitchen and see he gets something to eat and drink. I will call for him in a few moments."

Mr. Birchall gave no attempt to hide his irritation, but followed Amelia.

When he had gone, Graham got up from his desk and came around to take an armchair and asked Jackson and Sally to join him.

For a moment he rested his head against his hands that he had locked together in what looked like a temple.

He raised his head and looked at his new young friend and his baby girl.

"I assume since you are holding hands, you are not angry with one another?"

Jack and Sally nodded.

"You've both heard the saying: I have good news and I have bad news, which do you want first?"

"Daddy I have some news that you might think is good or maybe bad, but we need to tell you. Jack and I love each other," Sally said simply.

"It hasn't been much time, but I think everyone around here knew it, but you Jack!" he smiled and added, "If it makes you happy baby girl, it's good news indeed."

"Graham, Sally is also privy to almost all of what we talked about and as you said she is a very intelligent girl. She guessed most of the rest."

Sally walked over the Graham and sat on the arm of his chair and said, "I'm so proud of you. You could have just flowed with the tide, but instead you did what was right for Argentina and our family," she then kissed the top of his head.

Graham thought and frowned. Finally, shrugging his shoulders he said, "That's slightly disconcerting that you know all, but it is more comfortable having things in the open."

No one said anything so Graham continued, "I think bad news first and get it out of the way. That little man, Birchall, is FBI. He's a very suspicious man. He wanted to see the crate and the rest of the contents. I gave him a few of the pamphlets and told him the rest had been burned. As he put it, he now 'wants to ask Jack a few questions about his escape.' I told him that was up to you, Jack. Right now he's not a very happy person that is why I sent him away, to cool off.

"Now the good news; the currency is now converted to Argentine Pesos and deposited in your name at the Banco Hipotecario branch in Buenos Aires. There is a new leather brief case with 100,000 pesos in cash, the exchange ratios used and your bank books in your room. It has been arranged by my banker that the gold will be turned to cash and deposited next week. He found a buyer and negotiated a 10% discount because of the questionable ownership."

Jack thought for a moment, turned to face Sally and said, "Sally, will you marry me?"

Sally and Graham were both shocked at the question.

"Don't answer, let me explain. Unless something goes terribly wrong I will ask you again, but as you said earlier, 'this is not the place or time.' I ask because if the FBI and, for that matter, everyone else thinks we're engaged we can explain much of my past and upcoming strange behavior.

"Graham, when Sally kissed the top of your head and said how proud she was of you I made up my mind to do what I could to help. Not very scientific, but it feels right. I assumed I would be traveling, being away for extended periods and spending money like every other future groom does."

Graham and Sally sat in silence, then looked at each other and laughed until their sides hurt.

Jackson just stared. He couldn't think of what could be so funny, unless he had been tricked all along. He started to get mad.

Graham walked over to the desk touched something under the edge and within two minutes Miss Ada walked in.

"What is so damn important that you used that damned buzzer? I told you I hate that thing," said Miss Ada angrily.

"What did Sally say the day after Jack arrived?" asked Graham.

"She said a lot of things, what kind of nonsense is this?"

"What did she say when she came to our room that night?"

"Oh, you mean that she was going to marry Jack, everyone knows that except maybe Jack," she chuckled.

"Thank you, Momma, you saved us from having Jack being angry with Daddy and me, because we laughed at him when he asked me to marry him!"

Miss Ada walked over to Jack, kissed his cheek and hugged him. "I know it seems like a very short time to know someone before getting engaged, but Sally is very determined and she usually gets what she wants, you never had a chance."

Jackson sat there. Not knowing what to say. Everyone was smiling and staring at him.

"Now that my future is all settled and before we start making wedding plans," laughed Jackson changing the subject, "I guess I better talk to Birchall and get it over."

Deadly Marriage

Amelia brought Birchall in to the study and asked if anything else was needed. Graham asked for a bucket of ice to be brought in immediately and that champagne be chilled for later.

"I was wondering if I might have a word in private with Mr. Stevens?" asked Birchall.

"There's nothing about my escape my fiancé and her parents don't already know."

"Congratulations, I had no idea" said Birchall.

He continued, "I understand you're an American?"

"I understand that has nothing to do with my escape!"

"I thought, as an American, you would want to help the FBI."

"Help the FBI do what?"

"Help us find who was responsible for the plates."

"The only people I saw with the crates were two middle aged blond women, who the mate said were German and who are now shark shit on the bottom of the ocean. I gave that information to the local police and the Port Captain when I climbed off the crate. Now, what do you really want to know, Mr. FBI?"

"I think you had better come back to the embassy with me, until I check you out."

"Well, he finally said what he was really after."

"Come on, smart guy, let's go," demanded Birchall.

Jackson moved to face Birchall and said, "Thanks for offering the free trip to Buenos Aires, but I'm not going anywhere with you. And so we understand each other, I'm not doing anything that would harm America in any way, never would. But, if you or your hired thugs try to contact, intimidate or kidnap any of my new family, I will find you and believe me that would not be a good thing for you."

"Are you threatening me, Mr. Stevens?" said Birchall looking angrily into Jackson's eyes.

"No threat, Mr. FBI, I am just making you a promise," Jackson said calmly staring back. Birchall backed away.

Graham stepped in and said, "Birchall, you're no longer welcome on my property. Please leave now and do not return," said Graham.

Birchall glared over Graham's shoulder at Jackson. He then gathered his hat and started for the hallway.

He turned and said, "We will be seeing each other again soon, Mr. Stevens."

"Just remember my promise," said Jackson. An angry Birchall spun his tires as he left.

"That was interesting. I don't suppose I'll be receiving anymore intelligence information from Mr. Birchall in the future," said Graham.

"I was wondering, what type of info you actually received from him?" asked Jackson.

"Nothing of any real importance, mostly I was told what the FBI wanted and after today I don't think I could trust even that," said Graham.

"I don't think you lost a great deal, Graham. He's too far down the food chain to know much. I'm sure he has a boss at the embassy that keeps him on a pretty short leash. He is too easily manipulated to be trusted with anything important."

"I guess we'll see. I think it's time for a drink or two, Jack, and the ladies will have a lot of questions."

"I have a lot of questions too, but not very many answers, I'm afraid," said Jackson.

As they walked into the study Sally handed them both glasses filled with ice and Scotch. She then pulled Jackson's arm and led him to a couch where they could sit together. Graham sat next to his wife.

"What do you think of Mr. Birchall, Jack? Why is he so interested in you?" Sally asked bluntly.

Jack thought for a moment then answered, "The only thing I know for sure is that Birchall is a police officer. The FBI is a policing agency asked to do intelligence work in the Americas. I believe the reason he is interested in me is that he has an unidentified American arriving in what he feels is his sphere of influence, with German counterfeit U.S. currency printing plates. He knew these plates existed before I arrived, I don't know how. Any ideas about how he knew, Graham?"

Deadly Marriage

"He never told me how he knew, but he asked me to watch for the crate or the plates a couple of days before you arrived."

"I don't think the policeman in him will allow him to let this be without investigating. I do know, for sure, we'll be seeing him again," said Jackson.

Everyone sat in silence with their own thoughts. Drinks were refreshed and the radio turned on in the background.

Graham broke the mood by saying, "I think Jack needs to get away for a few days. Do you ladies think he's ready to see the seedier side of the Mac Arthur clan's lifestyle?"

Chapter 8

26 December 1939
Office of Obergruppenfuhrer von Richter
Danzig Germany (Poland)

Von Richter was becoming unnerved. He was sure he was being investigated, but by whom and why now? He had no way of contacting SS Major Felix von Krieg-Rupold, except through the Embassy in Buenos Aires. This was a risky option, but the only one available.

He called his aide Obersturmbannfuhre (Lt. Colonel) Zimmerman into his office.

Without preamble he ordered Zimmerman to send a radiogram to the Embassy in Buenos Aires asking SS Major Felix von Krieg-Rupold to report as soon as possible and sign it yourself.

Zimmerman didn't understand why von Richter would want him to sign his own name instead of the Obergruppenfuhrer's. He hesitated, starring at von Richter.

"That will be all, Zimmerman."

Zimmerman followed the order, but didn't like it. A few days before, he had been approached by the Gestapo. They had asked about von Richter's operation, if he had seen anything suspicious? He had answered truthfully that he believed von Richter to be a fine officer and was affective in his duties. He had noticed nothing out of the ordinary. The Gestapo had sworn him to secrecy and given him a number to call if something unusual occurred.

As Zimmerman was walking home to his tiny apartment he stopped at a café and called the number.

Estancia Mac Arthur
Rio Gallegos
Argentina

"Sally, I think you should take Jack to the house on Avenita Del Corrico. Now that he has money, make sure he buys some suitable clothing and then show him the sights, but keep him busy and out of trouble until his passport is ready. In fact, you may want to leave immediately. Birchall may be trying to talk the police into coming out here to investigate as we speak," said Graham.

"Daddy, that is a splendid idea, I'll go get packed. Jack, pack what little you have, there should be a valise in your closet."

"Do I get to ask where I'm being taken?"

"No, it's a surprise," said Sally.

After Sally scampered up the stairs, Jackson looked at Graham, "Hiding out until I'm legally an Argentinean citizen is a great idea, but won't you be putting yourselves at risk?"

"Please don't worry, Birchall and the police can't cause me any trouble, but without a passport and identification you are at risk staying here. Just relax and enjoy yourself."

"If you're sure, I don't want to cause you any trouble. I guess I should follow my orders and get packed. Do you think she's trying to see if I'm trainable?"

"She's just like her mother. You will be trained without even knowing it. Like I said relax and enjoy your trip."

Miss Ada poked Graham in the ribs and they both laughed.

Jackson filled the valise with all his worldly possessions. He was worried how things were progressing so quickly, but deep inside it felt like everything was happening as it should. He decided to relax and enjoy the trip.

He met the family in the kitchen. Amelia had put a picnic basket together, including the champagne that had been chilling. Sally was dressed in knee high leather boots, straight legged wool trousers, a white front buttoned blouse, a leather jacket and topped it all off with the bright yellow scarf around her neck.

Graham handed Jackson a wool coat and said, "I guess you're all set."

"Now I'm really confused, why the coats, it's over 90 outside?"

"They're just in case we need them or we might be going to the mountains," said Sally.

They said their goodbyes and headed out the backdoor. Jackson noticed the sound of an engine running. Sally put her arm through Jack's and guided him through the same gate Graham had used the night before. They turned left and went toward the building Jackson thought of as a hangar.

When they rounded the corner of the "hangar" Jackson saw a diminutive yellow airplane being warmed up and checked over by Umberto and Jasper.

"There's not enough room in that little thing for the two of us, and a pilot," stated Jackson.

"This is your first surprise. For your information, that little thing, is a J3 Piper Cub. It is capable of flying two people, in comfort, at a blazing 80 mph. To complete this phase of your education, the Cub was my 18th birthday present from my parents and came, you'll be happy to note, with flying lessons. I have been a licensed pilot since and you are in for a wonderful ride," smiled Sally.

Sally thanked Umberto and Jasper, did a "walk around inspection," and said

"We're good to go," as she motioned Jack to take the back seat.

Umberto and Jasper were standing back from the plane, obviously to watch the takeoff; or, was it to watch the look of fright on Jackson's face?

Jackson climbed in with as much dignity as he could muster, but couldn't hide the fact he was scared to death. He had never enjoyed his flying experience, which was all on military transports. The flights had been bumpy, cold, and totally uncomfortable. Furthermore, you couldn't see anything that was taking place, either in the cockpit or outside of the plane.

Jackson couldn't hear anything inside the cockpit over the engine noise. Sally made motions for him to put on the headset that was dangling in front of his face. She pointed out the "talk button" on the panel in front of him to his right. He followed her orders.

Sally came over the intercom, "All comfy and ready for takeoff?" she asked.

Deadly Marriage

Jackson pushed the transmit button and said, "Not really all that comfy, but I guess I'm ready," Jackson didn't like not having any control and this was one of those times he had none.

"The first rule is, don't touch the stick between your legs or the pedals by your feet until I tell you. I'll let you know when you can fly," said Sally giggling.

"I can't fly this thing."

"We'll see."

******

Agent Birchall drove angrily back to his office. His office was above the harbor and looked over it out to sea. The office was small but served the purposes of the U.S. Assistant Agricultural Attaché. It was in a row of similar offices in an old building that had seen better days.

Above the office was his small apartment. It consisted of a single bed, a chest of drawers, a bath with shower, a two person table and chairs and a small kitchen. The only redeeming quality was it had a view of the sea.

The agent climbed the stairs to his apartment, went to the cabinet over the sink where he kept his liquor bottles and made his first drink of the day.

He sat at his window and stared out at the Atlantic. He asked himself why he had let that smartass get to him. He had acted like a new agent without a brain. I have to remember that I'm in the intelligence business, not the law enforcement business and that I'm not in Chicago, but in Argentina. I had no authority to take him anywhere and he knew it. Was I just pissed, because I am now the lowest rung on the ladder?

As he made his second drink of the day he started to dwell on how his life had gone downhill. He had fallen from investigating murders, kidnappings and bank robberies in Chicago to wasting his time sitting in a hole-in-the-wall office in no-where Argentina. He gazed around his room and thought how he had fallen from a nice house in the suburbs to this hole.

He knew the answer and it stared back from his glass. He had started drinking heavily when his wife of fifteen years left with his children and moved to New York City. He had tried to convince her to come home, but she wouldn't hear of it. She said she had had enough of being a cop's wife and that he had changed. His job was now his life, not his family.

He had thought he was just passionate about his job, but she was probably right. The job had come first for some time, he confessed to himself. He knew he was here because he was an embarrassment to the Bureau.

He thought if he really gave a shit, he would call the police and get Jackson brought in and questioned. But, he really didn't give a shit! He made another drink, looked out his window and fed bread crumbs to the circling gulls.

******

Sally taxied onto the grass runway, did one more run up and started applying the power. The plane was shaking violently when she released the brakes.

Umberto and Jasper were standing next to the runway, where they could watch Jackson. They tried not to laugh as they crossed themselves in the Catholic manner. Jackson didn't think that was very funny and raised his middle finger in the international sign of affection!

Jackson tried to concentrate on the gauges as they bounced down the runway. He was startled when the tail began to rise; he had gone this fast in an automobile, then seconds later the Cub lifted off. The Cub was close to its maximum takeoff weight, so Sally put the plane in a slow climb.

Jackson was still scared, but was fascinated with how things looked from above.

"That wasn't too bad, was it Jack," asked Sally?

"I'm still not comfy, as you put it, but I have to admit the view is wonderful," answered Jack.

She swung around and flew over the compound giving Jackson a new appreciation of the layout and the building's locations. She then headed north.

Deadly Marriage

Sally came on the intercom, "Just so you know what our plan is, we will be flying at 3000ft, at 80 miles per hour and stopping for fuel and bathroom breaks every two hours. It's a long trip to our final destination, so I hope you can relax and enjoy the view."

As they climbed through 1500 feet, Jackson said, "Are all those cows yours?" He could see hundreds, maybe thousands, stretching out to the horizon.

"They belong to our family. Twenty years ago, before I was born, father brought the first cattle to this region from Brazil. The books say we have about 3,300 head now."

"I can barely see the sheep in the grass. How many sheep does the Estancia have?"

"We really have no way of counting all the sheep accurately. The herders move them around the property constantly and we lose some to predators daily. We carry over 40,000 head on the books."

"I'm very impressed, this is quite an operation!"

"This is the part of the Estancia Father and I love the most. My brothers are studying to handle the business side of things."

"What do you mean "business side?" asked Jackson.

"We have a meat processing house and a tanning business in Rio Gallegos. Also there is the winery you'll see later today and other smaller interests in Buenos Aires. Daddy believes in Argentina and keeps investing."

"Let's see, I'm not only robbing the cradle, but I'm going to marry money too. Is that about the situation?"

"Not quite. You now have money, maybe not as much as our family, but you're not a poor man either. You ARE OLD, but there's no way around that. As you heard from mother, I took control of your love life before you knew what was going on. I know what I want and what I'm getting, so unless you have doubts, just relax and be happy!"

He said, "Yes, dear," without thinking about it.

"That's better. Remember that response. It will make life much easier," laughed Sally.

Jackson just shook his head.

They landed on a grass airstrip about an hour later. The strip was located near the small village of Canadon Leon near the Rio Chico. A pickup truck with two 55 gallon barrels in the back pulled up to the Cub and a man in greasy overalls with the name Jose on a patch on his chest pocket greeted them with a smile as they stepped out of the plane.

"Hello, Miss Sally, how are you?" said the man.

"I'm well, Jose, how about you?"

"I'm surviving. Should I fill up your little yellow bird?" smiled Jose.

"Please do Jose and I'd like you to meet my fiancé Jack Stevens."

Jose wiped his hand on a rag and then held it up and shrugged. Jack chuckled and shook his hand dirty or not.

"Very nice to meet you, Jose," said Jack.

"It is my pleasure, Mr. Stevens. You're a very lucky man," said Jose formally.

"To quote her father, 'She has her moments'."

Sally punched him in the shoulder and they all laughed.

He then started to fill the gas tank. By the time both Sally and Jack had used the primitive bathroom facilities and returned to the plane he was finished.

Jose gave Sally a slip to sign and the transaction was done. They had only been on the ground fifteen minutes. They said their goodbyes and Jose drove away.

"I have money to pay for fuel," said Jack.

"Daddy set up a monthly system with Jose, because he never has change and I don't carry much either. I'm just about the only customer he gets from outside the village; most other planes have the range to bypass his little airport."

"Before you climb back in, will you get Amelia's basket out?" asked Sally.

Jacks said, "Yes, dear," laughed and climbed over the rear seat to retrieve the basket.

They stood next to the plane enjoying having their legs straight. They drank a cup of wine each and shared one of

Amelia's huge beef sandwiches. When they had finished they inserted themselves in the tiny plane and made ready to take off.

As they were taxiing Jack noticed Jose driving towards the village. His small hangar and office had been left open. He must have something very important to do, thought Jack. He, then, held on while the Cub bounced down the runway.

They flew for the better part of an hour without talking. Each lost in their own thoughts. The silence was broken by a radio call.

"Cub 79441, do you read me, this is Lockheed 78256?" asked a voice Jack couldn't identify.

"Lockheed 78256, I read you loud and clear, over," said Sally into the microphone.

"Sally, this is Eduardo Rueda. Your father called and spoke with the Colonel. It was decided between our fathers that we needed to talk, so I'm heading for your destination, so we can taste the wine. Did you catch all that, over?"

"Eduardo, I don't understand it, but it's always a pleasure to see you. I will be there to taste the wine in about three hours. Will that work, over?"

"I'll look forward to it, see you then. Lockheed 78256 out," said Eduardo.

"Cub 79441 out," Sally signed off.

"What was that all about," asked Jackson.

"I'm not sure. Edward is the son of Colonel Don Chano Rueda the leader of the Argentine Calvary and a close friend of my father. The colonel and my father sent Eduardo to meet us at the winery. I don't know why, he was talking strangely over the radio, like he didn't want to be overheard. He doesn't usually speak so seriously, he's kind of a clown sometimes. Does it make any sense to you, Jack?"

"Nothing makes much sense to me these days. I don't know if it means anything, but Jose rushed off towards the village as we were leaving. He left the airport wide open. He was in a big hurry for some reason."

"That's strange; he usually watches the planes takeoff. I think he's a frustrated pilot."

Jackson thought for a minute and said, "I believe you said we have another fuel stop before reaching the vineyard, let's be a little more careful when we make that stop, agreed?"

"Yes, dear," said Sally. They both laughed then both became silent.

On this stop, Sally circled the field and Jackson looked for any movement or danger, but found none. The fuel stop came and went uneventfully. After they departed, the cockpit of the Cub became silent. The banter and laughing were gone and would stay gone for the rest of the trip.

******

Birchall woke with a world class hangover. He thought, "another shitty day in purgatory." He had nothing to do all day, so he thought the day had a chance to improve. He dressed in casual attire and walked down to the corner café.

He was greeted by Luisa as he was every day. He took his usual table by the window; he never tired of watching the sea.

She brought him a very large mug of steaming black coffee and took his breakfast order like any other day.

He was feeling better after he had eaten and was sitting quietly drinking his third coffee when in walked a large strong featured Mediterranean looking man in seaman's garb. He sat at the bar and ordered coffee. He picked up his coffee and walked over to Birchall's table. Birchall knew his day was shot.

"May I join you Mr. Birchall?"

"Do I have a choice?"

"Surely you have a choice. I can leave now and take my money with me."

Birchall knew there was a statement left unsaid, "If I leave now, you will be dead by sunset."

"Please, join me Felix, I was just joking," replied Birchall lamely.

"How did your meeting with Mr. Mac Arthur go yesterday?"

Deadly Marriage

"Splendidly, I have your plates, but that's the only thing that ended well. I pissed off Mac Arthur, his visitor and got thrown off the Estancia. Oh yes, I was also told the crate had been burned."

"Another opportunity squandered," said the man, his eyes ablaze. "First the gun happy U-boat sinks the ship with our cargo aboard. We were extremely lucky when it showed up in Argentina and now it looks as though you've let it slip away?"

Birchall knew he had to think fast, Felix was not a man to disappoint.

"I don't believe the crate was really burned. I think I can try to go back, apologize and see what I can find out. Don't give up yet!"

"If the crate was really burned, I'm afraid, neither of us has a very long life expectancy. I hope you're correct. Beg forgiveness and see what you can do. I'll meet you here in two days. I'll send Quinn over to pick up the plates this evening," said the man as he rose and left the café.

"I don't need your threats or your orders, Felix von Blah Blah," thought Birchall.

But he did as he was told. He got in his car and headed for the Estancia.

Chapter 9

Mac Arthur Winery
Mendoza, Argentina

Fifteen minutes before they landed Sally called the Mac Arthur Winery to announce her arrival and to see if there were any problems they should know about before landing.

She received an "all clear" from Mariano Pijkovic, the winery manager. He also stated Edward Rueda had arrived 20 minutes earlier and was awaiting her arrival.

The vineyards covered the rolling hills for what seemed to be miles around the buildings and airstrip. Jackson could see "Mac Arthur Winery" painted in white letters on top of the largest building.

They landed just as the sun was setting behind the Andes. It was a rough landing compared to Sally's earlier landings. Jackson wondered if it was nerves or fatigue.

As they taxied toward the large building, Jackson saw a young man about his height and build leaning on the fender of an old stake bed truck. Jackson assumed this was Edward Rueda. Next to him had to be Mariano Pijkovic, the manager. He was a small thin man, with dark hair and a pencil line mustache.

Sally shut down the Cub's engine, the men walked toward the plane and the taller of the two opened the door.

"Hello, Sally, no problems I hope?" he asked seriously.

"The only problem is I'm not sure I know a serious Eduardo Rueda. What's going on?"

"I'll explain when we get this bug tied down and get in the house."

Sally made introductions and they shook hands. Eduardo Rueda knew how to tie down an airplane and the task was done in just a few minutes. They threw their bags into the stake bed and all climbed into the cab.

The building they drove to looked like a rustic hunting lodge. When they entered the ambiance proved to be the same.

Deadly Marriage

Rough wood floors, braided wool rugs, large comfortable furniture and a huge rock fireplace completed the scene.

Mariano Pijkovic asked if he could be of further service and when Sally responded negatively he said goodbye to Miss Sally and "Lieutenant Rueda" and told Jackson what a pleasure it was to meet him.

Jackson and "Lieutenant Rueda" stood and stared at each other.

Finally Jackson said, "What are you a lieutenant of, Eduardo?"

Eduardo smiled and said, "You'll be surprised. But, can we get some wine and something to eat before we start our conversation?"

Sally said, "That's a great idea, I'm starved. I'll go to the kitchen and see what Celia can come up with. You two make yourselves a drink and don't start without me."

Edward knew where the sideboard was located and started to make drinks.

"Would you like Scotch, Steve?"

Jackson couldn't keep his mouth shut, it just hung open.

"I don't know what you've told Sally, but I thought it a good idea we understood each other. I am an Argentine Army Air Force fighter pilot and a U.S. citizen. So we're both on the same side."

Jack couldn't grasp what this all meant. Finally he said, "Scotch will be fine, but make it a double."

They got their drinks and moved to two large armchairs next to the fireplace.

"I was told your father is a Colonel in the Argentine Army and now you're a U.S. citizen. I'm lost," said Jack.

"I guess Sally won't get mad if I explain how this happened before she gets back, she already knows the story."

"My father was a dashing Argentine Calvary officer and my mother was an oil heiress from West Texas. You probably know the little town, Midland?"

"Sure, I've been there. It's just a little bigger than Rio Pecos, where I'm from."

"As the story goes they met in Buenos Aires and were married for just a short period, before my grandfather forced my mother to move back to Texas. Neither of them ever got a divorce.

"Anyway I was the result. I was born in Texas and didn't know about my father until a few years ago, when my mother passed. She left me a letter explaining who my father was and what had happened.

"I came down not really knowing why or what I would find. My father turned out to be a great man, with honor and pride. He had kept in touch with my mother all those years and had a scrap book of photos of me. He had watched me grow up from a distance."

"I am also an Argentine citizen. I hold dual citizenship. My father arranged it before I was born and since I was born in Texas; I was also a U.S. citizen."

"How do you know about me?"

"I think we had better wait for Sally before we go much further. How about another drink, you seemed to have finished that one?" Eduardo chuckled.

Sally yelled from the kitchen, "Come and get it you two!"

"You get fried steak, fried potatoes and a very good Cabernet Sauvignon; and Celia says if anyone complains they cook next time. I thought it best if she left for the evening. She'll be here for breakfast in the morning."

Sally filled their plates and there wasn't much conversation until they finished.

"That was delicious. You must thank Celia for us, Sally," said Jack.

"I agree," said Eduardo.

"Now that we've been fed and you two have been in the Living lubricating your tongues, what's going on?"

Sally and Jack both looked at Eduardo who took a sip of wine and began.

"I'll start with what happened today. Someone informed Mr. Birchall of the FBI that you had taken off with Jack in your Cub. So someone is keeping an eye on your movements."

"My father also received a message from the U.S. embassy by top secret courier today, which contained Jack's military and FBI files.

"Before you ask, I don't know how the Colonel got this information. I do know the FBI has a man working as Agriculture Attaché named Sanford, who my father thinks is the head spook in Argentina. My father saw the high risk implications of Jack not knowing if the FBI had this information.

"He did know that the Germans wanted their gold back and were keeping an eye on Jack. He called your father, found out where you were headed and they agreed we needed to get word to you two.

"Also my father and Graham agreed that if the FBI had this information, so probably would the Germans. They have spies everywhere. So, I was volunteered to fly down here to meet you."

"I assume the men walking the perimeter are yours then, Lieutenant?" asked Jack.

"Not mine, they are my father's. He wants me to bring you to his Estancia in the morning; and Jack, please call me Eduardo, Ed or Edward. I'm not on official business and I'm trying to keep as low a profile down here as possible."

Sally asked if Eduardo had the files with him and the answer was no.

"I did go through them briefly before I left. There wasn't much that made sense in your Marine file. Model Marine, worked his way up the ranks and good evaluations from all your commanding officers. Then I read about the incident with the three officers?

Jack sat back in his chair. He had been leaning forward with his elbows on the table taking in everything Edward had to say.

"The real story probably reads a little different. I was having dinner and a few beers at a friend's place, when the three pup lieutenants came in and proceeded to get falling down drunk. This guy named Decker I reported to came down and started to harass me. I replied civilly, if not respectively. He swung at me twice before I laid a hand on him and then only to knock the wind out of him. He went down and then the other clowns charged me. I was just defending myself."

"You're right, it does read somewhat different. But why did you run?"

"It may look different from an officer's point of view, but I didn't think my word against two officers would account for much in front of a JAG board of inquiry."

"Here's a question for you: why is your father trying to help me keep out of the clutches of the FBI?"

"I'm sure he will explain his motives tomorrow. I'm sorry I don't know any more. I don't know what they will ask of you. I just hope you can trust Mr. Mac Arthur and my father enough to listen to what my father has to say. Sally knows my family and I don't believe Graham would send his daughter into harm's way."

"I know you're right intellectually and I'll meet with the Colonel and listen to what he says, but things are changing all around me and everything is out of my control. Feeling trust in my gut is proving to be much harder."

Sally sat looking concerned. The world had gotten serious very quickly in the last thirty minutes. The risk her father, Colonel Rueda and now Jack would be taking was real and people would die before this was over.

They all agreed to call it a night and that they would leave at 0600 in the morning. No questions as to sleeping arrangements were voiced. Edward went to his room. Sally led Jack to theirs, along with another bottle of wine.

Sally turned on a lamp on a night stand and asked, "Could we have a glass of wine and talk for a little while, Jack?" as she pulled two armchairs together in front of a large window overlooking the vineyards and poured the wine.

"I don't feel comfortable with all that's happening. I trust Colonel Rueda and Edward with my life, but I don't know what the GOU wants with you."

Jack sipped his wine, covered Sally's hand in his and said, "I think I know a few things you might not." He sat back, still holding her hand and rubbed his forehead with the other. After a few seconds he continued.

"One, the FBI can't arrest me in Argentina," and then added "not legally, except within the embassy grounds.

"Two, I wouldn't put it past the FBI to hire someone to try to abduct me and take me to the embassy, where they could arrest me. I can't let that happen.

"Three, my Marine file shows I'm a qualified sniper and a hand to hand combat instructor. Those skills would be very valuable to any military operation they are contemplating. Your father even mentioned training, I don't know who or what he wanted trained, but he mentioned it with a wave of his hand, as if it wasn't important, which now I question.

"Four, if the colonel convinces me that what they plan is the right thing to do for Argentina, your family, the U.S. and if there is something I can contribute, then I'll commit to the cause. As the old English saying goes, 'In for a penny, in for a pound.'

"Five, all the scenarios I can come up with are dangerous and I don't like the idea of my future bride being in harm's way."

After a period of silence and contemplation, "Is that all that's bothering you?" asked Sally sarcastically.

When Jack didn't answer she turned his way and said, "One, I agree with you completely.

"Two, I also agree with, I don't trust Birchall to give up any time soon.

"Three, I think it would be naïve to think that they didn't want you for some type of operation.

"Four, when I became aware of what my father was doing, I became committed. I think you will be too.

Five, I too think this is dangerous and don't want my future husband in harm's way either, but I think that decision has been taken out of our hands, hasn't it Jack?"

"I guess all the questions will be answered tomorrow."

"We could ponder the questions all-night and not come up with a real answer, right Jack?"

"That's about it."

"Well then I think this is our time and our place, don't you?" Sally said smiling.

She pulled him to his feet, put her arms around his neck, leaned into him and kissed him passionately. When she could feel his passion rising she gently broke free and told him to get in bed. She then stepped into the bathroom.

Jack did as he was told, but his mind would not settle down. He had a basket full of emotions, worries and concerns he couldn't just put away.

When Sally came in she was wearing just a black velvet choker with a pearl cluster and an allover tan. Standing in the soft light, Jackson thought she was the most beautiful creature he had ever seen. His mind was now clear and focused.

They made love three times that night. The first time was raw lust and sexual release. The second was slow and loving. The third was fun and playful.

They both got very little sleep that night.

Chapter 10

Rio Gallegos Harbor
Rio Gallegos, Argentina

   SS Major Felix von Krieg-Rupold smiled as he walked back to the dock where his boat was moored, thinking how pleasant it would be just to slip a blade between Birchall's ribs and pierce his heart. But he still needed him; his agents from Buenos Aires would arrive the next day. Then he could take over the retrieval of the Reich's property himself and eliminate Birchall.
   He had been sent from Germany to take possession of the cargo from the *John's II* and hide it in Argentina. When he had reported the sinking to von Richter, he was told he would be sent four agents from Buenos Aires as soon as possible. He was ordered to utilize the agents to make a thorough search for the cargo. It was his responsibility and he could use whatever means or resources were available to complete his assignment.
   He didn't trust Birchall and would feel better when the plates were in his possession.
   When he had been made aware of the agents being assigned to him he had bought a forty foot wooden sailboat in fair condition, which had adequate quarters for the six members of his team. He had climbed the mast soon after he moved aboard and installed a long range antenna, late at night and in the fog so he would not be observed. With the antenna up he could now contact Buenos Aires when needed. After the scuttling of the Gaff Spree and the internment of its crew, coordination of Axis activities in the Southern Atlantic had become a priority in Berlin. It was a new clandestine war being fought in the "neutral" countries of South America.

Mac Arthur Winery
Mendoza, Argentina

   Jack and Sally awoke to Celia pounding on their door and telling them breakfast was ready.

"What time is it, Celia?" asked Sally.

"It's 5:30, Miss Sally"

"We'll be right down and thank you, Celia," said Sally.

Jack tried to pull her to him, but she slapped his hand.

"We don't have time for that right now, but I look forward to tonight," she smiled lovingly.

"I guess us rebel warriors must make sacrifices for the cause," said Jackson getting out of bed.

Sally came to him and put her arms around him and asked, "Please don't make jokes like that Jack. I'm a little touchy about thinking of myself as a rebel."

"I'm sorry, Sally. That was a stupid attempt at humor."

She smiled, kissed him lightly on the lips and turned back to her packing.

They went downstairs to the kitchen, where Eduardo was just finishing his meal.

"Good morning, children, how did you sleep?" asked Edward smirking.

"We slept just fine thank you, Mr. Smarty Pants," laughed Sally.

Jack smiled and stayed out of the word play.

"You both do look sort of, how can I say this tactfully, refreshed this morning."

Sally walked over to Eduardo, threw out her hip and slapped him lightly on the face. They all laughed. Then Eduardo thought for a moment and said, "That might be my new record, slapped by a beautiful woman before 0600!"

As Sally and Jack sat down, Eduardo stood up and said, "I'll go and hide your little yellow bug and do my preflight. Come along when you're finished, no hurry."

After the exercise of the previous evening they were famished. Celia kept bringing coffee and more food, while smiling knowingly.

They finished, thanked Celia and walked out to the big bright polished aluminum Lockheed 12-1 Electra Junior. The Electra was an eight passenger, low wing, twin engine air plane capable of 225 mph, with a ceiling of 22,900 ft.

Deadly Marriage

One of the soldiers waved them aboard. They climbed the fold down steps and found a comfortable cabin with room for six passengers and a crew of two. The stairs were pulled up and the door locked. Then Edward came on the intercom and said in Spanish, "We are set to depart, please fasten your seat belts."

Jackson was surprised he understood what Eduardo had said. He was picking up some Spanish without really trying.

The roll down the grass runways was smoother and the sensation of the tail rising was more subtle, thought Jackson, as they left the ground. After they had leveled off at 18,000 feet Eduardo gave the plane to this co-pilot and came back to visit with Sally and Jack.

"Are you two doing okay back here? The troops are snoring like they took their duty seriously last night."

"This is a beautiful aircraft, Eduardo," said Sally.

"Again, like the soldiers here, it belongs to my father. He lets me play with it sometimes. Our co-pilot, Lieutenant Ocomo, was up all-night on guard duty and is a little tired. How about sitting in the right seat, Sally, and let him get some sleep? Jack, there is even a little fold down observer's seat, so you can keep an eye on your girlfriend here."

"I would like that, how about you, Jack?"

"Yes dear," for which he got a laugh from Eduardo and a punch from Sally.

Lieutenant Ocomo wasn't too excited to give up his seat to a young lady, but Eduardo insisted. When he fell into a seat in the back, his snoring was soon heard above the rest.

Edward explained all the instruments and gauges and how everything worked, Jackson thought for his benefit, because Sally knew what was what and was flying the plane at that very moment. He suspiciously thought, "Why is Edward giving me a flying course?"

The five and a half hour flight was uneventful, except for more flight training for Jackson. He even took a turn in the right seat when Sally had to use the facilities.

As they descended, the troops started to stir. Soon Lieutenant Ocomo came forwarded wanting his seat back. Sally thanked him formally, though she would have loved to land the plane herself.

They returned to their seats in the rear and looked out their windows. The compound on the Rueda Estancia was larger and the countryside was greener than the Mac Arthur Estancia. Jackson wasn't sure why, but it looked older. The trees were taller, the roads more defined and buildings gave off an aura of permanence.

As they taxied to the hangar, they were met by a beautiful black 1938 Buick Road Master convertible, driven by a very large man in an Argentine Army uniform. As they deplaned Jack noticed the man was armed.

"Hello, Enrico. I'm sure you remember the beautiful Miss Sally Mac Arthur?" said Edward.

"Of course, it's wonderful to see you again, Miss Sally."

"You still look smashing in your uniform, Enrico."

Enrico stood a little taller and beamed at the compliment.

"And this is her boyfriend Jack Stevens," said Edward.

"Welcome, it's comforting to have a real soldier visit instead of all these officers," smiled Enrico looking from Jack to Edward grinning.

A kindred soul thought Jackson.

"Suboficial Major Rodriguez that will be enough of your impertinence," said Edward in mock seriousness.

"It is an honor to meet you, Enrico, and I understand your discomfort at being surrounded by officers, they do have an odor of arrogance about them," laughed Jack.

While they shook hands they both grinned at Eduardo, who was doing his best not to smile.

They were driven to a large house similar to the Mac Arthur's, but more functional. No landscaping, lawn or flowers. Jackson thought of it as masculine.

Enrico ushered them in to the Colonel's office.

Colonel Don Chano Rueda rose from behind his desk and came forward to greet them.

Deadly Marriage

He introduced himself, shook hands with Jack and kissed both of Sally's cheeks. He returned to his seat at his desk, asked everyone to be seated and pulled out two folders from his center drawer. He then asked Enrico to order coffee for everyone. This was going to be a business meeting, thought Jack.

The Colonel began, "Welcome to Estancia San Franco. Please accept my gratitude for agreeing to meet with me."

"Mr. Stevens, is there anything in these folders that you would not wish Miss Sally to know about?"

"No Sir," said Jack simply.

"If you will indulge me, may I ask about the altercation with the officers in Maine?"

Jack told the truth of the incident without flourish.

"My son said the report didn't make sense to him and I have to agree. Thank you for explaining. The remainder of your record is very impressive."

Jack just nodded. He was tired of being swept along; not knowing what was going on. He wanted to know why this interview was being held.

The coffee was served by an orderly and everyone gathered around the large conference table that dominated one half of the Colonel's office.

"I'm sure you have a plethora of questions and I'll try to answer the obvious ones first."

"I received copies of your files from a contact at the FBI office in the U.S. embassy in Buenos Aires. Argentina has an intelligence agency, named the Presidential Security Department, PDS for short, which functions much like the FBI and they have sources within the embassy."

Again Jackson just shrugged. He had expected something along those lines.

"Graham and I are part of a growing organization of Military Officers and prominent business leaders, called the Grupo de Oficiales Unidos (G.O.U.), who feel Argentina is being pulled into this war in support of the Axis powers. We believe that Argentina would be better served by maintaining the neutral status it now enjoys and not to be subservient to the Nazi regime. We have been applying political pressure on the Ortiz/Castillo administration for months without much success.

"We have decided it is now the time to get organized in the event military action is required at some point to correct this situation."

"Colonel, with all due respect Sir, is it wise to tell me these things without my committing to help?" That was what he said, what he thought was I either join up or I'm never leaving this office alive.

"You ask a very appropriate question. I took the risk based on Mr. Mac Arthur's belief that if I could convince you of the "right" of our cause and the benefit it would be to the U.S., that you would commit to helping us. Was I wrong in this belief?"

This Colonel is one smart SOB thought Jackson. He's turned my question around and put me on the spot. Sally put her hand on his and brought him out of his thoughts. The conversation had turned into a one on one negotiation.

"You are correct Colonel in that belief, but I still don't understand just how this benefits the U.S.?"

"The main reason is that if Argentina were to align itself with the Axis powers, the Nazis and their comrades in arms would have a major deep water port in the Americas, a port from which they could supply and maintain their vessels and submarines. At the present time Germany has a foreign flagged vessel anchored in the Rio de la Plata which rendezvous with U-boats at sea and provides them with supplies. The present administration allows this to take place in violation of our neutral status.

"Furthermore, having such a port would allow the Nazis to control the east coast of South America, which in turn would allow them to eventually control the waters off the eastern United States.

"The Rio de la Plata would provide them a waterway into the continent allowing them access to the natural resources of Argentina, Uruguay and, eventually, the surrounding countries. As I'm sure you know obtaining oil is a major logistical problem

Deadly Marriage

for Germany. Having Argentina under their control would solve a multitude of problems for the Axis."

"Thank you for the explanation, Colonel. May I assume Germany understands the situation and has setup an underground network in Argentina to help Ortiz/Castillo?"

"Of course, a very large and powerful organization of spies and operatives," answered the Colonel.

"Sir, I am a Marine. There is a saying 'once a marine always a marine.' I'm sure you have a similar saying in the Calvary. I understand the risk and the potential benefit to both our countries, but still I have two more questions before I commit."

"How can I secure Sally's and her family's safety and what role did you have in mind for me?"

"Graham needs your help securing his Estancia. He has good men at his disposal, but no military leadership. He is a natural leader, as I'm sure you noticed, but other than Umberto, no military experience. Umberto is a good man, but how do the Americans say it, 'he is a little long in the tooth' and it's been many years since he's seem any action.

"What Graham and I had envisioned for you is training and leading our supporters on the Pampas."

"Why me?" asked Jackson.

Colonel Rueda rose and went to his desk to look through Jack's Marine file. He came back and handed a sheet of paper with Marine emblem emblazed on the top.

It was written to the Judge Advocate General's Office, Washington D.C. and dated December 26th, 1939.

Subject: Marine First Sergeant Jackson, Steven N.
Court martial Proceedings

Sir,

I respectively request that a full investigation of the matter before your office concerning Sergeant Jackson be instigated.

It has been my honor to have Sergeant Jackson in my battalion for six years. As you can infer from his record he has been an exemplary marine.

W.R. Ziegler

I have read the transcripts from the charging officer's testimony in this matter describing Sergeant Jackson's actions and find them totally out of character.

I humbly make this request for the benefit of the Corps. If we are to enter the hostilities abroad I would like to have all the leaders of my company have the skill and devotion to duty that Sergeant Jackson has displayed during his career.

Signed Colonel Roberts, Alvin T. USMC
Co-signed General Dawkins, Dwight NMN USMC

"Your Colonel Roberts is a brave man. This letter could be considered insubordination. I assume that's why General Dawkins signed it. They speak very highly of you Sergeant," stated Colonel Rueda.

"Colonel Roberts is the best officer I've ever served under, Sir. As you say, he is brave; I've been in action with him. He's fair, supportive of his troops and intelligent. This letter means a great deal to me. Thank you for sharing it with me, Sir."

"Graham was also impressed by you and when we received this letter and your file, we decided to ask your help.

"I think you should think on this, at least for a little while. Enrico, would you please take the Sergeant and Miss Sally to the dining and have Angela fix them some lunch. You two can talk while you dine alone, I can make some calls that need my attention and Enrico and Edward can find something to do elsewhere. Please return after you've eaten. And I hope you agree to our proposal."

They had been dismissed. It was a familiar experience for Jackson. He wondered if all officers, in everyman's military establishment, after reaching a certain rank learned how to dismiss underlings without the possibility of further discussion.

They were taken to a large rectangular room with shiny wooden floors, red and gold tapestries on the walls and the largest dining room table Jackson had ever seen. Enrico excused himself and went to the kitchen.

Deadly Marriage

Sally grabbed Jackson's hand and looked at him expectantly, but before anything was said, a pretty young girl with short black hair and sparkling eyes entered.

"Hello, Miss Sally. It's good to see you again," said the young woman.

"Hi Angela, this is my fiancé, Jack Stevens."

"Congratulations to you both. Now, what can I prepare for your luncheon?" said Angela as she shook both their hands.

Jack didn't have a clue what to order, but Sally understood his dilemma and spoke up.

"Whatever you planned for today will be fine," said Sally.

"May I fix you a drink before lunch?"

Now Jack knew how to answer.

"How about two Scotch with a splash of soda?" said Jack?

"Angela, I think he meant to say two double Scotch with ice and the slightest bit of soda," corrected Sally.

The young lady smiled and said, "No problem," then left.

"I'm not used to having people do for me. I feel like a turkey in a chicken coup."

Sally chuckled "I've never heard that expression before, but don't worry, you'll catch on and being pampered is easy to get accustomed to."

Angela brought the drinks, set them on the table and went back to the kitchen without comment.

They tried their drinks and leaned back in their chairs. Sally broke the silence.

"What are you thinking, Sergeant?" she asked.

"Well, I was just now thinking I don't like you calling me Sergeant, but I don't think that's what you're asking.

"I was thinking how my life is like a wave or avalanche carrying me along with no effort on my part. It just takes me where I'm supposed to go. I get worried I have no control and then when I get more involved in what is occurring around me it feels like I'm where I should be, doing what I should do!"

Sally listened, watched his eyes and held his hand. She knew he needed to talk it through and make his decision on his own.

Jack enjoyed a healthy sip of his Scotch and finally looked at Sally.

"I think there's something they're not telling me, but I don't know what it is. Your father could protect you by any number of means. I don't think that's really what they want me for."

"Colonel Rueda is a very respected and powerful man. If the GOU does take over the government, I imagine he would be president. I don't think he would mislead you, but he might omit something he didn't think you were prepared to hear," said Sally.

"Spoken like a diplomat."

At that moment Angela brought in steaming bowls of soup and a basket of hot bread. She smiled and pointed to Jack's drink. It was empty.

"I think that was enough Scotch for me. May we please have some wine with lunch, Angela?" asked Jack.

Angela grinned and left for the kitchen.

"In Argentina we always serve wine with lunch and dinner," said Sally.

"I'm still that turkey we were discussing earlier."

Sally smiled and kissed his cheek.

Jack asked, "What is your take on all this?"

"I think you need to figure out what you want, Jack."

"I think I need to know what you want and believe, Sally. This is not a question I can answer on my own, unless you're having second thoughts about us?"

Sally stood up and threw down his hand and said, "Damn you Jack. Do you think I just throw myself at every old man that comes along?"

Jack quickly stood up and wrapped his arms around her. Holding her as she tried to pull away he said, "I am so sorry. I'm just scared."

"What are you afraid of?"

"I'm afraid of you getting bored with me. We come from different worlds. When this crisis is over, am I going to be able make you happy? I love you so much; I guess I'm afraid of losing you!"

Deadly Marriage

"Well Jack, that's the least of your worries. I don't know how our relationship happened, but I'm sure you could never bore me or not make me happy. Just being with you makes me happy. Remember I love you too and if I have my way we will be together for as long as we live. So please never have a doubt about me again."

He smiled and said, "Yes, dear. Let's go tell the Colonel I'm committed."

Chapter 11

The Colonel was pleased with Jack's answer and asked him to return to the Estancia Mac Arthur. He was to secure the compound and surrounding buildings. "I will get in contact with you there," said Colonel Rueda.

Jack felt he had been dismissed again, without the word dismissed having been said. They left without comment.

Outside of the Colonel's office they ran in to Eduardo. "Welcome aboard, Captain Jackson."

"Was I that predictable and what is this Captain crap, I work for a living?"

At that moment the Colonel came out of his office. "I'm glad I caught you. In Argentina you will find it much easier to accomplish your tasks as an officer. So within our organization you will be a Captain. You may never get paid, if we are not successful, but you will be listed as a Captain."

Jackson hesitated then said, "Thank You, Colonel." Then the Colonel disappeared into his office.

"Do you understand the 'Captain Crap' now Captain?" asked Eduardo.

"I heard what he said, but I don't know why it would be easier being an officer?"

"Do you want to explain or should I, Sally?"

"The caste system in Argentina is rather stringent. In some ways we imbue wealthy people with assumed intelligence they may not have and to be an officer you must come from an upper class family. So, to deal with other members of the upper class and to lead members of the lower echelon it is much easier as an officer. Did that make any sense, I seem to have rambled?" asked Sally.

"Yeah, I guess it's the same in America. If you know the right people and go to the right schools, it is much easier to accomplish anything. We just hide it better."

"You're right about that, Jack," agreed Eduardo.

"Now, if you two are ready, can we fly back to the vineyard?"

Deadly Marriage

"Hold on, Eduardo. My father gave me an order and I think we should follow it. The Captain here doesn't have a wardrobe suitable for his rank and Daddy wanted me to get him fixed up while we're in town," said Sally.

"Your daddy is a wise man. I'll stay with Father while Enrico and a few men take you to the city and we can fly back tonight."

"Do you think that's necessary, Ed," asked Jackson?

"Yes, I insist. Buenos Aires is a dangerous place these days and if anything were to happen to the lovely Miss Sally I would never forgive myself," said Eduardo with his best gallant expression.

Jackson smiled and Sally stuck out her tongue at him.

Jack and Sally drove into the city in Edward's new Buick convertible followed by Enrico and three armed men in a Cadillac limousine. The procession found the clothing store Eduardo had recommended in a very upper class commercial area. Jackson, Sally and Enrico walked in. Enrico entered first, like a bodyguard, thought Jackson.

Then Sally and Jack entered and introduced themselves to the owner. The three men stood outside. One stood at the door and another on each side of the building. Jackson noticed their positions and thought these guys know their business.

Sally orchestrated the buying of his new 'appropriate" wardrobe. Jackson thought it would never end. It was much more complicated than he had expected and even included a tuxedo. When she was finished dressing Jack he paid the proprietor, who would not need another customer to have a profitable day indeed. Enrico filled the trunk of the Buick with the packages.

Jackson caught Enrico as they were entering the cars and pulled him aside, "Enrico, would it be possible for me to buy some outdoor gear suitable for crawling through dirt and grass, some combat or hunting boots and fire arms?" asked Jackson.

"Yes, Mi Capitan. If you will allow me drive, I believe we can find what you want."

Jack nodded agreement and Enrico spoke to the men in the limo.

"Where are you taking us, Enrico?" asked Sally.

"The Capitan needs some military type gear."

"Now, do you think this is necessary, Jack?" questioned Sally.

"I hope not, but like the old saying, 'I'd rather be safe than sorry!'"

Enrico drove them to a much lower class neighborhood and stopped at a surplus store. Jackson was surprised at the variety of items, some dating from the First World War. He found a simple British compass on a watch band, a black watch cap, wool and dungaree pants and shirts, web belts with ammo pouches and British army combat boots. Further searching found a set of desert camouflage binoculars and backpack. Jack paid the owner much less than one of his new suits had cost. The packages filled the trunk of the limo.

They had only driven a few miles when Enrico pulled in front of a small building with no signs.

"Miss Sally, I would suggest you stay here with one of my men. This is not a safe place for a lady."

"Sally, please take Enrico's suggestion. I would appreciate it," said Jackson.

Sally frowned and pouted, but said, "Yes dear."

No one laughed this time.

Enrico opened the door to the building and went in, making a sign for Jackson to wait. He returned and waved for Jackson to enter.

Behind an old glass display case stood an elderly, white haired man. The man was introduced as, "The Gunsmith," by Enrico. No further names were given.

The old man said with a heavy German accent, "How can I be of service, gentlemen?"

"I need three firearms. I need a 1911 .45 ACP automatic pistol, a Thompson 45 machine gun and a 1903 Springfield 30-06 rifle with telescopic sites and an excellent barrel."

The old man smiled "I see you know your weapons. The automatic I have here, you can take it with you today. The Thompson is almost impossible to get, but I'll try. All the

Deadly Marriage

Springfield's I see have worn out barrels. Telescopic sites are available, but expensive." He turned and entered a store room.

He brought out the automatic, still in its original box and laid it on the counter. Jack disassembled the pistol and inspected every part. It was new.

He then brought out a Springfield with a new barrel, sporterized stock and a large scope already attached.

Jack picked up the rifle, looked down the barrel, checked the action and checked the adjustments on the 6X18 long range scope. The old man did beautiful work, thought Jackson.

"Do you make ammunition for the Springfield?"

"I have some hot loads I'm sure will be adequate," he said smiling. Jackson was sure they would be, this guy was good.

"Okay, how much for the Springfield, with one hundred rounds and a traveling case, the 45 with 400 rounds and a belt holster and no questions asked?" asked Jackson.

The old man did some arithmetic on a pad and said, "500 US or 66000 pesos."

Jackson looked at Enrico who shrugged and said, "It's a high price, but The Gunsmith doesn't ask questions or give out information and he does excellent work."

Jackson counted out the money and The Gunsmith started wrapping everything in brown butcher paper. When he was finished Jackson asked him if ammunition loading gear was available. The old man said he wasn't sure, but would see what he could find, while he checked for the Thompson. They shook hands and the deal was done.

As the packages were being loaded in the back seat of the Buick Jackson asked Enrico, "How will I know if he finds the other items I want?"

"I will search him out once a week, until he has an answer for you. He moves around and doesn't contact his customers. You must know who to ask to find out where he is and go see him, Mi Capitan."

"Buenos Aires does seem like a dangerous place these days, Enrico."

"It is true, Mi Capitan."

The ride back to the Estancia was uneventful. Jack and Sally talked continuously in the open air, while Enrico and company kept vigilant watch in the limo.

When they arrived at the Estancia Enrico drove around the Buick and waved to have Jack follow him. He led them directly to the Lockheed Electra.

"I will load your packages in the Electra if you would like to go in and say goodbye," said Enrico.

"Thank you, Enrico. You are very kind and have been very helpful today," said Jackson.

"It is nothing, Mi Capitan."

Eduardo came out of the house and said, "I thought I heard the cars drive up. Were you successful getting "fixed up", Captain?"

"Yes, thanks to Enrico, I'm much more 'fixed up' than anticipated."

"My father has been called away and told me to present his apologies for not being here to say goodbye. If you don't mind I'd like to leave as soon as possible, you see I have a hot date tomorrow night and need some sleep," said Eduardo with a grin.

Chapter 12

Jackson's knuckles were not quite as white as when Sally had lifted off in the Cub for the first time, but he was still nervous when Edward took flight in the Electra. The sun had just dropped behind the Andes and the sky was beautiful.

"I'll be right back, I need to ask Eduardo something," Sally said and walked up to the cabin.

Sally tapped Eduardo on the shoulder getting his attention. He removed his head set and looked at her expectantly.

"How about swinging over the city and showing Jack the lights?"

"I'll swing in close, but not over the city. Without a flight plan we could get our hands spanked or our butts shot off."

"Thanks, Eduardo."

Sally came back and took her seat. She smiled at Jackson and held his hand.

"What are you up to now?" asked Jackson.

"You said you had never been able to look out of a plane, right? So, you've never seen the city lights at night then?"

It was just moments before Eduardo made a wide easy turn allowing Jack to see a view of Buenos Aires that was breathtaking. Sally sat and grinned while Jack had his nose pressed to window like a child.

"What are the lights across the river?"

"That's Montevideo, Uruguay. It's almost as large as Buenos Aires."

"How far is it across the Rio de la Plata?"

"It's over one hundred miles."

"You can see forever from up here."

Sally laughed; Jack was acting like a small boy with a new toy.

Jack stared out the window until the lights were just a bright glow. He turned to Sally and said, "That was one of the most impressive sights I've ever seen. Thank you for thinking of it. I'll have to thank Eduardo for the detour."

"Have I told you how wonderful you are today, Sally?"

"Not today, but I appreciate the thought."

The flight to the Winery was without incident and quiet. Sally went to play co-pilot and Jack fell asleep.

Jack awoke when the plane started its decent. He looked down to see burning smudge pots, lining what he believed was the runway. This time Jack was able to actually enjoy the sensation. That landing sure seemed smooth or I'm getting more comfortable in an airplane, thought Jack.

Eduardo was in a hurry to leave, so by the time they had unloaded their packages and gear into the manager's old stake bed truck, he had refueled and was ready to leave.

"Thank you for the trip and your little detour, Eduardo," said Jackson.

"You're welcome, it was my pleasure. I'm leaving for my base in the frontier at the end of the week, so I probably won't be seeing you for a while. I think the brass has plans for me. Be careful, cover your ass and take this mess down here seriously. It's dangerous."

"I'll make sure he's careful, but who is going to make sure that you are careful?" said Sally as she kissed his cheek.

"I've got the entire Argentine Army to keep me out of trouble. I better get going. I'll see you when the Army tells me I can see you," said Eduardo and walked back to the plane.

Mariano Pijkovic regaled them with the happenings at the Winery as they drove to the house.

Sally asked, "Have you heard from my father since we left, Mariano?"

"Your father called this afternoon and said Mr. Steven's paper work is finished and you can pick it up as soon as you get there. I hope that is good news?"

"Very good news, Mariano, thanks," said Jackson.

His new wardrobe and gear was stacked in the Living. Angela had cooked dinner and served it as soon as they were settled.

After dinner Sally said, "If you can wait a while I think I need to soak in a nice hot tub. I enjoyed flying the Electra, but the landing was a little nerve racking."

Deadly Marriage

"No problem, I have some things to do downstairs. I should be up in about 45 minutes. By the way, I thought the landing was perfect."

"Thanks, but I think you're prejudiced. Don't be too long, I may fall asleep," Sally said teasingly as she went up the stairs.

Jack found the box containing the .45 automatic and some ammunition for it. He then found the web belt and holster. He filled two clips and put the rest of the 50 round box of ammo in the pouches on his new web belt.

He then searched for and found a pair of dungaree pants and shirt. The boots were harder to find, but after fifteen minutes he found them. He took his new clothes and pistol upstairs. He put the pistol on the nightstand and his clothes in the chest of drawers. He went down the hall and found another bathroom. He took a quick shower and made his way back to their room.

Sally was curled in a fetal position, with her hair spread across the pillow. Jack looked at her with a feeling of happiness just being with her. He crawled in bed as quietly as he could, making sure he didn't wake her.

Jack was lying on his back thinking when Sally rolled over and put her arm over him. She barely opened her eyes and asked, "Are you too tired old man?"

They didn't get much sleep this night either.

The next morning Sally wasn't too pleased when Jack informed her that, because of the limited space in the Cub, he wanted to take the brown paper wrapped packages back to the Estancia and leave his new wardrobe to be picked up later. He tried to reason with her.

"Sally, I know I won't need the city clothes until we can go back to Buenos Aires, right? But, right now we may need my gear, so please don't be too angry with me?"

"Oh, all right, I just wanted to show them to my mother. I'll ask Mariano to bring them when he comes next month to see my father."

Graham watched from the window in his study as Mr. Birchall drove towards the house with a white flag waving from his window. "The bastard thinks he's cute," thought Graham.

Graham walked out and stood on the veranda. When Birchall parked and got out of his car he asked, "Didn't I make myself clear the last time you were here, Birchall?"

"Yes, you did, Sir. I just wanted to apologize for my overzealous actions to you and your visitor."

"Fine, you've apologized, now please leave!"

Birchall was furious, but kept calm, "May I apologize personally to your visitor?"

"I don't think that's a good idea, Birchall. He gave you a promise and might think your visit amounts to harassment."

He bit his lip as he walked back to his car. He forced himself to smile and wave as he drove off. Graham watched until he was out of sight.

******

Quinn knocked on Birchall's door. Birchall answered with a drink in his hand.

"Hello Quinn, how about a drink?" slurred Birchall.

Birchall thought Quinn was a local who just ran errands for Felix. Felix had introduced him as just Quinn to Birchall.

"No thank you. I understand you have a package for me?"

"That I do me boy."

He walked to the table and retrieved the box containing the engraving plates.

"Here you go. Come back again when you can stay longer," laughed Birchall and slammed the door.

"Well lieutenant, was he drunk as usual?" asked Felix.

"I suspect he is well on his way to passing out, Sir. He slammed the door in my face when he gave me the plates," replied SS-Obersturmfuhrer Christian Quinn.

Quinn was an Argentine national who had studied in Germany, joined the Nazi party and eventually the SS. He was actually SS Sturmbannfuhrer Felix von Krieg-Rupold's aide.

Deadly Marriage

"Are the bunks ready for our guest Obersturmfuhrer, and have the supplies been delivered?"

"Yes Sir, just as you ordered. I was able to store the food stuff in the galley, the generator and refrigerator are under the transom cover, Sir."

"I'm sorry I questioned you, Christian. I'm just anxious to get this operation going."

"No problem Sir, I understand. I too, am anxious as well."

"I think our Mr. Birchall has outgrown his usefulness, Obersturmfuhrer. I think we will pay him a visit later tonight, after the fog arrives."

******

The flight back to the Estancia turned out to be exciting for Jackson. They had just reached their cruising altitude of 3,000 ft. and leveled out when Sally said, "Jack, see that stick between your knees? Rest your hand on it lightly."

"I assume you mean the one attached to the airplane?"

"Smartass, yes I mean the one attached to the airplane."

"Okay, I'm massaging it softly."

"Get serious Jack, you're about to learn to fly."

Jack pulled his hand away as if the stick was red hot, "I don't think that's a good idea."

"I think is a necessity and you'll enjoy it after you get used to it. Down here the distances are so great; flying is the only way to travel."

Jack thought for a moment, "It's over a thousand miles from the Estancia to Buenos Aires and Buenos Aires seems to the center for everything, but agriculture. What the hell, you only die once."

"Okay, my hand is on the stick, now what?"

"I'll tell you what I'm going to do and you can feel what I do in the stick."

Sally said, "I'm going to pull back towards me and the plane will rise."

She pulled the stick back and Jack could feel how just a slight movement could change the attitude of the Cub.

"Now, I'm going to push it forward and the plane will go down."

The plane descended to their cruise altitude and then Sally leveled off.

"Now, you do it. Watch your gauges and take us up 500 feet."

Jack pulled back, but too hard. The Cub shot up and Jack couldn't stop it at 3500 feet.

"Easy Jack, push forward softly and bring her down very slowly."

Jack barely moved the stick and the plane descended slowly. He was able to stop the downward momentum and stop at 3000 feet.

"Very good, I'll take control now. Are your palms sweating?"

"Yes dear," though until that moment, he hadn't realized they were.

Sally had Jack practice taking the Cub to 3500 feet and back down to 3000 feet and then she asked him to maintain that altitude. The practice continued until Sally took control to land for the first fuel stop.

When they had refueled and were ready to take off, Sally said, "Now Jack, put your feet lightly on the pedals, just to feel them, don't push."

As they taxied he could feel when Sally pressed on one pedal harder than the other and the plane turned that way.

"Do you see how we steer with the brakes, Jack?"

"Yeah, they seem pretty touchy."

"They're like the stick; you must use very little force to make a big correction."

Jack was starting to like learning to fly.

They rolled down the runway with Jack taking mental notes of every nuance of the takeoff. After they cleared 500 feet and turned to the proper heading for the Estancia, Sally told Jack to take them to 3000 and try to keep them on the heading she had established.

Deadly Marriage

On this leg of the trip Sally demonstrated how to slew and correct the aircraft with the rudder and ailerons. She had him practice all he had learned until the Estancia was in sight.

"I'll take over now, Jack. You are doing excellent, but landing is the hardest part. Keep your feet on the pedals and your hand on the stick, but in no circumstance apply any pressure, Okay?"

"I'll do as you order, but could we make a quick circle, maybe a half mile, around the Estancia? I need to understand what is outside of the compound."

"No problem, Captain. Should I call you Captain when you get all military on me?"

"Now who's the smartass?"

Jack was making a mental picture of the terrain. He saw a stream bed or a ravine, some scattered trees and the trails/roads leading out of the compound.

"Seen enough, Jack?"

"I think so, I'll probably have to get Rico and ride all the trails before dark."

"Are you ready, here we go and remember no pressure, no matter what."

Sally landed smoothly and Jack felt all the movements, he was a good boy and didn't apply any pressure.

They taxied to the hangar and were met by Jasper and another young man Jackson hadn't met before. Jackson realized he needed to meet every one that should be in the compound.

Jackson and the two boys put the Cub in the hangar, and then the boys took all the gear inside the house.

They met Graham just inside the compound wall.

"Hello, Children. How was the flight?"

Sally ran to her father and gave him a big hug, "Jack will be soloing in a week or two, Daddy."

"Hello Graham. I think your daughter has too much confidence in me, but I have to admit I enjoyed it."

"I got a call from Colonel Rueda last evening and I'm glad you saw fit to join us, Captain."

"Thanks, I'll do what I can. I don't know about this officer thing, but everyone seems to think it's required."

"It is and the longer you stay in Argentina the more you'll agree."

"Oh yes, instead of Mariano bringing your clothes down next month, Umberto and I will fly to the winery day after tomorrow. We will bring them home with us," said Graham.

Jasper came back from the house with the other boy in tow. "Your packages are in your room, Mr. Stevens; and, Miss Sally's are in her room. Is there anything else I can help with?"

"Who is this young man?" asked Jackson.

"This young man is Sebastian, little Juan's older brother," said Sally.

Jackson said, "It's nice to meet you, Sebastian" and shook his hand.

"It is my pleasure, Sir."

"Jasper, there is something you can do for me, if you have an hour or so, I'd like to saddle up and show me around the Estancia?"

"Sebastian and I will go saddle the horses and be back in fifteen minutes."

After the boys had gone Graham asked, "What is that about, Jack?"

"I thought I better start earning my Captain's pay and take a look around outside the compound. I told the Colonel that I would secure your family and the compound, so I better get to it."

"Come inside and say hi to Momma and get something to eat before you go," said Sally.

"Yes dear," laughed Jack.

"I see you're learning Jack," smiled Graham.

******

At three am the two German officers left the boat. They walked in the fog, didn't speak and made very little sound as they made their way down the water front. The seaside

Deadly Marriage

boulevard was empty and even the drunks and ladies of the evening had called it a night.

They walked by the front of the US Agricultural Attaché's office and noticed no lights either upstairs or downstairs. They went down the boulevard and around the corner by the café into the alley behind the office.

Quinn stayed at the bottom of the stairs while Felix climbed to Birchall's door.

Felix quietly tried the door and found it unlocked. He thought "you would think he would have enough common sense to lock his door." He turned on a pen light, stuck it in his mouth and pulled a silenced pistol from under his coat. He pushed the door inward and shown the light around the room.

The pistol was not needed. Birchall was sprawled on the unmade bed, still in his clothes, passed out. Felix put the pistol back in his coat and removed a long thin dagger from a sheath on his left forearm. He then moved to the side of the bed and covered Birchall's mouth with his gloved hand. The knife went easily through the ribcage and into the heart. Birchall's eyes flashed open, but it was too late. Felix turned the knife around in Birchall's chest and smiled.

Chapter 13

Miss Ada had a special dinner prepared. They were served lobster with drawn butter, asparagus and baked potatoes. Good wine and fine conversation made for a memorable homecoming.

Graham and Jack retired to Graham's study where they poured themselves cognacs and sat in the comfortable armchairs facing each other.

"Well, Captain, what can I do to help with the security around here?" Graham asked smiling.

"There are a couple of things I can think of just off the top of my head. Is there a list of all the people who normally live within the compound walls?" said Jack with a straight face.

Now more seriously, "I can make one up for you tomorrow. Do you really think we might be in danger here at the Estancia, Jack?"

"The Colonel seems to think so and more I learn about German activity in Argentina, I believe he might be right. Is there some occasion where I might meet the people of the compound?"

Sally and Ada walked in, "Are we interrupting anything, gentlemen?" asked Miss Ada.

"Nothing you can't hear about. Jack was just asking if I could think of an occasion where he could meet all the people who live in the compound."

Sally perked up and said, "We could have a wedding."

"Sally dear; let the man catch his breath," said Miss Ada.

"Sorry, but I was just trying to help. You didn't have to look so scared Jack," laughed Sally.

Jack had turned red at her comments and could think of nothing to say.

"Jack, I'll try to save you. Would you ladies like a drink?"

"Not for me, Graham, and you don't have too many either."

"Yes dear," they all laughed.

"I'll take one Daddy; I'll stick around and enjoy the conversation. It's fun seeing Jack squirm."

Deadly Marriage

"I can take your harassment, but right now we need to talk seriously."

"Yes Sir, Captain!" said Sally.

Jack looked at her calmly, but with intensity she was not comfortable with. She had seen it with Mr. Birchall and now she knew she had gone over some mysterious invisible line.

"Sorry Jack. I'll try to control my smartass mouth."

"I'm sorry I have to be serious, Sally."

"What else is there we should be doing, Jack?" said Graham trying to lighten the mood or at least change the subject.

"It seems I have more questions than answers. How many men do you have living in the compound that I could train and can you trust them?"

"Eight, not including Umberto, you and me. As far as trusting them, I do completely. Many of them were born here and have spent all of their lives with us. The others are related in some way. It's more a family than a business."

"Could you let me have them for a couple of weeks for preliminary training?"

"We would have to pull replacements from other areas of the Estancia to cover for them. It might take a few days."

"Jasper seems like a bright young man; could he help me for about a month?"

"That would work out well. Sebastian is being trained to help Jasper and knows most of what is required. That shouldn't be a problem."

"One last thing, I need to go to town and pick up my passport tomorrow. It might be safer if I had company."

"Will Umberto, Jasper and I do?"

"From now on I would rather either you or Umberto stay in the compound. I know it causes you to change the way you handle your business, but this way there is a leader always here if something should come up."

Before Graham could comment, Miss Ada said, "If it was only for a short time, I can handle the compound, especially with Sally's help. Everyone listens to us."

Jack thought on this for a while. They both were strong, aggressive women and held sway over all that was the Estancia. Maybe this would work.

"Graham, if it's all right with you, let's give it a try, heaven knows they're strong, resourceful women. I wouldn't like to argue with them," Jack said chuckling.

"That is true. They are both probably meaner than either of us."

Everyone laughed. Maybe the men louder than the women, but they all laughed.

Since the mood had lightened the conversation turned to lighter subjects and soon Ada drug Graham off to bed.

"I'm getting a little tired myself. Let's go to bed," said Sally.

"I'll miss you in my bed," said Jackson.

"You'll be okay. You're probably tired of me already."

"Not true," said Jack.

Sally reached for his hand and led him upstairs. She kissed him when they reached the upstairs landing and they both retreated to their own rooms.

Jack was in bed thinking and feeling sorry for himself when his door opened.

Sally walked in wearing a housecoat and a cotton night gown. She looked down at him and said, "Do you know it's an acceptable practice in some countries for the betrothed to sleep together before the wedding in her parent's house?"

"How about in Argentina?" asked Jack.

"That practice is not yet widespread in Argentina, but I think we should start a movement to make it commonplace. Move over."

Jack thought someday they would need to get a full night's sleep, but not tonight.

Graham drove the new Ford "woody" down to the harbor and went directly to the Port Captain's office.

Umberto went for a walk to the back of the building and Graham sat in the car utilizing the car mirrors to keep watch.

Jackson went in and greeted the Port Captain.

"Hello, Mi Capitan, how are you?"

Deadly Marriage

"Hello, Herr Stevens. I have a package for you." He reached under the counter and brought out a plain manila envelope and laid it on the counter.

Jackson laid out 2000 pesos on the counter and said, "I hope it was not too much of a problem, Mi Capitan?"

"It is nothing. I'm glad I could be of service. You would not have liked to be around the harbor today without a passport. The US Agricultural Attaché was murdered last night and now the police are questioning everyone. They even stopped in here to see if I knew of any strangers in town."

"That is tragic news, Mi Captain. I wish them success finding his murderer. I hope you will excuse my being rude, but I feel I should get out of the city as soon as possible.

"Thank you again for your assistance. You have been a great help to the cause."

Jackson didn't wait for a comment; he turned and went out the door.

Graham started the car when he saw Jack coming. They drove around back and picked up Umberto.

"The Port Captain says the Birchall was killed last night. He also said the police are checking everyone, especially strangers, so if it's all the same to you could we go back to the Estancia?"

"Who would want to kill that little weasel?" said Umberto.

Jackson thought to himself, "The same people who urged him to pick me up and find the crate."

"I don't know for sure, but I'd wager it was someone interested in my crate, probably German agents."

"I agree. Let's get home and make sure everything is okay," said Graham.

*****

Felix and Quinn waited at the train station for the overnight train from Buenos Aires. They both fidgeted in the front seat of Felix's Packard. They had been waiting for over two hours and finally they could see the train coming slowly into the small station.

The ancient train was always breaking down and was in need of constant repair. Townspeople said with questionable pride that the train held the Argentine record for never being on time. Nevertheless, the overnight train was the most convenient way to get from Buenos Aires to Rio Gallegos, if one couldn't afford to fly commercial or didn't own a plane.

Local people rushed from the train to the waiting arms of their relatives, their big adventure to the city over. Businessmen walked slowly towards the taxi stand or their parked cars. Finally, four European appearing young men stepped down from the train. They quickly looked around until they saw Felix. They walked up to the German officers and greeted them.

"Hello Sturmbannfuhrer, we are your helpers from Buenos Aires."

"Welcome gentlemen. Let's retire to my car where we will not be so conspicuous."

Quinn opened the trunk and their small cases were stored away. They exchanged pleasantries until they entered the harbor area. Quinn pulled to the side of the road. A few hundred yards further the road was blocked by the police.

"This is not good, gentlemen. Quinn, let's take our friends out to the country for the day and after the police calm down we can return to the boat."

Quinn drove south down the coast to Puerto Nuevo, a small fishing village with a beautiful view of the waves crashing on the rocks and a small harbor filled with small colorful fishing boats.

They stopped at a small restaurant and sat outside on picnic benches. A waiter appeared and took their drink orders. When he had left Felix introduced himself and Quinn formally and asked the men to introduce themselves.

"Sturmbannfuhrer, my name is Herman Kohler; I am the leader of our little band."

Kohler was a large, heavily muscled, large boned man with light brown short hair and fair skin.

Kohler introduced his team members and all hands were shook.

Deadly Marriage

Kohler handed Felix a file folder which contained a dossier for each member of the team. Felix took the time to read the folders contents completely, while the waiter brought their drinks, took their meal orders and went back to the kitchen. Quinn asked harmless questions about home (Germany) and Buenos Aires until Felix had finished.

"Gentlemen, your dossiers make for interesting reading. You seem to be very accomplished men."

The waiter brought their meal and left.

"Let's enjoy our meal and I'll begin to explain what our mission is," said Felix.

******

There was a police car in the yard when Graham and Jack reached the Estancia. Jack thought this was going to be rough.

Graham said, "I guess we will see how good your passport is, Jack."

"Oh good, I can't wait," said Jack.

They walked into the Living and found Ada and Miss Sally having tea with Police Captain Suarez.

"Hello Captain. What brings you out here?" asked Graham as he gave Miss Ada a peck on the cheek. Jackson walked over to Sally and followed suit.

"Hello Mr. Mac Arthur, I'm sorry to say I'm here on official business. May I ask who this young gentleman is?"

"Captain, this is Sally's fiancé, Jack Stevens." The Captain stood and offered his hand and said, "Hello, Mr. Stevens, and congratulations. Sally is a lovely girl."

"Thank you, Captain. It is very nice to meet you."

"Mr. Stevens, I apologize for asking, but we have had a murder in our little town and must check everyone we don't personally know, may I see your passport?"

"Surely, Captain, I understand. I was sorry to hear about Mr. Birchall. I had the pleasure of meeting him a few days ago."

Jack handed him his passport. Jack and the Mac Arthur clan waited with bated breath as the Captain inspected the passport.

"This appears to be brand new, Mr. Steven. Why so?"

"I lost the original and had to get a new one. I was on the freighter *John's II* when she sank and my passport went with her. I just picked this up this morning."

"I see. Where were you last night between midnight and six this morning?"

"I was here with the Mac Arthurs all evening."

"Can someone vouch for your staying here all-night?"

Sally did not hesitate.

"Sorry Momma and you too Daddy, but I stayed in Jack's bed all-night. I can vouch for his never having left the bed for over two minutes."

The Captain blushed, Jack blushed, but Sally just stared at the Captain defiantly. Graham put his hand on Ada's hand and shook his head.

"I'm sorry for causing this embarrassment. Please forgive me; I was only trying to do my duty. I will leave you to enjoy the rest of your day."

The Captain blushed again and hurried out.

Graham stood up and walked into his study. Sally put her arms around her mother and they started to whisper between them.

Jack followed Graham moments later and found him at the sideboard pouring Scotch. He held up a glass offering Jack a drink. Jack nodded.

After they had sat down in their usual armchairs Graham said, "Jack, I'm not naïve enough to think we could have kept you kids apart, but it still comes as a shock when your baby girl announces it to the world."

"I'm sorry you had to hear about it that way, Graham."

"I'm not sure there is a good way, Jack."

They sat there sipping their drinks still comfortable in each other's company, even after Sally's announcement.

A short time later Ada and Sally walked in. It was obvious they both had been crying.

Sally was a little girl again. She stood by her father and asked, "Do you hate me, Daddy?"

Deadly Marriage

Graham patted his lap. Sally sat in his lap, put her arms around his neck and started to cry.

"I could never hate you, Baby Girl. It was just a shock that's all."

Ada sat on the arm of Jack's chair and put her hand on his shoulder.

"I told you once before, you didn't stand a chance, didn't I, Jack?"

"That you did, Miss Ada."

"Well, no one is blaming you or Sally. It was mother nature's way."

Jack reached up and held the hand on his shoulder.

"Sally, you've been acting like a woman lately, so quit your crying on Daddy's shoulder. It's not the end of the earth."

"You're right, Momma. I never wanted to hurt either of you, I'm sorry."

Graham lifted Sally up as he stood.

"My glass is empty; could I make anyone else a drink?" said Graham awkwardly changing the subject.

Sally came to Jack's chair and climbed on his lap. She nuzzled his neck and rested her head on his shoulder.

Ada followed Graham to the sideboard.

"How are you holding up, Daddy," asked Miss Ada?

"I'm Okay, just a little shell-shocked."

"Let's see, if I remember correctly, there was a young man who snuck into my bedroom more than a few years ago. You could say she comes by it honestly."

"Oh, you have a memory, but we didn't get caught!"

"We were lucky." They laughed.

They came back holding hands and smiling. Jack looked up and put a finger to his lips. Sally was sound asleep in Jack's arms. All the emotion and tension had been released and Sally was totally spent.

Ada petted Sally's hair and Graham touched Jack's arm and pointed upstairs.

Jack picked up Sally and carried her up to his room, laid her on the bed and covered her. It wasn't dark yet, but Jack felt like lying down beside Sally. In minutes he fell asleep. They would finally get a good night's sleep!

Deadly Marriage

Chapter 14

A few hours later Quinn walked towards the harbor from the highway. Felix had just dropped him off. The fog had not settled in as yet and Quinn could see the stars overhead. It was a pleasant evening and he was enjoying the walk.

He was stopped twice by the police, who didn't have anything better to do. To them he was just another Argentine with all the right papers and passport. Quinn had the same story for both policemen; he had had too much to drink and was walking it off. They both had sent him on his way.

He made his way back to the highway and reported that the police were still in the area.

"Gentlemen, I hope you were able to get some sleep on the train. It looks like we will be kept from our boat for a while. I suggest we drive out and I will show you the target of our mission, the Estancia Mac Arthur."

During the drive Felix told them what the actual objective was, the retrieval of a large crate. He described how it had reached Argentina, but not what it contained. He told them of the crate's passenger and the mystery surrounding him.

He pulled off the road short of the gate and parked in small clump of trees. They climbed through the strands of the barbed wire fence and walked down the road leading to the Estancia.

When they could see the courtyard lights within the Estancia Felix assigned each man a side of the compound. They were to look for anything that would aid in their entry and exit, while keeping the size of the crate in mind.

Felix followed Kohler towards the front gate. They were walking parallel to the road crouching down in the long grass.

They came within fifty yards of the main gate. It was a large double door affair made of wrought iron with a single lock where the two halves met. Kohler drew a rough picture of the gate complete with estimated dimensions in a small pocket notebook. He then motioned for Felix to go to the left while he went to the right.

Felix walked to the end of the fence noting that the fence was solid with no other openings and the trees were planted too far from the wall to help them get inside.

He walked back and met Kohler where he had left him. They retraced their path back to the car. Felix was thinking how Kohler had assumed control once they had reached the Estancia. Though he had used hand signals, Kohler had given Felix an order which he had followed. There was more to this young man than just muscles.

After they had walked about 500 yards, Kohler spoke.

"Sturmbannfuhrer, may I suggest that during the actual insertion and retrieval that you allow my team and me to work alone? We are well trained and there is no need to put the Sturmbannfuhrer at risk," said Kohler diplomatically.

"I will consider your suggestion, Kohler, and make my decision after we rest and you explain your plan in detail."

******

Jack awoke to find Sally sitting in a chair staring out the window. The sun was just starting to bring the Estancia to life.

"Good morning, Beautiful. What are you doing?" said Jack.

"Jack, I'm so embarrassed about last night. I was thinking about how hard it was going to be to face my parents."

Jack walked over and she put her arms around his waist and he stroked her hair. After a few minutes Jack said, "Then I suggest we go downstairs and get it over with."

They walked down holding hands. When they entered the kitchen Sally's parents were sitting sipping coffee.

"Hello you two, how did you sleep?" asked Ada, maybe a bit too brightly.

"Good morning. I, for one, got the best night's sleep I've had in a while," said Jack.

Sally just stood there looking very uncomfortable.

Graham stood up and walked to Sally, taking her in his arms and whispered in her ear.

Sally began to smile and then giggle. Graham released her from his bear hug and they all sat down. Everyone was smiling.

Deadly Marriage

Just before they finished a great breakfast of steak, eggs and homemade biscuits with fresh butter Jasper knocked on the door jamb.

"Good morning, Jasper, come join us," asked Ada.

"No thank you, Senora, I must speak to Captain Jack."

Jack walked through the door way and spoke in whispers with Jasper.

"Come back in and tell us what's going on boys," said Graham.

Jack motioned for Jasper to join the family and give them the same message he had just given Jack.

"Captain Jack asked me to ride the perimeter of the compound each morning. This morning I found tracks where four, maybe five men had moved through the grass. It looks as though they were inspecting the wall."

"Thank you, Jasper. You did well," said Jackson in dismissal.

Jack chuckled at how easy it was to act like an officer.

Sally said, "What's funny about visitors in the middle of the night?"

"Nothing at all, Sally, I was just laughing at myself acting like an officer. I used to wonder if they gave a class on how to dismiss people to officers and I just did it to Jasper without actually thinking about it.

"What do you think about our visitors, Jack?" asked Graham.

"A couple of things come to mind. They will be back and I assume tonight. We have a lot of work to be ready for them and the only thing they would want from the compound is the crate."

"I'll go gather the men," said Graham.

"Wait a minute, Graham. Have them report to the garage in ones and twos. If I was planning on breaking in here and did a "sneak and peek" like they did last night, I would have left a man watching in case something changed. Let's let them think we didn't notice the tracks. If there is a man out there hiding he saw Jasper and probably knows we know, but we might get lucky."

"What are we supposed to do, sit on our hands?" barked Sally.

Jack sat back down and thought. He was thinking of all that needed to be done to protect the compound. He wished he had more time.

He started thinking out loud, "If they come with only four or five men, it's one thing, but if they know we are expecting them they may come with more. We have to plan for a larger siege."

"Miss Ada, would you please get what help you need to turn the house into a fort? By that I mean, block the windows and entry doors, except the front and backdoors. Bring whatever food stuffs you have from the storehouse to the house. Prepare for losing the generator and the water supply. Set up a first aid station. And keep in mind, if we get hit badly we will want all the compound residents staying here inside the house."

"Couldn't we just call the police, Jack?" asked Ada.

Graham interrupted, "They would only send out someone to make a report. The report would read that they had found signs of something or someone moving through the grass around the compound."

"Another reason is we don't know if the police are aligned with the Germans and I assume our visitors are German agents."

"I see" said Miss Ada. "I better get to work then." She left to find Amelia.

"Sally, would you please find some scissors, writing pad, pen and some burlap bags and meet us in the garage?"

"Yes dear," she said and trotted off laughing.

"Were you such a smartass when you were her age, Graham?"

"No, but Miss Ada could give her a run for her money," laughed Graham.

******

The Germans finally made it to the boat just after the fog had settled in, one man short. Kohler had suggested that they leave a man to watch the compound so they would know if something important happened, something that would require a change of plans.

Deadly Marriage

Felix showed the agents to their bunks and they started to get settled in. He came back to the saloon and found Quinn sitting at the radio with head phones on. He watched impatiently while Quinn wrote down the coded message. It would probably take Quinn a half hour to decode, so Felix took a bottle of wine from the cupboard, poured two glasses and gave one to Quinn. Quinn looked up and smiled.

"Would it be presumptuous to ask to join you, Sturmbannfuhrer?" asked Kohler.

"No not at all, Kohler. Maybe you can share your thoughts with me about tonight's adventure?"

Felix retrieved another glass from the cupboard and filled it for Kohler.

"Thank you, Sturmbannfuhrer. If they do not expect us, we may be able to get in and out with the crate without alarming the compound. May I ask you a few questions, Sir?"

Felix nodded his accent.

"Do you know how heavy the crate is, Sturmbannfuhrer?"

"For planning purposes I would assume an empty crate, about two hundred pounds."

"Do you have a layout of the interior of the compound, Sir?"

Felix asked Quinn for a tablet and a pencil and started drawing. As he drew he explained what he was drawing to Kohler.

"I received this information from the poor man that was killed the night before last. He had gone to the Estancia on many occasions." Kohler had his note book out and was taking notes.

"He estimated the area of the compound at 500 meters on each side. He only found two openings in the wall, the entry gate and a small garden gate in the rear. There was a row of apartment-like houses, attached together along the north wall. The big house sits near the center of the compound and is very large. He thought it to be over 200 meters square on each of two floors."

"I assume, Sturmbannfuhrer, that the building with all the doors is an automotive garage?"

"Correct, that was his belief, but it was never confirmed."

Felix finished his drawing and turned it toward Kohler. Kohler removed his team's notes from his pocket and laid them on the table.

From the notes he added the tree line, the hanger, the stables, the power generator building and various other items. He also added where the farm equipment and trucks were stored or parked. When he was finished he handed the layout to Felix and asked, "Does this look fairly accurate to you, Sturmbannfuhrer, based on all you know?"

"Based on what I was told and what we saw tonight I believe it is."

"I need to know if anything inside of the crate is fragile or easily damaged, Sturmbannfuhrer."

Felix thought for a moment. Kohler is a pro. He has probably already figured out what's so important in the crate.

Before he had a chance to answer Quinn handed the decoded message to him.

Felix

We have discovered the identity of the American you asked about. He is a US Marine named Steven Jackson, Rank First Sergeant. Special Skills assessment shown: "Sniper" and "Hand to Hand Combat". He killed an officer 12/01/1939 and has been missing since.

Happy Hunting and Good Luck
Krantz

Felix thought for a moment trying to determine what Kohler needed to know.

"Yes to both. It is fragile and easily damaged, especially by fire or water."

"I just have one more question, Sir. Would it be possible for my team to remove the items from the crate and bring them to you?"

Felix thought, that would work, but then I would be forced to kill all of you.

"It would be possible, but you would have to be very careful. The items are priceless."

Chapter 15

The mysterious crate sat where Jack had last seen it. He walked around it feeling it rock in the waves. Jasper arrived and together they started to figure out how to disassemble the crate.

The supporting frame was first. Jack used a pry bar to take the boards off one end and Jasper held the end in place. When that section of the frame was removed Jack pulled out a package 3x4 feet wrapped in the same water tight wrap he had used as a catch basin. For some reason he laid it gently on the ground.

Sally entered the garage and asked, "How's it going?"

"You will tell us the answer in a few minutes. Will you please very carefully cut the outside wrapper from that package on the ground?"

Sally knelt down and inserted the point of a very sharp set of small scissors through the wrapper. She slid the scissors down the length, being careful to not penetrate the inner package. She performed the same operation on the remaining sides and pulled back the layer of outer wrapper.

Jack and Jasper got on their hands and knees to watch. Sally wiped her hands on her pants, she was sweating.

The next layer was heavy cardboard taped to a backing, also of heavy cardboard. She cut the tape on all sides until the next layer was free. She removed the cardboard. Something flat and wrapped in what appeared to be a bed sheet was next.

"Someone really wanted to protect whatever this is," she said.

"Someone is willing to kill for whatever this is," said Jack.

She slowly removed the sheet. Her movements were those of a surgeon performing a delicate operation. Finally she pulled back on a corner.

Sally said, "My God, do you know what this is?"

Jack, not understanding, said, "It's a painting."

"Not just a painting, Jack. It's a Monet. The Nazis must have stolen it and are now trying to hide it until after the war."

"Or some high ranking officer stole it and is hiding it from the world. But this explains why they were willing to kill to get it back and why they would tear the compound apart looking for it."

"Jack, I think there are two more paintings in here."

"Jasper, go get the woody and back it in here. We can stack the paintings on the cardboard just like the Nazis did," ordered Jack.

While they were repacking and loading the first three paintings, the Monet, a Degas and a Ruben, Graham came in the garage with Umberto and the first two of his men.

Jack thought he should limit who knew about the paintings. Everyone who knew was in great danger.

"Can you two finish taking this thing apart and keep it behind the Ford? I don't want anyone else to know about this," said Jack.

"Sure, Jack, but this is so exciting. How can you leave now?" asked Sally.

"Duty calls, sweetheart. Have fun and be careful. Jasper, keep an eye on her, when she gets excited she does some crazy things and make sure no one else sees the paintings," said Jack smiling.

Sally stuck out her tongue at Jack and went back to work. Jasper chuckled.

"Graham, may I have a word in private?"

Jack pulled Graham aside and told him about the paintings.

"That's a horse of a different color, as the saying goes."

"Yes it is, Graham. Whoever is behind this will not stop until they get them back."

"We need to get them moved as soon as possible. I think Sally will be done in 3 or 4 hours. Do you have any ideas on where to take them and how, Graham?"

They began walking to the house after asking the men to wait a few minutes, so they could talk without being overheard.

"If we could package them well enough that a moist environment would not harm them I have the place. I bought a large track of land years ago which has an old abandoned coal mine. It's been closed for years. It's about 70 kilometers away by four wheel drive road."

"There isn't another way to get there? No airfield or surface flat enough to land an airplane. "

"No, the sheepherders say it's very rugged."

"That's probably 5 to 6 hours and Sally has, say four hours, we could have the paintings there before morning. Let's go talk with the men," said Jack.

Graham introduced Jack and explained the visit of the previous night. Jack asked them if they were ready to fight to defend the Estancia. They all were.

Jack asked Umberto to take the men out at least 5 miles and see how they could shoot and what they had to shoot with. Jack really just needed the time to think.

Umberto shrugged and went to get a truck. The men came back with a wide variety of weapons ranging from an ancient single shot shotgun to western style .45 carbines. None of them had much ammunition.

After Umberto left, Jack and Graham went to the study. The furniture had been moved around by Ada and her helpers. They had done a good job. Graham and Jack pulled armchairs together to make talking more comfortable. Graham went to the sideboard which had stayed in its original location and made two stiff drinks.

Jack started talking without preamble, "We now know why, but we don't know who or how many.

"I see one thing that has changed, we can't let those bastards to get their hands on those paintings," said Jack.

Jack sat there deep in thought without having sipped his drink.

"What's on your mind, Jack?"

"I think we need to talk to the Colonel and explain what we found. He may have an idea of what to do with the paintings. We can hide them for a while, but we need a plan to dispose of them permanently."

"I think this may be too dangerous to discuss on the phone, Jack. Do you want to fly the paintings to Estancia San Franco?"

"Is your plane large enough to lay the paintings flat and seat the ladies?"

Graham looked away. He had just had a disturbing thought.

"I have another problem besides the phone being safe. I trust the Colonel to do what's best for Argentina, but what he may feel is best for Argentina may not be the best for our family, especially you. If he just hides the paintings, the Nazis will still think they are here somewhere on the Estancia and come for them. When they don't find them they will be forced to find you. You're their only obvious link to the paintings."

"It's not just me they will want to find, Graham, it's the entire family. We know they are capable of killing and they won't flinch at torture to find those paintings either".

With that chilling thought they both went silent with their own thoughts.

******

Felix woke with a sour taste in his mouth from the wine. He also had an uneasy feeling in his gut.

He quietly shook Quinn, motioned for him to dress and come outside. They reached the dock and started walking towards the café through the thick fog.

They entered the café and sat down at Birchall's table by the window. Felix hadn't said a word since they had left the boat. Quinn could see the Sturmbannfuhrer was in deep thought.

"Good morning, Gentlemen, may I get you some coffee?" asked Luisa handing them menus.

Felix finally spoke, "Please. That would be most welcome."

After she had brought their coffee and taken their orders and she had returned to the kitchen Felix said, "How are you this morning, Christian?" surprising Quinn.

"I am well thank you, Sturmbannfuhrer, and you?"

"I'm concerned about a couple of things and wanted to talk them over with you before the operation tonight."

"I am always at your service, Sturmbannfuhrer."

"Kohler asked permission to lead the operation without my being there. He feels I am too important to take the risk. What are your thoughts on his taking this responsibility?"

Quinn gave his answer some thought before saying

"They seem to be a very capable group. I wasn't there to watch them at the Estancia, so I am not in a position to comment on Kohler's leadership ability. I do agree that you are in a command position and should think seriously before allowing yourself to get in harm's way."

Luisa brought their breakfast and warmed their coffee.

When they were alone Felix said, "Well said, Christian. Enjoy your breakfast."

They ate in silence, both thinking of the upcoming operation.

They paid their bill and started walking back to the boat. The fog gave the dock a sinister eerie feeling. It made them both ill at ease.

"I have made my decision. Kohler will lead the group during the actual operation. You will remain in the car and be in command at all other times. I will stay on the boat and worry."

******

After a long period of silence, in which both Jack and Graham pondered the issues facing them, Jack said

"We need to convince them that the paintings have been moved and that we know they are coming," said Jackson. "If we can do that, they will need to regroup and come up with a new plan. And, if they believe the paintings have been moved, they may not attack the Estancia."

"They will still know all of those who know of the paintings will still be in the compound," said Graham.

Just then Ada came in, "Mission accomplished, Captain," and did a mock salute."

Jackson smiled and said, "Thank you, Miss Ada." He then turned to Graham and said, "I see what you mean, Graham."

"What did you say, Graham?" asked Miss Ada.

"I told Jack, that Sally came by her smart mouth naturally, that's all."

"I was just trying to lighten the mood around here. Sorry if my smart mouth was inappropriate, Jack."

"No problem, Miss Ada. It has been a couple of hours since we smiled and it was needed."

"Can I get you something to eat? I see you have something to drink."

Jack glanced at his drink. The ice cubes had melted. He hadn't touched his drink.

Graham looked up from his drink which was in the same condition as Jack's and laughed.

"I could use something to eat, Miss Ada, thank you," said Jack.

She started to say something smart, thought better of it and said, "I'll see what I can find," and then she left the room.

"Graham, I have an idea. Do you have some paint in the compound?"

"Sure."

"This is really simple, I hope it works. I'll take a part of the interior cover, hang it on the gate and sign it, 'Jackson.'"

"Why sign it, 'Jackson?'"

"I would rather have them chasing me than the whole family."

Umberto came in and announced, "I have dismissed the troops and are awaiting orders, Mi Capitan," laughing.

Jack shook his head and said, "Another smart ass I see. Do they amount to much besides cannon fodder, Umberto?"

"As it looks right now they are more dangerous to each other than any enemy. Most are lousy shots and the weapons they have are likely to jamb or misfire at any time. And they all need training."

"Graham, would you please tell Umberto about the paintings? I want to go check how Sally is coming along. I'll be right back. Don't let Miss Ada throw my food out."

Jack walked out to the garage and was happy to see Jasper look his way when he entered. The young man was following his orders.

"It's about time you came back to help," said Sally.

"Sorry, I'm not here to help. I was just seeing how much more you had to do."

"We just have the end left to disassemble."

"How many paintings do you have so far?"

"Eleven and they're all important works of the Masters."

Jack decided that asking if there was any damage was a bad idea. He said instead, "It seems like you're taking excellent care of them."

Jack kissed her cheek and asked, "Any idea how much longer you'll be?"

"I'd guess about an hour."

"What do you want us to do when they are all loaded in the car?" asked Jasper.

"Just lock it, come in the house and get something to eat."

Sally was so involved with another painting she didn't notice Jack leave.

"How's it going out there?" asked Graham.

"It looks like about another hour and they'll be done."

Jack noticed Graham and Umberto had finished their lunch.

"I suppose I should have known you would eat my lunch, Umberto. How was it?" laughed Jack.

Umberto just laughed and rubbed his big belly.

"I hope that will sustain you for a while. I need you to take the four wheel drive up to the old abandoned coal mine. Do you know where it is?"

"Yes Captain. I had to pull a sheepherder's wagon out of the mud just past the mine last winter."

"If you're done with my lunch, would you please have the men wait for me on the veranda in back as soon as possible?"

"Right away, Captain," said Umberto much more seriously.

"Let's hear it, Jack, I assume you do have a plan?" asked Graham.

******

Kohler woke his crew and assembled them in the saloon.

Deadly Marriage

"The Sturmbannfuhrer doesn't totally trust us. I asked him to allow me to lead the mission and he still hasn't responded. We will do our best in any case.

"I believe the best point of insertion is the main gate. Based on your report, Umsted, the rear garden gate would seem to be more liable to have people moving around it. Also, if we must remove the target as a whole crate we would need to use the main gate, we wouldn't have a choice."

He waited to see if anyone had a comment before continuing.

"Hans has been lying in the grass all-night and will continue to do so all day. We can't expect him to be as able as usual. I will have him stationed outside the gate in case someone shows up.

"Remember, if possible, we go in undetected and leave undetected. Is that clear?"

"Yes Sir," said the team almost in unison.

"Find something to eat and check your weapons and gear. Try to get some more rest before this evening."

Felix and Quinn returned to the boat to find one of the agents cooking breakfast, while the rest cleaned and checked their weapons.

"Good morning, gentlemen. May I have a moment, Mr. Kohler?" said Felix.

Kohler followed Felix up the steps to the cockpit.

"Mr. Kohler, I have decided to agree to your suggestion concerning leading the operation. With one caveat, Mr. Quinn will be command while in route and when returning here. He will remain with the car during the operation."

"Yes Sturmbannfuhrer, thank you Sir."

******

"Well Graham, the plan is a bluff. We paint the sign and hang it on the gate. That should confirm that we have the paintings."

"I'm sure if the FBI found out who I am, they have also, so my signature will add credibility and make them follow me, I hope. We need to turn on every outside light within the compound walls and I'll have the men walk guard duty around the fence and act like they're talking and gesturing to other guards inside the compound. I'm trying to make them think there are more of us and we're more prepared than we really are."

"What if they still try to enter the compound?"

"At the first sign of an attack I want all our men to run for the back gate, come inside and securely barricade the gate. Once they reach the house they should barricade the two remaining open doors. We will all then be in the house and we will defend it. We will have a man at each entrance. You and I will be on the roof watching the front gate. Do you have a hunting rifle?"

"I have an old 303 British rifle we use for predators and three shotguns, but I only have about 20 rounds of ammunitions for the 303."

"I would suggest distributing the shotguns in the house at likely points of entry."

Jackson thought for a few minutes and continued.

"Also, we need a good man with a shotgun with Miss Ada at all times."

"I like that idea Jack. What about Sally?"

Without answering Jack asked, "How long till sundown?"

"It's six now, so probably three and a half hours."

"In answer to your question, I'll have Sally with me until we settle in for the night. After that she should stay with Miss Ada."

"I have some things to take care of, Graham. Would you please explain the plan to the men and have them rest up until dark?"

"Sure. Where will you be if something comes up?"

"In Sally's Cub," said Jack as he headed for the garage.

As he entered the garage he saw Sally, Jasper and Umberto loading the paintings in the 4x4 pickup.

"Your timing is impeccable, Captain," groused Sally.

"It couldn't be helped and we're running very short on time, so bear with me if I just give orders. Jasper, ask Miss Ada or Amelia to pack up 4 or 5 days' worth of food and drink for two

Deadly Marriage

people. Then you pack a small bag with clothes for that long and come back here."

While Jasper trotted off, Jack went on with assignments.

"Umberto, you had better tell your family you won't be back until dawn. Make sure they know to come to the big house before dark also. We need you to leave for the mine within the next half hour. Jasper is to stay at the mine with the paintings until we can relieve him. Understood Umberto?"

"Yes, Mi Captain," said Umberto seriously this time.

When they were alone, Jack pulled Sally into his arms and kissed her as if it was the last kiss they would ever have.

Sally broke free and caught her breath, "Is it really that bad?"

"I'm not sure. The whole plan is a stack of cards, a bluff."

"Jasper, Umberto and I were talking and we all have confidence in you. You really are good at this sort of thing."

"I hope I'm good enough. How about taking me for a plane ride?"

"See, I'm getting better, I'll just say, 'Yes Dear', but can I get something to eat first?"

"Good idea. Would it be asking too much for you to bring me a sandwich also? Umberto ate my lunch."

"Yes dear."

******

29 December 1939
USMC Training Center
San Diego, California

Colonel Roberts was sitting at his desk reading his company's "combat readiness report" when Sgt. Rucker stuck his head in and waited to be recognized.

"What's up, Sarg?"

"I thought the Colonel would want to see this ASAP. Seems Jackson's been cleared," He then handed the Colonel the JAG communication.

Roberts read the communication three times, making sure he understood the legalese.

He dismissed Rucker and started pacing the floor. The communication stated that an autopsy had been performed and the lieutenant was found to have a heart abnormality which, along with the heavy drinking, caused his death not the punch. When the other officers involved were interviewed again, after this development and after being told that the investigation would continue, one finally gave in and said Decker had started the fight without provocation.

Roberts thought the JAG had really come through this time.

"Now, where the hell are you Jackson?" he said out loud to no one.

******

When Jasper returned Jackson told him to watch the paintings and to get on the road as quickly as possible. In the meantime he went to the hangar. He rolled the little plane out into the sun, checked for fuel and oil. That was all he knew to do.

When Sally approached the plane Jackson said what he had done and that he needed to go get something from the house.

Sally started the Cub and put Jack's lunch in his seat. She walked around the Cub performing her normal preflight and had just finished when Jack returned with his "sniper rifle."

He also had one of Graham's felt hats.

"Sally, dear, would you please put your beautiful hair up under this hat?"

"Why Jack?"

"Because we are going rat shooting and I don't want the rat to be able to recognize you."

"Why did I ask?" She motioned him into the plane.

The rat was Obergerfreiter (Corporal) Hans Scholz and he was having trouble staying awake. He had been awake for over 24 hours. He had learned during his career that stakeouts were pure boredom with bits of adrenaline thrown in. This one had been worse than most.

Hans was a street smart resident of Hamburg's city center. He had joined the Nazi party in 1931, thinking that the party was Germany's salvation. His father had been killed in WWI and his family had lost everything in the ensuing years since the armistice. He had bought into the party, heart and soul. When he had joined the party he moved quickly up in rank until he was assigned to the Gestapo. He had been trained in every aspect of espionage and was second in command of his team and a true professional. He would be hard to scare.

They took off and started circling the compound expanding the circle each time around. After the fourth trip around Jack said, "I've got him. He's good, but from up here, not good enough."

"On the next trip around I'm going to scare him. The odds of me hitting him are nil. This rifle hasn't been sighted in, so he's safe. I will open the window and shoot towards him, so don't' be startled. I hope he takes off running for the road."

When they came around Jack fired in the general direction of the discolored patch of grass. It hit the grass 10 feet from the target. Nothing moved so he chambered another round and fired, trying to walk the shot closer. A puff of grass and dirt showed that this shot missed by only a foot. Now the grass exploded and a man ran towards the fence as fast his legs would carry him.

"Come around and buzz him, Sally. We need to make sure he keeps running."

Sally brought the Cub around and dropped just off the top of the grass. She followed the path of the running man. When they got within range Jack fired a four shot burst from his Colt. Hans fell to the ground, rolled to his back and returned fire with his Luger.

Jack shouted, "Break off!"

Sally banked hard right and started to climb. As they climbed they could see the man running again towards the highway.

"Good job that should keep him running for a while," smiled Jackson.

******

Obergerfreiter Hans Scholz ran from bush to tree to bush until he came to the fence surrounding the Estancia. He walked to the clump of trees where Quinn had parked the car the preceding evening. He crawled between two tree trunks where he was shielded from the sky and caught his breath.

Now that the sound of the airplane was gone, he prepared for a follow on attack by foot or horseback. He was surprised when none came.

He spent the rest of the day deep in thought about his life at home in Hamburg, his beliefs and of his dying in a foreign land for an unknown prize. While he thought and rested he watched the road, he was still a professional.

******

As Sally had retreated out of harm's way she asked, "What now, Jack?"

"Let's check on Umberto and Jasper. Make sure they made it to the mine."

Jasper and Umberto had pulled off of the main trail and had driven the last half mile in four wheel drive through the grass. As they approached the knoll they could finally see the boarded up mine opening. As they were pulling up to the mine entrance Umberto remarked, "I'm glad you're the one staying here and not me. I don't like tight dark places."

"That part doesn't bother me; it's just one of those things that must be done."

"You were always smart growing up Jasper, but you're turning into a wise man!"

Together they removed a couple of boards to allow entrance to the interior of the cave. They entered and shown their flashlights on the walls, floor and ceiling. The interior surfaces were soil at the mouth of the cave, supported by wooden beams, but soon turned to a black flaky coal and soil mix. Further in, the surfaces were solid coal. The cave only went 30 feet into the small knoll. The end wall had turned back to soil. Jasper thought that the mine was abandoned, because the vein of coal was too small to be profitable.

Deadly Marriage

The paintings were moved to the back of the cave, placed on boards, brought along for that purpose and covered with water proof canvas.

Jasper put his gear just inside the entrance.

"If you're all set, I better get back. Our visitors may return and I wouldn't want them to be disappointed when I wasn't there to greet them," Umberto chuckled.

As he was climbing in the truck he heard the sound of the Cub approaching.

Sally was waving and giving a "thumbs up" signal. Umberto thought that crazy Captain must at the controls.

Jasper held up his hand in the "Okay" sign.

"Be careful, mi amigo," said Umberto as he started the old truck.

"If you see the visitors say hello for me, Umberto," replied Jasper smiling.

Jasper watched as the truck drove off and then as the Cub headed back for the Estancia.

Jasper felt proud that Umberto had talked to him like a man and not a child. He knew he had been given a great responsibility guarding the paintings. With the trust the Captain had shown in mind, he got ready to settle in until he was relieved.

He marched out through the grass tearing handfuls at a time and carrying them back inside the cave. He made sure he hadn't left a pattern of damage to the grass that might be seen. He kept bringing in grass until well after dark.

He lit the lantern he had brought and looked around his temporary shelter.

He tied a handful of grass near the base and made a broom. After sweeping out the debris, he made a bed by stacking grass five inches deep and lying his bedroll on it. He then pulled the boards from the entrance back in place. He was set for the night. He thought tomorrow he would camouflage the entrance with grass.

The sun cast the longest shadows of the day when it dropped behind the Andes. At that moment Jackson landed the Cub.

No sooner had they had fueled and stored the Cub in the hangar, then all the compounds exterior lights came on.

When they approached the garden gate they were met by the first four guards that would patrol the compound fences. They seemed to be in a festive mood and greeted them warmly. Jackson thought, "I hope to hell nothing happens tonight. We wouldn't stand a chance."

They entered through the backdoor with the kitchen on the right and the dining room on the left. The kitchen was filled with people eating and cooking. Amelia had taken charge of the kitchen. The dining, which had been turned into a first aid station, was empty except for Miss Ada relaxing with a glass of red wine.

"Hello you two, I'm glad to see you made it back. We heard the gunshots, but then saw you heading east; we were hoping you were not hurt?"

"Hello, Mamma, we're fine. It's been an exciting day."

"Hi Miss Ada, I'll let Sally tell you about our day, but I should talk to Graham. Do you know where I might find him?"

"He should still be in his study. He's been making everyone as comfortable as possible and working with the guards. He's also making sure everyone who should be here is."

******

Kohler was restless. He would calm down once his team was in place, but the waiting was hard on him. Felix wanted them to wait until midnight to leave the boat, then not make the insertion before 2 am and get back before the fog lifted in the morning. He would be glad to get away from the SS officers.

He called the team together and went over the insertion/search/extraction plan for a final time. Everyone answered correctly. They were professionals and knew the plan. There was really nothing left to do, but he had them check each other's equipment in their knapsacks anyway. He was unable to think of anything else that needed to be done, so he did what he always did, he went up on deck and exercised.

******

Jackson found Graham in the study working at his desk. He had the appearance of a tired and concerned man.

"Hello Graham, are we set for visitors yet?"

"We are as ready as can be expected, Jack. I'm praying for your bluff to work."

"As am I, Graham, as am I. Anything new happen today I should know about?"

"No, today went smoother than we could have hoped for. All the people are now in the house except for Umberto, who should be in before midnight. I'm worried about the men being used as guards. They seem to take this as an exciting change of routine or a play they are actors in."

"I met the first shift and got the same feeling."

"By the way, Graham, Umberto and Jasper made it to the mine and Jasper is settling in."

"That's good news. I made a slight change in your plan. I'm having Sebastian and another boy climb as high as possible in the trees adjacent to both gates at midnight. I thought they would be able to see our visitors if they decide our hoax is just that a hoax."

"Great idea, sorry I didn't think of it. How are they going to alert us without becoming targets?"

"I was talking to Sebastian about that and he came up with an ingenious idea. He climbed up the tree trailing a long rope. Then he found where he could see clearly and tied off the rope within reach. When he got down he tied a bucket to the rope and put it on an empty 55 gal drum he had placed underneath it. When he pulled the bucket up a few feet and let it drop on the drum, it made one hell of a racket."

"Smart kid," said Jack.

Jackson made a tour of the house and its preparations before getting something to eat. Then he carried pillows and blankets to the roof. The pillows were to rest his rifle on and blankets were to keep as comfortable as possible.

******

Right after midnight Felix called the team together, wished them luck and shook all their hands. They put their gear in the Packard and Quinn drove away.

Felix was left with a feeling of foreboding. He had had the feeling all day. There was not one solid reason for the feeling, but it was there none the less.

He went below and made a drink. He sat at the saloon table and tried to figure out what could go wrong.

They could know they were coming. That wasn't likely. They hadn't engaged anyone and they had made it out without disturbing anyone or anything.

He thought about Kohler leading the mission. He was capable and had the faith of his team, which Felix knew he would not have had. He should be able to handle anything that comes up. I would probably just be in the way.

The paintings could already be damaged. There was nothing he could do about that. If the Obergruppenfuhrer had a problem with that, it was between him and the damned U-boat skipper.

Felix had been proud of his assignment to safeguard Obergruppenfuhrer von Richter's stolen treasure. The general had picked him personally and told him of his faith in him. It had allowed him a certain level of autonomy and kept him out of the shooting war that was starting to rage in Europe. Felix made another drink and sat down to wait.

Quinn drove slowly through the deserted streets of Rio Gallegos. There was no nervous chatter as he had expected. The team members were calm and busy with their own thoughts.

They reached the road to the Estancia and Quinn turned off the headlights. With daylight it was a half hour's drive. With the lights out and only moon light to show the way it required twice that long.

Quinn turned into the small grove of trees he had used the previous day. When he turned off the engine they heard a hidden voice say, "Kohler?"

Kohler got out of the front seat and stood by the car. He said, "Hans, is that you?"

Hans walked up with his flashlight shining under his chin. Hans explained why he had left his position. He told Kohler about the airplane and the exchange of gun fire.

"What has happened?" Asked Quinn as he walked up to the two agents.

Hans explained again. Kohler surmised that the compound knew they were there and would probably expect them to return. In other words, they were expecting them and had prepared.

Kohler and Quinn discussed all their options.

Kohler believed that the Marine was the only person to worry about within the compound walls and that the rest would be farm laborers not fighters.

Quinn thought that was wishful thinking. They really didn't know who was in the compound, for all they knew the police could be waiting.

Kohler offered a compromise. He suggested that he go in alone, determine the situation and return for his team, if they had a chance of success.

Quinn reluctantly agreed.

Kohler ran off in a trot. Quinn didn't feel comfortable knowing the compound expected them. The team members had bunched up together and were asking Hans questions. SS Untersturmfuhrer Quinn felt completely out of his element and as alone as he had ever been.

Twenty minutes later Kohler returned. He was carrying a sign, the sign Jack had made.

Angrily Kohler said, "First Sergeant Steven Jackson left us a note," and handed the sign to Quinn.

Kohler continued sarcastically, "What high ranking officer or group of officers is smuggling stolen property out of Germany, SS-Untersturmfuhrer Quinn?"

"I don't know. I'm just following orders, same as you," said Quinn defensively.

"Whose illegal orders are you following?"

Quinn answered angrily, "Get in the car. I will let the Sturmbannfuhrer answer your questions!" He turned away from the agents and headed for the car.

Kohler pulled a silenced pistol from under his jacket and shot Quinn in the right calf, breaking the bone. Quinn rolled on the ground in agony, moaning and crying out in pain.

"I asked you politely twice, SS-Untersturmfuhrer Quinn. I would suggest you answer me truthfully before I'm forced to shoot you again. Oh, by the way Untersturmfuhrer, I should tell you that I'm Hauptscharfuhrer Wilhelm Kohler, Gestapo."

"I really don't know who issued the order. I was the Sturmbannfuher's aide long before he got this assignment. I wasn't privy to where the orders originated."

"That's not good enough. A smart young man such as you should have wondered about the origin of the orders. They were obviously illegal." Kohler then shot Quinn in the right knee.

Quinn was ready to pass out from the pain. He thought he would never walk normally again and if he didn't tell Kohler he would probably die where he was in the dirt of Argentina.

Trying to catch his breath and with tears in his eyes Quinn said, "The only name I've heard is Obergruppenfuhrer von Richter."

"Do you know the penalty for treason, Untersturmfuhrer, it's death?" Kohler then shot him twice in the face.

******

Graham awoke as the sun was coming up. He could see the fog bank towards the coast. Jack was sitting up surveying the outside of the compound with binoculars.

"You should have woke me up, Jack"

"No problem, Graham. There hasn't been any movement outside the compound since I relieved you. I called off the guard routine an hour ago, it didn't seem needed."

Deadly Marriage

"By the looks of things it seems like your bluff worked, Jack."

"I'll feel better after I take a few laps around the Estancia in the Cub and make sure we don't have any unexpected visitors. How about waiting up here and watching for another half hour or so, until I get back?"

"Sure, Jack. Do you think you can handle the Cub by yourself now?"

"Sally was shot at once, because I didn't know how to fly. I'm not going to let that happen again. Besides, all pilots have to solo sometime, right?"

"I wish you good luck. I wouldn't want to be your shoes if you bruise Sally's little Cub"

Jack sighed as he walked away.

By the time Jack had pulled the Cub out of the hangar and did what he thought was a preflight inspection the sun was completely up. He went through the preflight check list and started the engine just as he had been taught.

His take off was fairly smooth and he climbed to 1500 feet. He circled the Estancia in ever widening circles. When he reached front gate he could see his sign was gone. He circled and came around for a landing.

He realized he had a death grip on the stick and repeated Sally's words, "gentle small movements."

After he calmed himself as much as possible, he lined her up and brought her in, just like he knew what he was doing. As he taxied toward the hangar he was greeted by Sally and Umberto clapping and yelling.

He shut down the airplane and climbed out. Sally ran to his arms and gave him a congratulatory kiss. Umberto shook his hand and patted him on the back.

As they walked towards the house Jack waved Graham down from the roof.

Sally said, "That was a great landing, Jack, but why didn't you wait for me? I wasn't sure you were ready to solo yet."

"It was one of those things a man just has to do."

Sally stared at him not understanding, but Umberto grinned and nodded. He had recently heard much the same thing from another good man.

******

Kohler reversed the route Quinn had driven and parked the car near the dock. He walked quietly through the fog until he reached the boat.

Hans got on the boat first then Kohler came aboard. Hans called down the companionway, "Sturmbannfuhrer, Mr. Quinn has been hurt." Then he went below to find the Sturmbannfuhrer. Kohler and the rest of the team followed. They searched the boat from stem to stern and met back in the saloon. The realization that Felix had escaped reached Kohler. He charged up the steps, but didn't reach the cockpit.

Felix was standing in the shadows watching the boat. When the team had returned without Quinn or anything resembling the paintings, Felix knew that their mission had failed and they now knew what they were after. If they were loyal to Germany's present leaders and not Obergruppenfuhrer von Richter, they had to die. Felix pushed the plunger and the boat exploded, caught fire and sank.

Felix coiled what was left of the wire that had been attached to the detonator, the plunger and walked casually to his car.

Deadly Marriage

Chapter 16

Estancia Mac Arthur
Rio Gallegos
Argentina

Amelia had out done herself, the breakfast was delicious; or maybe I was starved, thought Jackson.

They had discussed the preceding evening's activities. What worked and what had not. Jack was trying to make decisions for the coming night, and not having any success, when Sally grabbed his arm and hauled him to his feet.

"No excuses, we're fine for now and you need some rest. You've been up for most of 48 hours!"

She grabbed him by the ear, as you would a child and marched him upstairs. He could hear the laughter from the kitchen caused by the manner of his withdrawal until they reached his room. Suddenly, he was unable to think or function. Sally got him undressed and into bed. She kissed his forehead and tucked him in. She then picked up a book and sat by the window to read. Jackson was sound asleep and snoring within 60 seconds.

When she was sure Jack was sleeping peacefully, she put down her book and went downstairs.

******

The light seeped through the cracks between the boards at the entrance to the mine, the shafts of light playing tricks in the dust hanging in the air within the mine. Jasper had had trouble getting to sleep. He heard sounds outside that he couldn't identify. He had checked outside the mine twice, searching for whatever had caused the noises.

He began to think of his feelings for Sally. Was it just a crush? She had always been there and been a constant in his life. Now she was being taken away by someone he liked and trusted. He decided no one knows where life will take them you just have to make the best of it. He finally fell asleep, listening to nature's sounds, but too tired to stay awake.

In the morning he chastised himself for letting his feelings for Sally occupy his mind. He rose and peeked out the entrance to the mine.

From atop of his little knoll he could see for miles in every direction. For the time being he was safe. He realized he was enjoying the solitude. He had been raised on the Estancia and still lived with his parents, three brothers and two sisters. He had never really been alone for any length of time.

He busied himself camouflaging the mine entrance, until he heard the sound of a plane. He turned and saw the friendly site of the bright yellow Cub coming his way.

The first time by Sally waved and yelled. He could see her wave, but the yell was lost in the engines roar. On the next trip by Sally dropped a small package out the window. She then waved and flew back towards the compound.

Jasper looked for fifteen minutes before finding the package. It had settled down into the grass and Sally wasn't too accurate a bombardier.

The package contained a note and pieces of candy. The note said, "All is well at home. Hope you're doing well? I bet you forgot to take something sweet? See you soon, signed S."

Felix found the sign in his car, signed by Jackson. He drove north out of Rio Gallegos not knowing where to go, but knowing he needed to get away from the site of his boat exploding. He hadn't seen Quinn's body, but was sure he had been killed. He felt some remorse over Quinn's death. He had been a faithful and obedient aide. He admitted to himself that over the last two years he had become a friend. Felix didn't have many friends, only acquaintances.

Was Obergruppenfuhrer von Richter a friend? He had been his mentor and guided his career for many years, but was he really a friend? Felix knew he felt a loyalty to him and that was enough for Felix.

******

Deadly Marriage

Sally shook Jack's shoulder, "Wake up or you'll be late for dinner."

Jack usually woke up instantly, but this time he was extremely groggy. He then realized what Sally had said, "late for dinner."

"How long did I sleep? We have to get ready for tonight!"

"You slept over 12 hours and we're all set for tonight. You just need to get cleaned up and come down. Take a shower and wake up, we'll talk when you come down," Sally kissed him tenderly and left him to do as he was told.

After Sally had left he said out loud, "Yes dear!"

Jack came down a half hour later. Showered, shaved and wearing clean clothes for the first time in two days, Jack felt refreshed and wide awake.

"Hello everyone thanks for letting me sleep in. I needed it more than I'd like to admit." Sally got up and hugged him. She then held him at arm's length.

"You sure smell a lot better and your eyes almost look rested. I guess you'll do."

"Thank you for your approval." And he kissed her cheek.

"You two had better sit down before you embarrass the parents," said Graham with a smile.

"Should I save all my questions about what went on today until after dinner or am I allowed ask them now?" asked Jack, glanced at Sally and saw she was grinning.

"Now would be fine," said Sally, as if Jack really needed her permission.

"Did anything occur today I should know about, Graham?"

"I should say quite a bit happened. Sally checked on Jasper and he's fine. Umberto and I rode around the compound looking for any sign of intrusion and then out to the gate. The sign was gone as we suspected and we saw buzzards sitting in a grove of small trees a few hundred yards down the road. At the grove we found a man's body picked over by the buzzards. He looked like he had been shot twice in the face. We had to turn him over to see the exit wounds to know he had been shot. The birds had made his face unrecognizable."

"Did he have any identification on him?" asked Jack.

"No, we found nothing on him, but he wasn't a working man, his hands were soft and smooth."

"It seems our visitors aren't playing nice with each other. Anything else exciting happen?" asked Jack.

"I set up a rotation of boys to man the tree lookouts where Sebastian set them up last night. We're going to have another clear night with a three-quarter moon, so they should be able to see anyone approaching. I made the executive decision that that would be all we needed now that they know the paintings have been moved. Also, everyone stay in their homes and come here if the bucket sounds."

"See Jack, you really weren't needed today," laughed Sally.

"I noticed the doors and windows are still barricaded. It seems Sally was right, I wasn't needed today. You've done a great job, Graham."

******

SS Sturmbannfuhrer Felix von Krieg-Rupold approached the small town of Puerto Santa Cruz and stopped in front of a small café. He had been thinking while he drove of his options for recovering the paintings. He did not relish the thought, but he felt he must report to Obergruppenfuhrer von Richter. The only safe way to make contact was through the German Embassy in Buenos Aires.

After a mediocre meal he decided to spend the night in Puerto Santa Cruz. He needed to rest his body and to relax his mind.

He found a hotel with surprisingly clean and comfortable rooms that had a view of the city square. It had a small balcony with wrought iron railing. He sat in the sun and watched the families and others enjoying the green grass and shade trees. There was a spattering of lovers lying on blankets hidden in the shade. He thought how it would be to live such a peaceful life. He had never known a peaceful life, he had always been driven to achieve. He could blame it on his parents, but that wouldn't be fair. He was driven from within.

He gave up on the peaceful line of thought and began to think of the task at hand.

He never thought again of his five dead countrymen in Rio Gallegos. He did think constantly of First Sgt. Steve Jackson and the Master's works of art.

******

After dinner Jack and Graham retired to the study, made drinks and sat in their usual armchairs to talk.

"You're better at securing the Estancia than you let on, Graham."

"I've learned a lot from you in the last couple of days."

"You know, I still haven't figured out what you and the Colonel have in mind for me?"

"Not that it's important at the moment, but I only have one task if the GOU takes over the government by force. That assignment is taking control of the naval base with as little loss of life as possible."

Jack sat back and looked at Graham. He had a calm steady stare that made Graham uncomfortable.

After a few minutes his expression softened.

"I assume the base commander is not a member of the GOU, correct?"

"It's somewhat worse than that. He has allowed German vessels to resupply and make repairs at the base in violation of our neutrality. He, like President Ortiz and Castillo, is pro Axis and makes no excuses for it."

"I also assume Colonel Rueda cannot send forces or even a few officers to help you with your task?"

"The Colonel is taking great risk already. He is constantly under surveillance. You see, Castillo has spies among Rueda's troops, they report his every move. If officers or troops, for that matter, went missing Castillo would know within a matter of hours. What needs to be done here will take months."

Jack stared at the floor, deep in thought. Graham was thinking that any action by the GOU was months if not years away. What needed to be done now was getting Jackson and the paintings safely hidden.

"Do you have any idea when this might happen, Graham?"

"I don't think anything will take place until after America joins the Allies. Argentina is now important to the Axis, but when America joins the war, Argentina will be vital. We feel if this happens and the Ortiz/Castillo government is still in power, they will force us to join the Axis."

"So everything the Colonel told me concerning my helping Argentina would also help America was fact?"

"That's very true, Jack. You have my word, Jack, you know all that I know now and if I should learn anything new I will share it with you."

"All the GOU members are taking a great risk; I don't blame you for being cautious. As Bogey said in that new movie Casablanca, 'this could be the start of a beautiful relationship,'" Jack stood and offered Graham his hand.

As Graham walked to the sideboard, after shaking hands, to refresh their drinks Sally and Ada walked in.

"As long as you're up, you can make a couple more of those?" said Miss Ada.

Jackson didn't even notice the ladies had entered the room. He was thinking if, by helping GOU, he would be helping America, why wouldn't entrusting the Colonel with the paintings help America? He was sure Colonel Rueda would no more profit from the paintings than Graham would. He could also hide them and use them as bargaining chips, if need be, in service to Argentina.

Jackson jumped when Sally put her arm around his neck.

"Down boy, relax," said Sally.

"Sorry, just deep in thought."

"What are you thinking so hard about?" asked Sally as she sat on the arm of Jack's chair.

"Something your father said a while back, that he trusted Colonel Rueda to do whatever was best for Argentina. But he wasn't sure the Colonel would do the best for the art world, if we entrusted the paintings to him."

Deadly Marriage

The phone rang; Jackson had never heard the phone ring before. Everyone looked at it with concern. Calls at the Estancia at night were few and far between.

Graham got up, went to his desk and picked up the phone, "Hello."

Graham listened for a few minutes then said, "He's been here all day and is still here, Captain."

After a couple of more moments he thanked the caller and hung up.

Graham walked back to his chair while everyone looked at him expectantly.

"It seems our Police Captain still doesn't trust you, Jack. There was an explosion on an old sailboat docked at the back of the bay. Four bodies or pieces of bodies were found in the wreckage. The boat had been bought recently for cash by a man with a German accent and he is nowhere to be found. He wanted me to vouch for your whereabouts for the last 24 hours."

"Someone is tying up loose ends in Rio Gallegos" said Jack. Then he continued, "I don't think the compound is at risk any longer. My thought is that the person responsible for receiving the paintings brought in help to check the compound. When they found out that the paintings were gone they didn't need the hired help any longer. I can't figure out where the body you found fits in with the other four, but I'm sure he's mixed in there somewhere."

"Why would he kill all those men?" asked Miss Ada.

"Because he still has a task to complete, to reacquire the paintings for his boss and he doesn't want anything to point to his identity or interfere with his accomplishing his task," answered Jack.

"Graham, what did you do with the body you found?"

"We left it out covered in a wagon behind the compound in case you wanted to inspect it. I planned on burying it tomorrow if not."

"Were there any labels in the clothes, tattoos or anything to help identify who he is or where he's from?"

"We didn't check, but I'll get someone to check now," said Graham, as he walked to his desk and pushed a button again.

Amelia came in the study.

"Si Patron?"

"Would you please ask someone to get Umberto for me?"

"Right away, Senor," Amelia replied.

"Why don't you use the damn buzzer you installed to call Umberto, you used it on me," asked Miss Ada?

"Because he hates it about as much as you do and I'm sure we're disturbing his evening with his family."

Jack was off in his own world of thought again. Sally got her parents attention and pointed out Jack's concentration to them. They all sat there waiting for Jack to join the party.

Jack came alive and started talking as if he was continuing a previous conversation.

"I don't want to be unfeeling or uncaring about the paintings, but I think we need to get them off of the Estancia and to the Colonel where they might be of benefit to Argentina and America." Before anyone could make a commit he continued.

"Graham, when you joined the GOU you entered the war weather you meant to or not. In war we must utilize all our assets. Right now the paintings are just assets, nothing more. The Colonel will know how to utilize this asset, we do not. I'm sorry, Sally, but that's how the marine in me feels. I would rather lose all the paintings then lose any one of you."

Jack stopped talking and stared at the door. Umberto entered.

"How did you know he was there?" asked Sally.

"He smokes the worst smelling cigars ever and I can smell him before I see him."

Everyone chuckled except Umberto, who tried to look angry.

"Did you invite me here to insult me?"

"No, sorry about insulting your fine smelling cigars. We would like to know if the on the body you found has any labels in the clothing or if the body has any tattoos that might shed some light of who he is. I know it's a grisly task, but it needs to be done," said Graham.

"Can I have him buried when I'm done? He's starting to stink as bad as my cigars," said Umberto grinning.

"Sounds reasonable to me, how about you, Graham?" asked Jack.

"Fine Umberto, please let us know what you find. Thank you!"

Chapter 17

German Embassy
Buenos Aires, Argentina

Oberfuhrer Wilhelm Krantz left his office for lunch. He was getting bored with playing spy games and putting on a show like he was really the German Embassy's Agricultural Attaché. As he walked to his favorite restaurant he wished the politicians would convince Ortiz/Castillo to join the Axis. Castillo always said that the military would fight him if he tried. If Castillo coordinated this with German intelligence, of which he was head, he could bring it off without conflict. Krantz would just have enough sea and manpower in the harbor to squelch any uprising. It would take time, but he could do it if the politicians in Berlin would allow it. If the war wasn't going so well he was sure he could have convinced them.

He was taken to a table in an enclosed courtyard shaded by large umbrellas at each table. He ordered a beer. He felt drinking beer really wasn't drinking, it was just being German. Because of his position and his image he didn't like to be seen drinking during the day.

"Hello, Oberfuhrer Krantz, how are you this fine day?" asked Yuri, the waiter.

"I'm well and how are you, Yuri?"

"I'm great. I love these beautiful summer days. What would you like for lunch, Colonel?"

"I would like a small steak, boiled new potatoes and a tomato and lettuce salad."

Yuri smiled, nodded and left. Krantz thought about Yuri. He was of Russian decent, his family had left prior to the Bolsheviks taking over Russia and he had been born shortly after their arrival. He thought Argentina really is a melting pot.

He finished his lunch and was relaxing with his second beer when Colonel Alejandro Bernardo Martin of the Argentine Bureau of Internal Security approached his table. Martin was

Deadly Marriage

the head spy for Argentina and as such a feeling of camaraderie, if not trust, existed between the two men.

"Won't you please join me, Colonel?" asked Krantz.

"Maybe for just a moment, I have some news for you. I just received a radiogram from Rio Gallegos. There was an explosion on a boat in the harbor; four European appearing men were killed. It looks to be a bomb. The owner of the boat, a man known only as 'Felix,' has disappeared. I just thought you might like to know."

"I appreciate the thought. If I receive anything interesting I will also pass it on. Thank you, Colonel," said Krantz.

"It is nothing for a friend, now I must be on my way. Goodbye, Oberfuhrer."

As Martin disappeared Krantz tried to decide what the news meant. That arrogant bastard von Krieg-Rupold requested my best agents and now they're dead, no doubt by his hand. Why was I ordered to send Gestapo agents instead of mine? I think he is working for someone or something other than Germany and the Gestapo is on to him.

As he walked back to his office he decided he would contact Berlin and inquire about SS-Sturmbannfuhrer Felix von Krieg-Rupold. I want to know everything about this man.

******

The conversation in the Study turned to lighter matters as they waited for Umberto to return.

Sally was telling the story about dropping the note and candy to Jasper. Jack thought that was very thoughtful of Sally, Jasper was pretty young and might be feeling a little lonely.

Miss Ada asked, "How old is Jasper now, Graham?"

"Let's see, he is two years younger than Sally, so he must be 18."

"Does he still have a crush on you, Sally?" asked her mother.

"He never had a crush on me, Mother," said Sally indignantly.

"Sometimes I think you are as oblivious to affairs of the heart as our Jack here. You don't remember his following you around trying to impress you since you were about thirteen?" laughed Miss Ada.

Umberto came through the door before the laughing subsided.

"I see you're having much more fun than I, but if you can quiet down, I do have news. His clothes are from German tailors. His belt and shoes are also from Germany. There was a SS emblem tattooed to the inside of his right bicep. I have my men digging a grave now and will bury him, if that's acceptable?"

"That's what we needed to know, Umberto. Would you like to have a drink with us and relax after this nasty business?" asked Graham.

"Thank you no, Patron. I want to tell my men that it's okay to finish the burial and then go take a shower. I don't know if I'll ever feel clean again after examining the body." Umberto didn't try to hide the fact he wasn't happy.

Umberto did a shallow bow before Graham could respond and left.

******

Felix didn't want to mingle, so he had his dinner brought to his room, along with a good bottle of Argentine wine. He had spent the afternoon going over all he knew about what had transpired since his arrival in Rio Gallegos.

Quinn would have returned if he hadn't been killed, that was obvious. Why had he been killed? Felix thought the answer was obvious also, they had found the packing material and sign and had the evidence they were searching for. He didn't know who "they" were, but most likely Gestapo. What would cause the Gestapo to investigate? By midnight he had come to the conclusion that someone highly placed within the Reich was investigating Obergruppenfuhrer Meinhard Egon von Richter and his operations.

Office of Obergruppenfuhrer von Richter
Danzig Germany (Poland)

On a chilly wet morning Obergruppenfuhrer Meinhard Egon von Richter was met by four Gestapo officers at the door to his office. He was told he was under arrest for treason, without conversation he was handcuffed and marched off to a waiting black 1936 Mercedes Benz sedan. He was driven to the airport, boarded a military aircraft, accompanied by one of the Gestapo officers and flown to Berlin. Minutes later newly promoted SS-Oberfuhrer (Brigadier-General) Zimmerman arrived at the same office to start his new assignment.

Nothing was said from the time of his arrest until he reached Gestapo headquarters in Berlin. During the flight his mind spun with the realization that he had been caught. He and Anna would not live a life of wealth and prominence in Argentina. He thought of his family and of his career. He had devoted his life to Germany and now Germany would take his life.

As they entered Gestapo headquarters von Richter was made to take off his uniform and put on a common set of gray overalls with a large P on the back and slippers. His teeth were checked for cyanide capsules. This was only the first humiliation of the day for von Richter.

He was placed in an interrogation room and handcuffed to the table. He waited for over two hours before anyone entered the room.

A small pale man with beady eyes and his hair combed over the top to hide his baldness came in escorted by two very large men, all in civilian clothes.

"My name is Vogel, Herr von Richter, and I'll be conducting your interview."

"Vogel, I've sat here for two hours, I need to use the restroom."

"I think not, von Richter. You will be giving no more orders from now on. If you must, just relieve yourself in your prison suit."

Von Richter straightened his posture and sneered at Vogel. The small man nodded to his comrades. They unlocked von Richter's handcuffs, but then relocked them behind his back. Each man roughly grabbed an arm and raised it until von Richter was standing on his toes staring at the floor. Then the interview really began.

By the end of the day, after being beaten, humiliated, hearing threats against his family and being shown that the Gestapo had solid evidence against him, he confessed. He would be hung or shot before a firing squad in disgrace, but with his confession his family would remain poor, but safe. After confessing and knowing he would surely die, giving up Sturmbannfuhrer Felix von Krieg-Rupold was easy. Felix didn't know it, but he was a wanted man and he was on his own.

******

The conversation in the study lasted for some time. Disposing of the paintings was the topic, different opinions made for lively debate.

Graham and Jackson had finally agreed that the paintings would be best utilized by Colonel Rueda. Sally was not convinced. She wanted the Master's works available to be seen by the world, not some collector's prize, hidden away.

"Sally, we can't afford the luxury of putting the paintings before people's lives. If the Colonel can save 100 or 500 Argentine lives by controlling and utilizing those paintings, wouldn't it be worth the risk?" asked Graham.

"You said to me 'that you trusted Colonel Rueda with your life,' remember? Your life is much more important to me than any paintings and I believe the family will be much safer if we don't keep the paintings," asked Jack.

"Okay, since you're ganging up on me and throwing my own words back in my face, I agree to let the Colonel have the paintings." She was acting mad, but couldn't quite pull it off.

Deadly Marriage

She punched Jack in the arm, stuck out her tongue and called him a "Bully."

Jack pulled her into his lap and yelled, "Quick, Graham, call the Colonel before she changes her mind."

Graham told the Colonel that he would like to come for a visit if possible tomorrow afternoon. The Colonel did not want to talk on the phone, "Your visit tomorrow afternoon would be most welcome."

******

Bright warm morning sun filtered into Felix's room. He awoke feeling physically better, but he still had a deep feeling of foreboding. He tried to package the feelings in his mind and put it aside, but it stayed with him.

He showered, shaved and dressed. He wandered around his room checking for anything he might have inadvertently left and went down to the lobby to pay his bill. The breakfast at the hotel restaurant was good and of large proportions. As he left he noticed a row of pay phones, but walked by them.

He had decided not to call Krantz. It would be safer to find him outside of the Embassy. Felix decided to drive the two days to Buenos Aires and do his best to enjoy it.

Oberfuhrer Wilhelm Krantz found two radiograms when he got back from lunch. One was an intercepted message to the FBI.

From the office of the Director Federal Bureau of Investigation
0230 GMT 04 Jan 40

To: Section Chief US Embassy Buenos Aries Argentina.

Responding to a request by the Secretary of the Navy:

You are hereby authorized to use all available means to locate First Sgt. Steven N. Jackson USMC. You are to inform

him he has been cleared of all charges and is requested to contact the SecNav's office through your office.
   Verification Question: Lieutenant Harsten's nickname
   Verification Answer: Miss Texas

Signed:
J.E. Hoover
Director FBI

   Krantz read the message three times. When he had decided there was no hidden meaning he questioned why the fuss over a First Sergeant.
   He glanced at the other message and realized he should have read it first. It was a letter from Reichfuhrer SS Himmler.

Nationalsozinlistische Deutsch Urbriterpactri

Oberfuhrer Wilhelm Krantz
German Embassy
Buenos Aires, Argentina

   This letter is to inform you of the arrest and subsequent confession of Obergruppenfuhrer Meinhard Egon von Richter to a charge of treason and theft of Reich property.
   He has provided the name of his accomplice, SS-Sturmbannfuhrer Felix von Krieg-Rupold, which I am told is of your acquaintance.
   You are to use all means to terminate or apprehend, detain and arrest SS-Sturmbannfuhrer Felix von Krieg-Rupold also on charges of treason and theft of Reich property. The properties stolen are works of art (paintings by noted "masters").
   Recovery of stolen Reich property is desired, but is to be considered a secondary objective.

H. Himmler
Heinrich Himmler
Reichsprotektor

Deadly Marriage

Krantz had never received any type of communication directly from the Himmler. He decided to frame the letter and put it on his office wall.

He reread the letter to glean out all pertinent information. He made notes on a pad at his desk.
- Von Richter will be tried and hung.
- Krieg-Rupold awaits the same fate. Bringing him in alive is not paramount!
- Krieg-Rupold is now my problem because Himmler knows he is in Argentina and has had communication with me in the past.
- "All means"
    - Locals?
    - My agents?
    - Request Gestapo?
- Paintings secondary = find and return if possible?

He then put the letter in a large manila envelope and placed it in the back of his filing cabinet. Krantz wanted to find a special frame for such an important letter.

Krantz asked his secretary to find SS-Hauptsturmfuhrer Huber and bring him to his office. Hauptsturmfuhrer Huber was an enterprising and aggressive young man. Since his arrival 18 months ago, he had developed contacts within the underworld of Buenos Aires and had been successful in completing every task to which he had been assigned. Huber is the man to find von Krieg-Rupold thought Krantz. A soft knock on Krantz's door brought him out of his reverie of dreams on meeting the Reichsprotektor in person.

"Enter."

"Hauptsturmfuhrer Huber reporting as ordered Sir," said Huber in a booming baritone voice.

Krantz was always taken aback at Huber's voice compared to his appearance. He was a small man with receding greasy brown hair, soft features that included a nose broken on numerous occasions and a slovenly appearance even in uniform and at attention.

"Relax Huber, have a chair. The Reich has a problem I would like you to handle for me."

******

Sally and Umberto were assigned to retrieve Jasper and the paintings. They left just after sunup after Sally had flown the Cub along the trail to the mine looking for visitors and found nothing out of the ordinary. Even with this knowledge they went heavily armed.

Miss Ada was returning her home back to normal from its fort configuration. It had been decided that the "tree boys" were adequate warning for the compound and that the threat had greatly diminished.

Jack and Graham were removing two seats from Graham's Fairchild 45-A to allow the paintings to lay flat. The Fairchild had a plush 5 seat luxury cabin and was powered by two 320hp Wright R-760 radial engines. It could cruise at 175mph and make the trip to Buenos Aires with only one fuel stop.

"I see why you bought Sally the Cub. You wouldn't want her banging up this beautiful plane."

"She really got the flying urge while flying in this and can now fly it as well as her Cub. There is some truth to your comment though, this is my baby."

Jack followed along while Graham did his preflight inspection.

They were interrupted by little Juan.

"Miss Ada says Captain got call from FBI," He then gave Jack a message.

Jack opened the folded note and read.

Jack,

An agent Treat Sanford from the FBI called asking for Sgt. Steve Jackson. I told him I didn't know him. He explained he had very good news if I could find you and left this message which doesn't make any sense:

Deadly Marriage

Lieutenant Harsten's nickname is Miss Texas.
You are to call the Embassy soonest.

Ada.

Jack just reread the message over and over. He obviously remembered Victoria Harsten and her being called Miss Texas by someone, but couldn't remember who.

Graham retrieved the note from Jack's hand and read it. Just then Jackson let out a whoop and a, "Holy Damn!"

"Graham, this message is from Colonel Roberts, my old CO, telling me to trust the FBI. I need to call now if that's okay?"

"If you're sure it's safe, Jack. I don't trust the FBI."

"Roberts is the only person who knew Vicki and he had called her Miss Texas the last time we were together. He wouldn't put me at risk even under orders. He's a good officer and friend."

"Let's go to the study and find out what this is all about then."

As they rushed pass the kitchen Miss Ada fell in line. Her curiosity was getting the best of her.

Jack was smiling and shaking with nervous energy when he took the phone from Graham who had gotten the FBI office on the line. He asked to speak to Treat Sanford and identified himself as Jackson.

The operator said, "I'll put you through to the Section Chief, one moment please."

"Graham, this Treat Sanford is the Section Chief?"

"Sgt. Jackson, I'm glad to hear from you so quickly. Mrs. Mac Arthur almost had me believing she didn't know you," He chuckled well naturedly.

"As you know, Colonel Roberts had his hands in getting this message to you. Before we get to the formal documents I have a personal note from Roberts for you:

Steve,

Hope this finds you healthy and living well.

All charges against you have been dropped. One of the little pukes gave Decker up during interrogation. You'll still have to explain about taking off, but the JAG says that's just a formality.

Now the strange part, I was contacted by a Colonel Donavon and ordered to report to Washington for a meeting. The meeting was held in the Whitehouse!

Donavon showed me his orders signed by the President. Basically it read "all military personnel are to provide the Colonel with anything he feels will help him complete his duties. These duties were not defined in any way?

He questioned me about you and how you and I got along for over an hour. He finally smiled and said he needed to contact you ASAP for a Top Secret intelligence assignment. He then asked me to help convince you it was safe to contact the FBI. He shuttled me off to the FBI building where an agent spent another hour explaining the workings of the FBI in foreign countries and ultimately Argentina.

I came up with the verification question/answer.

I hope this all works out well for you.

Sincerely
Roberts

PS

You were right. Kim has taken over as squad leader and is doing a fine job and Stiles is becoming a good officer.

"That's it, sergeant. Does all that make sense to you?"

"Yes, Sir, it does. Thank you for reading it to me."

"Is there any way you could come to the Embassy here in Buenos Aires, Sergeant? The paper work and instructions should be read in person. I've read them and believe they are in the best interest of Uncle Sam, but it's still your decision."

"Would 10:00 am tomorrow morning work, Sir?"

"I really didn't expect you to come in that fast, you do seem to make things happen, but I'll arrange it. Unless you have something else, Sergeant, I'll wait to see you tomorrow?"

Deadly Marriage

"I look forward to it, Sir," He had been dismissed. Jack hung up the phone.

Jack was explaining the phone call to Graham and Ada when they heard the truck pull up in the compound.

Sally came in alternately rubbing her neck and her bottom.

"Next time, Jack, you get to ride in that damn truck," but she put her arms around him and kissed his check. She then did the same to her father.

"Why do all of you look like you've taken crazy pills?"

"Sit down, Sally dear, and Jack will explain all," said Miss Ada still curious.

Jack went into great detail telling the story for both their benefit and his. Hearing him repeat it out loud helped him fully understand.

When he had finished they all appeared to have taken, "crazy pills" and they were working. They were smiling, but showing signs of concern as well.

Jasper came in and shattered the mood.

"The paintings are loaded, Patron."

"How was your stay at the mine, Jasper?" asked Jack.

"I have to admit, I was scared a few times."

"A wise man once told me 'When you're guarding something, that means someone might come and try to take that something from you,' you should have been scared Jasper," smiled Jack and patted his shoulder.

"Why don't you go see your family and get some rest, Jasper? We will see you tomorrow," said Graham.

"Thank you, Patron," said Jasper and left.

"Well, Graham, let's get packed up and get going," said Jack.

"You sound like you don't want me to go, Jack? That's not an option. I'm going and I'm staying with you from now on."

"I couldn't tell you how dangerous this may turn out to be or how I don't want you to get hurt or that it's just a bad idea. I don't really have a choice, do I?"

Sally said, "No, dear." Everyone laughed at her remark except Jack, but he was smiling.

Chapter 18

Felix drove north staying slightly over the speed limit. He was enjoying the day. The sun shone brightly and country was changing slowly, keeping his interest. He knew he couldn't accomplish anything this day and that thought allowed him to relax. He planned to drive until dark. That would allow him to reach Buenos Aires before lunchtime tomorrow.

German Embassy
Buenos Aires, Argentina

Huber walked slowly to his rarely used office in the Embassy. He was mulling over what Oberfuhrer Wilhelm Krantz had said and implied.
I am to apprehend or eliminate this SS officer Felix von Krieg-Rupold. The recovery of the paintings was not meaningless, but not a priority. I should use all resources available. What did that mean?
He unlocked the door to his small musty smelling office. A row of windows opened to a garden, one wall held empty metal filling cabinets and the only furniture was his wooden desk, a single wooden chair and an old fashioned coat rack.
He thought for some time before deciding the criminal element of Argentina would have the best chance of finding Felix. Huber didn't like aristocrats and their von names, so SS-Sturmbannfuhrer Felix von Krieg-Rupold was just Felix in Huber's mind. Once the decision was made he left his office heading for the seedier section of Buenos Aires.

******

Jackson had been converted. He was really enjoying this flight. Maybe it was anticipation of the forthcoming meeting or having Sally along, he didn't know. What he did know was the Fairchild was the nicest plane he had ever flown on. It was smaller than the Colonel's Lockheed, but much more luxurious. It had reclining leather seats, individual air vents and a small head back in the tail.

He gave up his relining leather seat to sit on a hard observer's seat behind the crew so he could watch what was going on in the cockpit.

Sally was actually acting like a real co-pilot! She radioed the Colonel's Estancia and reported they were an hour out. She also asked for help to secure the plane.

She glanced back at Jack, "That was so the Colonel would have troops to take charge of and protect the paintings."

Graham brought the Fairchild in smoothly and taxied toward the hangar. Six Argentine soldiers were standing with Colonel Rueda near the door. As Graham was shutting down the plane, a military 2.5 ton Ford truck pulled up as the engines died.

Everyone deplaned and was greeted warmly by Colonel Rueda. He then suggested the package be transferred to the waiting truck and taken to its new home.

Jack and Graham nodded agreement and with a glance from the Colonel his soldiers removed the package from the Fairchild and positioned it flat in the bed of the truck. Four soldiers climbed into the back of the truck with the paintings and the other two got in with the driver. When everyone was settled the truck drove away.

When they had reached the Colonel's study, all but the Colonel was surprised to see three large men in dark cheap suits.

"May I introduce Station Chief Treat Sanford, FBI? I believe you have spoken on the phone, Captain?" said the Colonel.

A middle-aged man with salt and pepper hair, kindly features and a vise like grip stood to shake Jack's hand.

"I'm sorry to surprise you, Sergeant, but tomorrow turned out to be a problem for me so I took advantage of the Colonel and asked him to allow us to meet here."

"It looks like you two have a good relationship," said Jack.

"We share information from time to time," said Sanford smiling.

"You've had a long flight. Would like to get cleaned up and can I offer you some refreshment or something to eat?" asked the Colonel.

Graham suddenly took charge, "You are too thoughtful, Mi Colonel. We would all like to clean up and meet back in fifteen minutes."

The Colonel waved and Enrico moved out of the shadows and led the way down the hall.

They chatted with Enrico until they came to the first guest bedroom when he opened the door he indicated that this room was for Miss Sally.

"There's no reason to soil two rooms Enrico, we can all use this room. Thank you."

"As you wish, Mr. Mac Arthur," said Enrico as he left and closed the door.

"What are you thinking, Graham?" asked Jack.

"I was just caught off guard. I also wanted to see if the two goons with Sanford would follow us."

"I understand the feeling and wasn't smart enough to check on the goons," said Jack.

"Well, what are we doing here?" asked Sally.

"Getting cleaned up and thinking," answered Graham. "You get the honor of cleaning up first."

"Sometimes you have to go by feel and for some reason this feels fine, but thanks for getting us out of there so I could think," said Jack.

When Sally came out, Jack said, "I'm next" and went into the bathroom.

"Sally, are you sure you know what you're doing? I just don't want you to get hurt, emotionally or physically."

"Daddy, I'm sure. I don't know how or why Jack came into our lives, but I'm sure how I feel. I've tried to figure out the reasons and I'm not sure they exist. I feel at a loss when he's not around. I really don't know how to explain it."

"You don't have to explain it, Sally. I feel the same way about your mother," said Graham as he hugged Sally.

"Your turn, Graham," said Jack coming from the bathroom.

Deadly Marriage

Sally put her arms around Jack and kissed him long and hard. When she released him he asked, "What was that for?"

"I just hadn't had the chance to kiss you properly today," she smiled.

When they returned to the study the Colonel and Agent Sanford had taken seats at the conference table. They both rose when they noticed them returning. Jack sat beside Agent Sanford with Sally next to him, the Colonel was at the head of the table and Graham sat across from Sanford.

"Would anyone care for some refreshment?" asked the Colonel.

"A Scotch with a splash," said Graham.

Jack help up two fingers and Sally held up three.

"I shouldn't, but bourbon neat sounds wonderful," said Sanford.

Enrico left the room to get the drinks. The other two agents had left the room.

Sanford opened the briefcase that had been handcuffed to one of the goon's arms. He removed five separate files and arranged them in some order that made sense to only him.

He opened the first file and stated, "The first thing I would like to discuss is your acceptance of Wild Bill's offer?"

"Who is Wild Bill, Mr. Sanford?" asked Sally.

"William Donavon, he's President Roosevelt's head spy," answered Sanford.

"I will try to simplify the legal mumbo jumbo, and then you can read it before you make your decision, okay?"

"Sounds good to me, Mr. Sanford," said Jack.

"Donavon wants you to be part of his intelligence team. To this end he has offered you a commission equivalent to your position with the GOU. I believe that is Captain, correct Colonel?" The Colonel nodded.

"You will be paid and service time will accrue at this rank or higher until you are released by Colonel Donavon or choose to return to the USMC or you retire, but you will be listed as Missing In Action on all of your military records. Since this is so extraordinary Donavon had Roosevelt initial off on the contract."

Sanford pushed the file in front of Jackson and asked Jackson to look it over.

Enrico brought in the drinks and everyone settled in for a long afternoon.

The papers in the file were shuffled between Jack, Graham, Sally and the Colonel. It actually surprised Sanford it didn't take longer.

After 45 minutes Jack asked, "Does anyone have a problem with me signing this contract, does anyone have any comments?"

Everyone nodded, except Sally.

"We still don't know what this, "Wild Bill" wants you to do?"

"Not exactly, Sally, but I have a good idea. It will be okay."

Sally nodded. Jack signed.

The rest of the afternoon was spent going over the other files. Some had to do with how his pay would be kept for him. His expenses would be paid by the Government, his Insurance benefit disclosures, how his activities would be hidden and finally Top Secret Security Agreements for Jack, Ada, Sally and Graham.

"Is there anyone else who you would like to get a clearance, but remember everyone who knows who you are and what you're doing is a risk and at risk?" asked Sanford.

Jack thought for some time. Sanford was telling the truth, his new family was at risk. He looked at Graham, "I was thinking Umberto and Jasper already know enough to be at risk. Shouldn't we get them cleared, so at least they know what they're up against?"

It didn't take Graham long to say, "I agree, Jack. They deserve to know the truth."

"I will need their full names and any other information you think is applicable," said Sanford.

Jasper was easy. He had been born on the Estancia and the family had known him since birth. Umberto was a little harder, but with the Colonel's help they were able to create an outline of his life as well.

Sanford busied himself providing Jack with copies of all the documents he signed. He then said, "I would suggest you put these in a safe deposit box, a very large safe or burning them. If they reach the wrong hands, well you know what could happen."

The Colonel held up a lighter and a large square ash tray. Jackson didn't hesitate. He burned the copies; some things must be taken on faith.

"You will receive your orders through me and only me. They will come from Washington and only I will relay them. I will help where I can, but personnel will not be available to help you. I will return to the Embassy and send your acceptance to Washington. I should have your orders by tomorrow evening. Would you please come to my office tomorrow at 7, we can talk then I'll take you to dinner?"

"Yes, Sir, that would be fine."

Agent Sanford and his men left. They ordered more drinks and sat thinking quietly. Finally Jack broke the silence.

"Well, I guess I'm officially a spy!"

No one responded. After a few moments the Colonel stood and offered his hand to Jack. Jack rose to take his hand.

"You are now truly committed. You have taken a very large leap of faith. I commend you on your courage. The gods smiled on Argentina when you stepped ashore."

Jackson could think of nothing adequate to say. He finally got out, "Thank you Sir."

Enrico stepped forward and shook Jack's hand. Graham got up and did the same. Sally got up and said, "You may be a US/Argentine spy, but you're my US/Argentine spy," and hugged him. The solemn mood caused by the Colonel's announcement was broken. Everyone laughed.

They retired early and went to their room. Jack and Sally talked well into the early morning hours and then took advantage of being alone. They didn't get much sleep this night either.

Chapter 19

Huber marveled at the difference between Embassy row and the ghetto. The ghetto was located high above the Rio de la Plata on a steep hillside. Flat land was at a premium. The ghetto was a huge and growing section of Buenos Aires where anything was available for the right price.

He had walked these filthy dirt roads before. He had seen the poverty and misery, but it had no effect on him. It was just the state of the world. There would always be ghettos and the poor people who lived there. He finally reached what he believed was the center of the ghetto.

Here perched on one of these flat areas was a large fairly clean looking home with a block wall surrounding it. He thought it had a semblance to a fort or small castle. He could see armed guards walking the wall.

He walked to a small door facing the street and rang a bell.

A small viewing window opened.

"Senor Huber to see Senor Ramirez, please," said Huber.

The little window was shut and locked without any comment from the guard.

Five minutes later the door was pulled open. Huber walked in.

He was stopped by two guards and checked thoroughly for weapons and recording instruments.

He was led upstairs to a rooftop covered sitting area where Julio Ramirez was holding court. He was laying on a large round pillow bed with a young, Huber thought very young, lady on each side with very little covering their bodies.

"Herr Huber, your visit must be of great importance for you to arrive unannounced and unprotected. You know the ghetto can be a dangerous place?"

"Thank you for seeing me, Senor Ramirez. Yes, it is of great importance. May we speak alone?"

"Surely, girls go powder something for a half hour," he could only reach one lovely bottom as they got up, but he squeezed

Deadly Marriage

the one he could reach. The girl smiled back at him and laughed as she left.

"What can this poor businessman do for the mighty Third Reich?"

Huber thought you are anything, but poor.

However, all he said was, "I need to find a German officer who is considered to be a traitor. If you could locate him and bring him in or eliminate him it would prove very profitable for you."

"I see. What information do you have on this traitor and how profitable?"

Huber handed Ramirez a file. In the file was a photograph and description.

"His last confirmed location was Rio Gallegos, but he could be anywhere in Argentina by now. Twenty thousand USD should cover your expenses."

"Make sure I understand you. You have a traitor somewhere in the vast land of Argentina and you expect me find him for twenty thousand USD?"

"I suppose I might go as high as twenty five thousand."

"Let's not haggle, it bores me. You will pay me thirty five thousand or our conversation is over."

This pushed Huber to his spending limits, but Krantz had said, "All means," even if this means was expensive.

"I agree, haggling is boring, so if you bring him in alive thirty five, if dead thirty."

"My regular terms, ten percent up front and if you don't pay when the job is done you will die slowly and painfully."

Huber nodded and removed his wallet from his coat pocket. He then counted out thirty five hundred USD and handed it to Ramirez.

Ramirez got up and shook Huber's hand, "Now that we are doing business together, please call if you need to visit and I will send someone for you."

Ramirez handed him a business card with nothing on it, but a number.

"I will have a car take you back to your office now. Thank you for stopping by."

Huber caught himself before he clicked his heals and just bowed slightly.

******

Felix was tired of driving when the sun set. He stopped at a German themed country inn which had a restaurant/bar downstairs and a few rooms upstairs. He had a delicious German meal and went upstairs to his room.

The bed was a four poster style with a white down comforter that dominated the room. There was a small chest of drawers and two night stands. The bath was small, but functional. He was comfortable. He had spent many nights in inns just like this one back home.

He stretched out on the bed and quickly fell asleep, fully clothed.

******

Enrico seemed to be the only one home when they left their room in the morning. He was sprawled out on a large armchair in the study, his mouth agape and he was snoring loudly.

Sally asked, "Do you think we should wake him?"

"If we don't we're stuck here. I don't want to steal one of the Colonel's cars. You wake him he won't hit you."

Sally tickled Enrico's ear. He swatted like a fly was bothering him. Then Sally pulled on his grand mustache, but jumped back as he snorted and sat up.

"Okay, I'm awake. Miss Sally you have had a mean streak since you were a child."

"Sorry, Enrico, we didn't know what else to do, but wake you," smiled Sally.

"I can't stay mad at you and you know it!" he continued.

Enrico rubbed his eyes and sat up.

"I was told to tell you that Mr. Mac Arthur left at first light to go home and asked you to stay safe. The Colonel is inspecting the hiding place for the paintings and won't be back for some time. And I am at your service."

"Would it be possible to have some breakfast and then give me a tour of Buenos Aires? We were in a hurry last time and I have until seven tonight to see the sights?" asked Jackson.

"If that is your wish, Captain, it would be my pleasure."

******

Felix was on the road before the sun had risen. He reached Buenos Aires before ten, and drove past the German Embassy two times checking for anything out of the ordinary. He then drove to a much lower class neighborhood eight blocks away from the Embassy and got a room in a small hotel. He left his car at the hotel and walked back to the Embassy.

He bought a newspaper and sat on the bus stop bench across from the Embassy. Every time a bus arrived he would wave it off as if waiting for another bus.

He had read the entire paper twice before he saw Oberfuhrer Wilhelm Krantz leaving for lunch. He followed Krantz at a discreet distance through the park and to the restaurant. The man is nothing if not predictable thought Felix.

When Felix had first arrived with his orders from Obergruppenfuhrer Meinhard Egon von Richter he had taken lunch with Krantz at this same restaurant.

Felix bought a different paper and sat on a bench in the rear of the park near the path Krantz would follow. An hour and fifteen minutes went by before Felix saw Krantz strolling through the park. Felix stepped behind some bushes until Krantz pulled abreast. He then slipped out behind Krantz his dagger firmly held in his right hand.

Felix grabbed Krantz by the arm and hustled him off into the bushes. Krantz was fumbling with the safety strap on his holster when Felix said, "Don't try it my friend, you will be dead before you can pull your Luger."

Krantz pulled his hand away and looked at Felix as if he had seen a ghost. Felix pushed him against a tree trunk and held the knife to his throat. He then removed Krantz's pistol and threw it into a bush.

"Have you heard anything from von Richter?" asked Felix.

Krantz didn't answer. He was thinking of how to escape this madman who would not think twice of slitting his throat.

"Can't you hear me, Krantz? If you don't answer you will be listening with only one ear."

Krantz thought for a split second about lying, but thought better of it.

"The only thing I've heard is that he was arrested for treason and theft of Reich property."

Felix had thought this possible, but wouldn't allow himself to believe it until now.

"Then if that's the case I assume I'm also wanted for treason and theft?"

"That is correct, but if you turn yourself in to me I'll help you all I can," said Krantz lamely.

"I think not, Oberfuhrer. We both know I would hang along with von Richter. Have you taken any steps to locate me?"

"No, I was just informed this morning."

"I think you're lying, Oberfuhrer." Felix then slid the dagger between Krantz's ribs and into his heart. He retrieved the Luger from the bushes, pulled Krantz's body behind two bushes and walked away deep in thought.

******

Buenos Aires held more beautiful examples of colonial architecture than any city in South America. It was laced with picturesque parks and statues. The history of Buenos Aires was much longer than any city in the US thought Jackson. It was older than any city he had ever been in. The tour Enrico gave them spent the entire day. Sally said the night life would take days to sample, but on another trip.

Enrico dropped Sally and Jack off at the Alvear Palace hotel not far from the US Embassy at four that afternoon. They had had a good day and Jack had a better idea of how Buenos

Aires was laid out and what it offered. Jack thought, "It really is a beautiful city, I could spend days just exploring."

They checked in as Mr. and Mrs. Stevens. A suite was secured that overlooked the park. This was the same park where Krantz had died a short time earlier. His body was still undiscovered.

Jack tipped the porter, closed and locked the door. Sally walked around the suite until she found the bathroom. It had a very large soaking tub with marble features, brass hardware and fixtures.

"Jack, I'm going to take a long hot bath."

"Would you like a drink while you soak?"

"You are a thoughtful husband," she giggled.

Jack wondered if they would be able to be husband and wife before one of them got killed. He couldn't keep from worrying about Sally and what he'd gotten them both into. He stalled until the water stopped running.

Jack was amazed how Sally looked sitting regally in a mountain of bubbles, her blond hair piled on top of her head. He set her drink on the edge of the tub then sat on the toilet lid. Romantic feelings of closeness and how special she was to him filled his body and soul. The mood crumbled when Sally asked, "Jack, I want to carry a gun in my purse and I want you to teach me how to use it." Jack was taken by surprise.

"What brought this on?"

"I want to be a helper not a hindrance. Whatever Sanford tells us tonight it will be dangerous. I just want to help my husband, Mr. Stevens," said Sally as she sat up to take a taste of her drink.

The bubbles were running off her shining breast as she sat up. Jack watched as she drank and sank back into the bubbles. He was sorry they were having a serious conversation.

"Are you going to answer me or just ogle?"

"If you're sure that's what you want I'll find something tomorrow and we can practice back at the Estancia."

"Quit fighting it, Jack. We are partners in this, no matter how it turns out. Just relax and enjoy it." Jack had heard this many times since he had met Sally.

"Yes dear."

"That's a good husband, now would you please wash my back?"

******

The bed had felt good and Felix thought he could get some sleep, but his mind wouldn't slow down. He realized the life he had known and lived up to this point was over. He couldn't go home or even meet with the few acquaintances he had in Argentina. He kept coming back to the same thought.

He knew it wasn't rational to blame his situation on Sgt. Jackson, but he couldn't change how he felt. He hated Jackson and wanted him dead. He felt he needed a purpose to his existence. He needed a goal to meet or a target to hit or an enemy to kill. Jackson was his enemy. He fell asleep thinking of how to accomplish his new task.

******

Jack and Sally walked to the Embassy from their hotel holding hands and acting like the young lovers they were.

The Embassy was a turn of the century mansion with eight foot block and wrought iron fences. They walked up to the gate and were met by two Marine guards.

"Hello, I have an appointment with Mr. Sanford," said Jack.

"May I see your passport and yours, too, Miss?"

Jack handed them the passports and started to smile. The Marine walked the passports into the entry and picked up a phone.

"What are you smiling about?" asked Sally.

"He's a good marine doing his duty by the book."

The marine returned and handed the passports back to Jack.

"Sorry for the inconvenience, Sir. If you would please follow me I'll take you to Mr. Sanford's office?"

They followed the marine down two flights of stairs to what Jack thought must be the basement. He knocked on the door and a quiet, "Come" came from inside.

"Hello, Captain. Miss Sally, would you please take a seat?" There wasn't much in Sanford's office but two wooden straight back chairs, his desk and a wall of full metal filing cabinets. Finding a seat didn't take long.

"I would like to remind you of something I said earlier. I am just the funnel for information going to and from you, that's all. If I receive information I think is warranted I'll get it to you as soon as possible, okay?"

Jack and Sally nodded agreement.

Sanford handed Jack a radiogram and said, "As you will see it's pretty loose in content."

Jack read.

To: Jack Stevens

First let me thank you for accepting my invitation. I sincerely hope our working together will be long lasting and fruitful.

You are hereby ordered to assist Colonel Rueda with all matters concerning the GOU and convey any information you feel is appropriate to me. The President and I hopefully feel that the Colonel is best for the future of Argentina and consequently the US.

You are to draw needed funds from Agent Sanford to accomplish this task.

Good Luck!

Sincerely,
Colonel W. Donavon

"You're so right, Mr. Sanford, that is loose," said Jack while Sally was reading.

"Did you notice he dropped the 'President card' on you? There is not much to add to that. Do you need funds now Captain?"

"No, Sir, I'll use my own funds until something unexpected occurs."

"Sir, is this copy the only copy of this radiogram?"

"Yes, I made sure of that. You can burn it here if you'd like?"

"Thank you, Sir, I would appreciate that."

"It's a little early for dinner by Argentine standards, but we could go early and get a great table?"

"Mr. Sanford, now that I'm officially a spy, it might not be advisable for us to be seen socially together. Please, no offense intended, but if you don't mind I think we will walk back to the hotel and order room service?"

"I understand completely, Captain. No offense taken. Can I ask you to be careful? I will hear from you when I hear from you. When I need to contact you I will leave a message at the Mac Arthur's and sign it 'Wild Bill'."

"I don't think we can forget that name. Thanks for your help, Mr. Sanford."

As they got up to leave Sanford said, "One more thing. Our country isn't in the war yet, but you are, Captain. Take care of yourselves."

They shook hands and left. A new marine escorted them out to the gate. They passed through the gate and into a new life.

They walked the three blocks back to their hotel, still holding hands. They stopped by the bell captain's station and ordered their dinner and a bottle of wine.

The ride in the elevator to their room was quiet. Sally had snuggled up under Jack's arm and put her arms around his waist. They stayed that way as they walked to their room. There was a note from the hotel manager under their door. Jack picked it up and read. Then he passed it to Sally.

The manager was informing all guests that the Agricultural Attaché from the German Embassy had been killed in the park. He was asking all guests that until the murder or murderers were apprehended to lock all doors and windows.

Deadly Marriage

Jackson thought that was foolish. If he had killed someone he would be long gone by now. He had no way of knowing he had walked past Felix's hotel room window while walking home from the Embassy.

They had just started their dinner when the conversation turned to their new assignment.

"Does this change your relationship to the GOU, Jack?"

"No, it just strengthens it. I'll do all I can for the GOU, the Colonel and your father."

"We will just watch out for any interference from any quarter, not just Ortiz/Castillo. I will inform the Colonel of my new status and he may have some ideas of how I can help."

"I think this an alive, growing assignment. I don't think we have any idea where this assignment will lead," said Sally.

"Of course you're right, no need to speculate, just prepare."

"Jack, I know you would rather I go home and just wait for you, but I'm not built that way. Hand and hand and all the other rot, we're in this together all the way! Please don't fight me on this."

"On one condition, Sally, this is that we get married as soon as it can be arranged." Jack wanted a chance to be married before something happened. He wasn't quite sure why, but that was what he was feeling. He realized he was doing a lot by feel these days. Sally walked around the table and sat on Jack's lap.

"I accept the condition and the proposal, Jack. Can I call Momma after dinner and tell her the news?"

"Will it have to be a big production?"

"Of course, you're not marrying a peasant girl you know?"

Jack shook his head and said, "Yes dear."

They finished their dinner and Jack was beginning to relax with a glass of wine when Sally ran to the phone.

Jack watched Sally talk to her mother with all the excitement of a school girl. She is young, thought Jack. But he added she is also smart, loving, beautiful, stimulating both mentally and physically and I love her. I'll just relax and enjoy it.

In the morning, Jack felt he needed transportation that wasn't borrowed. Jack knew what he wanted. They caught a taxi and went to the Buick dealer. Jack chose a V-8 Road Master Convertible like Eduardo's. Sally chose the color, bright yellow and the interior tan leather.

They haggled with the dealer, as was expected, and arrived at an agreeable price. Jack called his bank and had a certified check brought over by messenger. Jack signed the bank withdrawal form, gave the check to the dealer, worked out insurance and title issues and the car was his.

They drove to the Colonel's Estancia enjoying the beautiful day with the top down and the new car smell that emanated from the carpet and upholstery. Sally played with the switches and knobs alternately activating the lights, windshield wipers and horn. Jack realized he just enjoyed watching her.

A few hours before Jack and Sally had left the hotel Felix had checked out of his hotel and went prowling the streets. His car was known, so he needed another. Shortly, he found what he was searching for, a simple generic common automobile, an older dark green Renault sedan. In less than a minute he had it hotwired and driven off.

He drove downtown and into a parking structure. He parked next to another Renault, and then made sure no one was around and swapped license plates. He then headed south out of the city. He was now on a quest to find Jackson.

******

Enrico greeted them when they reached the house.

"Hello, Enrico, how's the mighty mustache?" asked Sally.

Enrico tried to put on a serious face and said, "Someday, when your Captain grows up, he will have a mighty mustache, too," but he couldn't keep from laughing.

"Don't pick on me, I didn't pull your mustache," said Jack.

"That is true. The Colonel would like to speak with you in the study, Mi Capitan."

Deadly Marriage

The Colonel was on the phone when they entered. He waved them to take a seat and Enrico joined them.

When he finally hung up he apologized for having to take the call. He didn't elaborate on who was calling or what was discussed.

Jackson told him of his meeting with Sanford and his "orders."

"Fascinating, Captain. How will you proceed?"

"I intended to go back to Rio Gallegos and complete your original assignment. If you feel it becomes necessary, I will be available to you on your command, Sir."

"Thank you, Jack. I will try not to interfere with your present assignment, but I'm happy to hear you are available."

"I am honored to serve, Mi Colonel."

"I'm sorry to be rude, but I really do have business to attend to."

"Goodbye Colonel," said Jack and they left, dismissed again, politely.

Chapter 20

Felix was staying under the speed limit. He didn't need to be stopped for speeding. The Renault was a giant step down in comfort and power from the Packard, but it was safer at least for now. He retraced his route and stopped at the same hotel for the night. He was comfortable again and got a good night's sleep.

The next morning, as he drove down the coast, his mind calm for a change, he noticed a bright yellow convertible coming up in his rear view mirror. The car contained a blond woman and a man. As the car quickly overtook him and passed, he would have sworn the man was Jackson. He tried to catch the convertible, but the Renault with its small engine could not keep up. He settled back into his safe speed and put Krantz's Luger back in the glove box.

As he drove he decided the Port Captain had to have greeted Jackson when he arrived on the crate. He would call on the good captain and gather any information he could. At least he had a place to start.

******

Jack was talking to the service station attendant that was filling his tank when he noticed a green Renault Juvaquatre sedan parked at a German Inn across the street. This was the same Renault he had passed, the same car that had tried to catch them. Jack watched the man who exited the sedan. He was tall and erect, and walked with purpose like a military man. Jack didn't think much about the man, just registered his impression in his subconscious mind. Felix had not noticed the Buick.

Jack drove for another hundred miles and stopped for the night at a small roadside hotel. Jack put the top up on the Buick and they went in to register.

After registering they had a modest dinner in the hotel restaurant and went to their room. They were both tired and wind burned from riding with the top down all day. They quickly got into to bed kissed each other good night and slept. They actually got a good night's sleep!

Jack woke up late to the sound of the shower running. He walked into the bath and said, "Good morning, Sweetheart."

"Hi, why don't you join me? I'll wash your back." When Jack took longer to answer than Sally thought necessary she added, "Unless the old man is too tired?" Jack pulled back the shower curtain, slapped her bottom and said, "I'm never too tired."

They played in the shower and then on the bed. They checked out just before noon. While they had been playing, a dark green Renault had passed by their hotel unseen.

******

Felix reached Rio Gallegos late that night and rented a room in a small hotel near the waterfront and checked in as Sergio Garcia. He opened the window and let the sea air fill the room. He enjoyed being by the water. He thought, "after this assignment is over maybe I'll become a fisherman." He laughed at himself when he realized that, "there is little chance of a life after killing Jackson." He would not allow himself anymore thoughts of a future.

By now they had found Krantz body and had made the connection to him. He was but a fly bothering an elephant. His countrymen would eventually send someone capable of finding and terminating him. It was just a matter of time. He only hoped he had time to take Jackson with him!

German Embassy
Buenos Aires
Argentina

SS-Hauptsturmfuhrer Huber had received orders to take charge of the Embassy's intelligence network until someone of sufficient rank and experience could be found to replace SS Oberfuhrer Wilhelm Krantz.

He knew if he handled the office well and made a smooth transition it would look very good on his record. He wished, without much hope, he would be promoted and allowed to become permanent Station Chief. He had set a goal of attaining the rank of Oberfuhrer before the war ended. Much of his success hinged on Mr. Julio Ramirez.

Ramirez knew that one must honor his contracts. "Anyone can be assassinated," was one of his favorite sayings; and this included himself. He also knew he was a big fish in a small pond compared to the Third Reich and shouldn't disappoint them. Besides, he planned to get future business from the little man with the big voice.

He called for his favored assassin Nester "Madman" Marquez. Nester was a vicious ruthless killer and enforcer, but much more intelligent than most of his kind.

Nester arrived at Julio's home in his armored panel truck. Driving was his back up man, Washington James. James was six feet seven inches tall and weighed over three hundred pounds. He was incredibly strong and dark black in color. He was wanted by US authorities for killing two policemen in a shootout while he was robbing a liquor store in Georgia. It had taken him two years of wandering, doing odd jobs and stealing before he had found a home in the ghetto of Buenos Aires. It had taken five more years to gain Nester's trust. He was inside now and wanted it to stay that way.

James stopped to visit with Julio's guards when they had reached the rooftop. They talked quietly and stood where they could all keep an eye on their charges.

"Good Morning, Julio, you wanted to see me?"

"Yes, Nester, thank you for being prompt, this is important."

Julio handed him a copy of the folder he had received from SS-Hauptsturmfuhrer Huber. He allowed Nester time to review the package of documents and pictures.

"You will receive five thousand USD if you can find this man and bring him back dead or preferably alive. You must be cautious; he is a dangerous man with many skills. He will be a formidable opponent."

"His last known location was Rio Gallegos," said Julio and added, "Yes, I'm sorry it has to be so far away. Do you have an idea about how to get there?"

"Without finishing my planning I would guess we will drive. I will need equipment and since I will not know anyone local I will need helpers to locate him."

"Thank you, my friend, and good hunting," Julio had dismissed Nester.

******

"Welcome home, children," shouted Miss Ada standing by her husband on the veranda.

"That's some fancy car for a mere Captain?" laughed Umberto trotting up to greet them.

"Hello everyone, it's good to be back," said Jackson.

"I always dreamed of being able to afford a Buick Convertible Umberto and I was tired of borrowing cars, so I went ahead and got one. It's the nicest car I've ever owned."

"Umberto, you can stay and gawk at the Buick or you can come inside and listen to them tell their adventurous story," said Graham, adding, "Come on in children, we want to hear it all."

After Jack and Sally had told their tale including Jack's status and orders, Krantz's murder, buying the Buick, Sally picking the colors and their drive home Graham nodded and Miss Ada shook her head.

"That's a flashy car for a spy," said Umberto smiling.

"It seems nothing has really changed, has it?" asked Graham.

"That's pretty much true, Graham. It does feel good not to be a wanted man anymore."

"Speaking of you being a 'wanted man' let's discuss our wedding," said Sally.

"Just tell me where to be, when to be there and what to wear," said Jack.

"Let us leave the ladies to decide your future and have a drink in the study," suggested Graham.

When they had settled comfortably in the study, Jack got serious and said, "Graham, I've tried and tried to convince Sally she isn't a part of my intelligence/spy career, but she won't listen. Do you think you might have better luck?"

Graham chuckled, shook his head and said, "You have much more influence over Sally now than I do, Jack. I know this may sound like surrendering and I guess it is, but I suggest you just give up. I told you before, once she makes up her mind, she usually doesn't change it, ever."

Now Umberto was laughing.

"Umberto, if you say, 'just relax and enjoy it' I'm going to punch you."

They all laughed and toasted each other.

******

James had built the panel truck from a 32 Ford sedan delivery. He had been a mechanic before he committed his first murder and took pride in his automotive skills. The truck was armored with ½ inch steel plate welded in place. The engine was a souped up late model flat head Ford V-8. The extra speed and armor had served their purpose in the past and would again.

The panel truck drove through the gate into a small courtyard. The courtyard surrounded a small house and a few outbuildings on the side of a hill above the Rio de la Plata. Nester had been born here thirty six years ago. Then it had just been a shack among thousands of other shacks in the worst ghetto in Buenos Aires. This was the only home he had ever known so, as he rose in prominence in his chosen trade, he built a home and base for his assignments.

Nester entered the two bedroom house and went to his large bedroom suite. The sitting room adjacent to his bedroom had been turned into a "war room." This was where Nester planned all his missions and kept track of his other businesses. James had his own room and bath in the other side of the house.

"I parked the truck in the garage. Is there anything I can do for you, Nester?"

Nester thought for a moment and said, "Would you bring in a bottle of red and join me?"

"I'll be right back, boss."

Nester walked to a school sized chalkboard and erased all the notes written there. He had only gone to school for two years, but he had been enthralled by the teachers writing, then erasing lessons on the board.

Nester wrote in the top center of the board "Find Felix." Under that, on the left side, he wrote, "Rio Gallegos" with a note, "unknown" next to it. He then added the words, "Long Drive." He finally realized he would have to plan on the run. He didn't have enough information to plan the entire mission.

James handed him a glass of red wine.

"Thank you, my friend. We need to find a man in a place called Rio Gallegos about 1200 miles from here. I don't have enough information to create a plan; we will just have to make it up as we go. Do you have any ideas, amigo?"

This conversation was common among the two friends. They would bounce ideas off one another for hours until a plan was formulated that took into account most or all of the possible contingencies.

"My first thought was to take some of the street kids along to watch the hotels. What do you think boss?"

"That sounds like a good idea. I don't think we can do much else until we get to this Rio Gallegos. How many kids do you think we'll need and how many can you get?"

"I think I can find maybe 5 or 6 kids we can take. A small place like that shouldn't have too many places he can hole up. That should be enough."

"Good. Have them meet us here at first light. We'll switch driving duty and go straight through. Let's have another glass of wine, then, while you find the kids, I'll load the truck, okay?"

"That works for me, boss."

Chapter 21

Jack and Sally didn't get much sleep their first night home. They rose after 8 and went to the kitchen.

"Good morning, Children," said Amelia.

"What is this, "Children" thing that seems so popular around here?" asked Jack.

"That is how Patron and Miss Ada refer to you. Don't you like it?"

"What do you say Sally, I can live with it?"

"We will probably be the, "Children" until we have children of our own Jack," smiled Sally.

"Okay Children, what would you like for breakfast?" smiled Amelia.

After they had finished breakfast Jack announced it was time for him to earn his pay.

"I need to get a layout of the harbor, where the base is, roads, buildings and everything else for that matter."

"We need to get a harbor layout, Jack," Sally emphasized the, "we."

"You can't kill a guy for trying. Anyway do you have any suggestions partner?"

"That's better. Let's go to the chandlery in Rio Gallegos and get navigational charts they should have restricted areas and the base marked. Then we can get Daddy's fisherman friends to take us around the harbor."

"You make it sound so easy?"

"With my help it is Jack. It really is."

"Okay, but I think we need to borrow a car or truck. I hate to agree with Umberto, but the Buick does kind of stand out. I guess I got caught up in the moment and didn't think it through."

"No problem Jack, we will soon be taking it on our honeymoon."

Sally and Jack were dressed like fishermen. Sally had her hair up under a Greek fisherman's hat and Jack wore a bright colored wool cap with earflaps. They both wore ponchos over their clothes and they were needed. It was before sun up the next day and cold.

They sat on the center seat of the motor boat that had towed Jack's crate to Rio Gallegos. Graham had arranged a harbor tour with same grizzled fisherman that had towed Jack's crate.

Sally had a chart of the harbor and was noting everything Jack saw as important. There was a restricted area around the Naval Base, but Jack was able to see the general layout. They had completed the survey in less than two hours.

They thanked the fisherman, filled his small tank with gas at the fuel dock and walked back to the old truck. Jack drove around the dock area while Sally continued to make notes. When they drove past the Port Captain's office something set off alarms in Jack. He drove another block before realizing what it was. Next to the Port Captain's Chevrolet Coupe was parked a dark green Renault Juvaquatre sedan. Jack drove back by trying to see inside the office.

He could only see the man talking to the Port Captain was approximately the same size as the man he had seen on the road.

Jack didn't say anything, but Sally looked at him with concern.

"What are you thinking Jack?"

"That I don't like coincidences. I think I've seen that green Renault that was parked by the Captain's office too many times for it to be a coincidence."

******

Nester and James arrived late in the afternoon the following day after stopping in Puerto Santa Cruz and checking into a small hotel.

James had found five boys willing to take the trip and work for a week for five dollars USD each. Nester explained what he wanted them to do. They were each to watch the hotel they were assigned to and look for the man in the picture. Either James or Nester would check on them every couple of hours. They had been memorizing Felix's picture off and on for a thousand miles. They all were sure they would recognize the man. James and Nester went driving around town to see what made up the town of Rio Gallegos. Felix entered the Port Captain's office and walked to the counter, "May I help you, Senor?" asked a pretty young clerk.

"Hello, I would like to speak to the Port Captain?
"I'm sorry the Captain is on the dock checking a ship that arrived last night. He should be back in about a half hour, if you would care to wait?"

"You may be able to help me. I'm searching for a friend that seems to have disappeared. Would you mind taking a look at his photograph?" He then handed her Jack's picture.

She shook her head and said, "I am not familiar with this man. But your friend is very handsome Senor."

Felix didn't think of Jackson as handsome. He smiled and said, "Sorry to have bothered you. I'll wait in my car for the Captain."

She just shrugged as he left.

Felix saw a man he thought might be the Port Captain walking toward the office from the dock. He carried an old battered briefcase and exuded self-importance. As he opened the door, Felix followed him in and blocked him from closing the door.

"Hello Captain. May I have a moment of your time?" asked Felix as he locked the door behind him.

Captain Sanchez stared at Felix with annoyance.

"What do you want, Senor?"

Felix took Jack's picture from his shirt pocket and showed it to Sanchez.

"Do you know this man?"

"No. I do not know this man."

Sanchez had taken a second too long to answer and his nervous eyes gave him away.

Deadly Marriage

As Felix pulled Krantz's Luger from his belt at the small of his back he said, "I think you are telling a lie my friend. Let's all go into your office."

The clerk looked at Sanchez, but only said one word, "Poppa," as if questioning whether she should do as she was told. Sanchez nodded.

They entered the small office, Felix took the seat behind the desk and made Sanchez and his daughter sit in the straight backed chairs facing the desk. The daughter was about 16, thought Felix, and was already built like a woman. She had sensual lips and a smooth complexion and deep brown eyes.

Felix laid the pistol on the desk, but pulled out his dagger.

"Now Senor, one more time, do you know this man? And think carefully before answering. Your daughter is very pretty, but a few scars would not leave her so," said Felix, playing with his knife.

******

When Sally and Jack returned to the Estancia Sally's parents were sitting in the Living with Father McDona.

"Hello Children, you remember Father McDona, Jack?" asked Miss Ada.

"Certainly, nice to see you again Father."

"And it's nice to see you also, though it would have been nicer to see you at Mass."

Jack shrugged and smiled. The Father smiled and shook his head.

"The request of Mrs. Mac Arthur's is highly irregular," said Father McDona.

Sally softened the mood with a peck on the Father's cheek.

"I'm sorry, Father, for asking and I'm sorry for the surprise, Jack, but Sally is in a great hurry and, frankly, so am I. That's why I asked the Father here to plan your wedding," said Miss Ada.

"Well, I'm glad I got back in time to have some say in these matters," laughed Jack.

Graham laughed, Sally, Miss Ada and the Father didn't.

Sally leaned over and whispered, "Say yes to every question."

"Jack, I've seen your passport and birth certificate. Is it true you were baptized a Catholic?"

"Yes Father," said Jack smiling at Sally while he lied.

"And you are ready to enter into this marriage without reservation or doubt?"

"Yes Father," said Jack not lying.

"Jack, you know this is a lifelong commitment, not like in America with their divorces."

"Yes I do Father."

"And if you are blessed with children will they be baptized and raised Catholic?"

"Yes Father."

The Father didn't like to rush as he was being asked to do, but didn't want to anger the Patron or disappoint Sally.

"Well, since I've known Sally all her life and you are, let me see how I should say this, more mature, I believe we can wave the Church's pre marriage counseling."

Jack just smiled; he didn't think saying, "Thank God" was appropriate.

"Okay Miss Ada I'll plan for Saturday noon," said Father McDona."

"Thank you, Father. The wedding would not have taken place without your blessing," replied Miss Ada. Jack wasn't so sure about that statement.

"I'll be in touch before Saturday, but I need to go see a sick parishioner now," said the Father as he got up to leave.

Sally rose and walked to the Father. Looking straight into his eyes she said, "Thank you Father, it means a great deal to me that you will officiate, you are part of this family."

"You are very welcome Sally, I understand how you feel, I feel the same way, but I really must be leaving."

Jack shook the Father's hand and thanked him. The Father walked to his car and left.

****

Deadly Marriage

Nester walked up to the Port Captain's office and tried the door. He found it locked, but the lights were on inside. It was strange that on a weekday the office would be locked, maybe he just stepped away for a while. I'll come back.

He noticed a dark green Renault driving away from behind the office building.

When Felix left the office twenty minutes later he noticed the giant black man behind the wheel of a panel truck parked in front.

Felix drove to the restaurant Birchall used to frequent. He took Birchall's table by the window and stared at the water. He was happy to see the waitress didn't seem to recognize him. He ordered and returned to looking at the water.

He was disturbed, not guilty just disturbed. Killing the Port Captain and his daughter didn't bother him in the least, he had killed many, but forcing himself on the pretty young girl was not like him. He had never forced a woman before, let alone make her father watch before killing them both. Maybe he was becoming sadistic as he neared the end of his life. Maybe he was losing his mind.

When he had finished he drove out to the Mac Arthur's Estancia, parked in the same clump of trees Quinn had used and waited. After a couple of hours, he got out to stretch his legs and found a large dark moist spot in the soil.

Chapter 22

"Two days isn't much time to set up a wedding is it?" asked Jack.

"Don't worry, Jack, the girls will make it happen. You can't get out of it now," laughed Graham.

"If we hadn't just had Christmas it would have been harder, but we'll make it on time. You two are now officially in the way, so why don't you go to the study and find something to do?" ordered Miss Ada. Sally was all smiles.

Graham said, "Yes, dear" and they left.

In the study, Jack spread the nautical chart on the coffee table. Graham got a detailed map from his desk and they sat down to compare notes.

"Jack, before we get started I just thought of something you do have to do for the wedding. You need to ask someone to be your best man."

"Oh shit, I hadn't thought of that. You can't be best man; you're giving the bride away. Umberto would do it, but he wouldn't be happy about it. The only two close to my age that I feel somewhat close to are Eduardo Rueda, who is somewhere in the wilderness near Brazil, and Jasper."

"I think Jasper would feel it a great honor and soothe his feelings about you marrying Sally if you asked him to be your best man."

"I'll go find him and ask him," said Jack.

"I think it would mean more to him if I called him in and you asked him formally Jack." Jack nodded.

Graham called the stables, but finally reached him at his parent's home.

When Jasper arrived there was champagne and three glasses on the side board and Jack and Graham in deep discussion.

He stood in the doorway waiting to be invited in.

Jack looked up and said, "Hello my friend, won't you join us?" Jack got up and offered Jasper his hand. "Would you like a drink?"

Deadly Marriage

"Sir, I've never had hard liquor, I don't know if I want one or not," smiled Jasper.

"I'll make you a short one and you can try it. Have a seat."

When Jackson returned from the side bar he asked, "I assume the compound gossip mill has already announced that Sally and I are getting married Saturday?"

Jasper couldn't keep the slight frown from his young features.

"No Sir, I hadn't heard, Congratulations."

"Graham asked you to come so I could explain something to you and ask you a question. I haven't known you very long, but I have trusted you, seen your bravery and strength and consider you a good friend."

"Thank you, Sir. I also feel you are a friend."

"Jasper, would you please call me Jack and honor me by being my best man?"

Jasper sat there for a few moments as if he had been shocked. Finally, he rose and offered his hand to Jack.

"It would be my great honor to be your best man Jack," Jack shook his hand and patted him on the shoulder.

"Now that that's settled, how do you like your drink, Jasper?" asked Graham.

"Sorry, Sir, it's a little strong for me."

"Then how about a glass of champagne to celebrate the wedding and your friendship with Jack?" asked Graham.

"Thank you, Patron that would be wonderful."

They drank their champagne and Jack learned more about Jasper. Eventually Jack excused himself to go relieve himself. Jasper took the chance to ask Graham.

"What is required of the "best man", Patron? I have never had the honor before."

Graham smiled and said, "Don't worry, Jasper, I'll help. Meet me here at 9 tomorrow, we'll go to town and get you set up. No problem, it would be my pleasure."

******

"Nester, I think we may have to take a more direct approach. The kids haven't seen anything and our discrete inquiries haven't netted us anything. I can show the picture around and see what pops up."

"Thank you, my friend, but everyone you spoke to would remember you. I don't want to lose you to a prison sentence or worse, just for money. Let's let the kids have another day and then I'll take a more direct approach."

******

Felix watched the road to the Estancia and as the afternoon wore on more traffic appeared. A florist truck, a catering company truck and others had shown up, stayed about an hour and left. It looked like they were planning some kind of celebration at the Estancia.

When the florist truck left Felix followed it back to his store front. He parked a block away and waited fifteen minutes. He then entered the store.

"Would you happen to know what is happening at the Mac Arthur Estancia? I'm an old friend and just got into town to surprise them, but I didn't want to disturb them if it was something terrible like a funeral."

"I understand, Senor. It is not bad, it's good. Miss Sally is getting married Saturday."

Felix thought he would take a chance. "Does she still have her beautiful blond hair?

"Yes sir, it is very beautiful."

"On a wonderful occasion such as this I don't think they will mind if I invite myself and surprise them. What time is the wedding scheduled?"

"I have to be there by ten, but I think it is scheduled for noon."

"Thank you Senor, you have been very helpful. I will mention your assistance to the Mac Arthurs." Felix was smiling as he walked back to his car.

******

Deadly Marriage

Later that afternoon Nester walked up to his boy standing by a small hotel. The boy was all excited.

"Slow down, Manuel, I can't understand you."

"Senor, the man in the picture went into the hotel, and then fifteen minutes later he came out with his bags and drove off in a dark green Renault. I didn't get the license, it was too far away."

"You've done a good job, Manuel. Wait here while I talk to the desk clerk.'"

Nester walked across the street and entered the hotel. He rang the bell and a small man with a paunch and thick, black rimmed glasses came from the back room.

"Good afternoon, Senor, may I help you?"

"Good afternoon. Would you happen to know this man?"

"Si Senor, but he just checked out."

"Did he happen to say where he was going?"

"He didn't explain, he just said he was going to a wedding."

******

Saturday arrived faster than Jack thought possible. He hadn't got too involved with the wedding, he kept getting shooed away. He had busied himself with the chart and map, making plans for taking the Naval Base. His biggest problem, he decided, was he had no way of knowing what naval ships may be in the harbor when the time came and what their officer's politics might be.

Sally had slept the night before the wedding in her own room and Jack in his. Jack had awakened early and gone for a ride with Jasper to release tension and get some exercise. Around ten Jack returned and started to prepare for the big day.

Jack was putting on his tuxedo when Graham knocked on his door.

"Come on in, you can get a laugh out of me trying to get into this monkey suit."

"You want some help? I just got Jasper into his tux; I can get you into yours."

Graham took over and had Jack squared away in just a few minutes. Jasper was standing at the door grinning. Jack looked over and rolled his eyes.

"I think we look like a trio of penguins," laughed Jasper.

"We had better go downstairs and get our final orders," said Graham.

As they walked towards the stairs they could hear laughter from the master suite. The girls were having a great time. Graham yelled through the closed door.

"We'll be in the study when we're needed!"

"Fine, now go away," said Miss Ada.

Graham shook his head and led the way to the study. He was at the side bar fixing drinks when Father McDona walked in.

As he walked up to Jack offering his hand he asked, "Are you ready my son?"

"Yes Father," said Jack.

"And what are you up to Graham?" asked Father McDona.

"I'm brewing up some liquid courage for us penguins, Father. Would you like a taste?"

"It is a little early for me, Graham, but I wouldn't want to insult you by refusing," chuckled the Father.

Once the Father had his drink he gave Jack his final instructions. Jack made sure Jasper had the ring and thanked Graham again for letting him borrow his grandmother's wedding ring for the occasion. He would buy whatever Sally wanted when there was more time.

******

That morning Nester had left the boys in their hotel room in Puerto Santa Cruz. He knew all that was required was to follow the florist truck to the wedding site. James had driven them back into Rio Gallegos early that morning. They parked a few doors down from the florist shop and waited.

They waited until a few minutes after nine when the florist delivery truck came out the driveway adjacent to the shop. He drove by the panel truck without noticing. He still didn't notice when James made a U-turn and started to follow.

******

    Felix had spent the night near the entrance to the Estancia in the clump of trees. He couldn't sleep. He had spent the time wondering how his life had crumbled through, what he thought was, no fault of his own. It wasn't rational, but he still felt it was because of Steven Jackson. He checked his weapons and rechecked them again just before dawn. The silenced pistol was his choice, but he carried Krantz's Luger as a backup.
    He cleaned up as much as possible with bottled water, dressed and waited for the cars to start arriving. He planned to join the trail of cars and act like all the rest of the guests.

Chapter 23

When the florist's truck turned on the Estancia road James kept going. He went another two miles and turned around and came back. They stopped and pulled off the side of the road where they could see the cars enter the Estancia, but not be too noticeable.

"Do you want me to move up to that clump of trees boss?" asked James pointing further in on the Estancia road. The same clump of trees which held Felix and the Renault.

Nester gave it some thought before he answered, "No, I think we are better off here. We're not on Estancia property. If the police come by we're just having car trouble. Let's say the truck was having vapor lock problems and stalled. If they find us up there we would have trouble explaining why."

******

At a quarter past eleven Felix noticed family type automobiles had started to arrive with finely dressed occupants. Felix started the Renault and joined the flow of traffic.

A young man pointed to where Felix should park. Felix smiled and waved thanks to the young man. He checked his gear one last time and got out of the car and joined a group of guests going into the main gate of the compound. He smiled and visited with the guests as he walked to a shaded area lined with chairs behind the house.

After they had been seated near the outer end of the second row the gentleman next to him asked, "How do you know the family?"

Felix was ready for this type of question. He had worked out his story in the middle of the night.

"I don't really know the family, just Mr. Mac Arthur. We have business dealings in Buenos Aires. I was scheduled to be here this morning to see him, so I was invited at the last moment."

Deadly Marriage

The altar boys arrived in the study; the Father rose and greeted them. He then, introduced them to Jack and Jasper and formed the wedding procession.

The recorded music started playing at precisely noon. The Father made a circular motion with his index finger and boys started to move, they had provided this service many times. The procession moved slowly between the aisles towards where a temporary altar had been erected.

Jack felt like an idiot smiling continually, but couldn't stop himself. He was a combination of impatient, scared, agitated and embarrassed all at the same time. He realized this was a beautiful occasion that he would cherish later in life, but right now he just wanted it be over.

Felix had to control his emotions and keep still when the priest led the bridegroom down the aisle. There was still something inside of him that wanted him to survive. He didn't understand it, but it now held sway over him.

There was a large man with a very macho mustache acting as an usher at the end of his row. Felix wished he would leave or at least move so he could slip away unnoticed towards the altar.

Graham walked into the master suite and saw his daughter dressed for her wedding for the first time. She was beautiful. His other daughter, Danielle, came and gave him a hug.

"I'm sorry I missed you last night, Daddy, but you and the boys seemed to be having a good time and I didn't want to interfere."

"I'm thankful you were able to come."

He picked her up and turned her around like a little girl then set her down.

"It's so good to see you; it's been way to long."

"Is Franco upset about babysitting for the weekend?"

"He whined a little. He was planning to play golf, but I didn't give him much chance to refuse. I told him Sally will only get married once, but he could play golf any weekend."

"I know he really didn't have a choice, but thank him for me anyway."

Miss Ada was fussing with Sally's long golden braid when Graham walked over.

"Sally, you look magnificent. For a tomboy, you're stunning. Actually, you are stunning for anyone."

"Thank you, Daddy. I'd hug you, but Momma would pull the braid out of my head."

"You two can talk while you walk, but I have to finish this before the music starts."

"Momma, I'll finish that. Why don't you go get seated and relax a bit? I've braided her hair almost as long as you have."

"Please, Momma, I want you to be able to enjoy today too, but you're getting too nervous," said Sally.

"OK. I'll go. But, Graham, if you muss her with one of your bear hugs you're in big trouble," said Miss Ada smiling.

Miss Ada then kissed his cheek and shook a fist at him.

"She's so nervous she doesn't know if she wants to kiss me or hit me," laughed Graham when she had gone.

"There, you're all done. And you really do look beautiful little sister."

"Thanks, Danielle. I could feel mom's hands shaking, I'm not sure she would have ever finished. Should we get this show on the road?" said Sally as she carefully picked up her bouquet.

They had only waited a few moments when the wedding march began to play. Sally took her father's arm and started to walk out on the veranda. The flower girl and ring bearer, who had been waiting on the veranda, took their places in front of Sally and her father.

Sally looked up at her father and realized he was looking at her with tears in his eyes.

"Daddy, if you don't stop, I'll start and make a mess of my makeup."

"These are happy tears baby girl. Though you know I'll miss you."

"You won't miss me for awhile. Jack and I haven't even talked about where to live. You're stuck with us for now."

"That sounds wonderful to me."

Deadly Marriage

When they stood before the altar, Sally kissed her daddy's cheek and took her position on the right. Danielle moved in beside Sally. Graham took his seat beside Miss Ada.

Sally thought Jack looked nervous while he stood there and stared at her, so she winked at him. This brought Jack from his zombielike state and he grinned. Sally thought it looked like some of the tension left his body.

The ceremony was moving along rather quickly thought Felix. The Mustache, as Felix thought of him now, had taken his seat at the end of the row. He knew he could make the shot from where he was, but he would be giving up his life. His will to live was still alive though intellectually he knew he was a dead man. He had to take his shot soon and try to make his exit.

The priest was pronouncing them husband and wife when Felix walked, bent over, down his row. He patted his stomach as if he were sick and excused himself as he moved. When he reached the Mustache he smiled at him and put his left hand on his shoulder. He leaned in as to whisper and his right hand plunged his dagger into Umberto's heart. Umberto was dead instantly.

The priest was starting to introduce them for the first time as Mr. and Mrs. Jackson Stevens when Felix took his shot. All that was heard was spiff sound.

The first shot hit Jack in the left side of his chest. Felix knew it would not be immediately fatal so he fired again, but the best man had gotten in the way trying to catch Jackson and took the bullet in the back.

Felix heard a shot and felt a searing pain in his right arm. He started to run towards the cars when another bullet flew by his head. As he ran waving Krantz's pistol with his left hand at anyone who tried to stop him, his silenced pistol dropped from his worthless right arm.

Graham sat there in shock for a few seconds before charging the altar. By the time he reached the altar Sally had fired her second shot. She held the pistol in two hands in the military manner Jack had taught her and she knew she had hit the man with the first shot.

Graham pulled Jasper gently off of Jack and looked at his eyes. He then felt for a pulse, there was none. He turned his attention to Jack.

Jack was bleeding profusely, so Graham yelled for Dr. Ybarra. Sally sat down and put his head in her lap.

Dr. Ybarra asked Danielle to call for an ambulance. The doctor had delivered both Danielle and Sally. He was their long time physician and friend. He had Graham hold a pressure dressing on the entrance wound and he gently turned Jack so he could see the exit wound. He couldn't find an exit. He laid Jack back down, shook his head and said, "The bullet is still inside, so we must move him very gently. Leave him here until the ambulance gets here."

Little Juan was standing off to the side crying. The doctor sent him inside for a blanket and pillow. He then went to check on Jasper, but returned shaking his head.

Felix made it back to his car and was able to start it and get it moving in second gear with one arm. He drove as fast as he could back to the highway. He slid around the turn and accelerated as fast as the little engine would pull the sedan. He never saw the panel truck start following him.

When Jack came to, he heard Umberto's wife screaming, Jasper's family crying and people yelling all around him. He finally opened his eyes and looked up at Sally with tears in her eyes. She was sobbing.

"Why the tears Mrs. Stevens?" asked Jack weakly.

"Oh, Jack, you've been shot," was all she could think of to say.

Jack slipped back into unconsciousness.

Deadly Marriage

Epilog

James had run the Renault off the road after only a five mile chase. Nester had fired his shotgun pistol at point blank range just as the Renault plunged down into a ditch. James skidded to a halt and backed up to where the car had exited the road. He then went down the slope to get the body. Nester scared off the other cars that had joined the chase by peppering them with .410 shot.

James found that the shotgun blast had removed much of the man's face on the left side. As he pulled the man free of the car he noticed a Luger and a dagger lying on the passenger seat. He pulled the still moaning man up to the road and loaded him in the panel truck. Felix would die as he had expected within the hour on the road to Buenos Aires. When they stopped to pick up the kids at Puerto Santa Ana, Nester and James rolled the body in a large canvas tarp and tied it securely. The kids used the body for a seat for the trip home. Julio Ramirez gave Nester a nice bonus.

Hauptsturmfuhrer Huber was promoted to Oberfuhrer and made Section Chief based mainly on his handling of the Obergruppenfuhrer Meinhard Egon von Richter case. The paintings were never recovered.

The next time Jack awoke he was in the small hospital in Rio Gallegos. He thought he was alone in his room, with tubes running everywhere and feeling drugged. He thought, "I really must be doped up because I don't hurt."

Suddenly Sally loomed over him. She was repeatedly pressing the nurses call button. Without stopping her button pushing she kissed his forehead.

"Hi husband of mine." That was all that was said before the nurse ran in. She looked at Jack's eyes, turned right around and ran for Dr. Ybarra.

Jack was still gathering his senses when the doctor arrived. He checked Jack's vital signs and the machines and then noted his findings on Jack's chart.

"Hello Jackson."

"Hi doc.," replied Jack drunkenly.

"You were shot in the chest and the bullet lodged near your spine. I called in a surgeon from Buenos Aires to take it out, it was too complicated for me to handle. You were in surgery for three hours; we've kept you sedated so you wouldn't move and until your blood work was close to normal. You lost a lot of blood my boy. If Sally hadn't shot the man you might have been hit again."

Sally asked, "What are his chances now doctor?"

"If we see no infection he should be able to go home in a few days. I think he will make a full recovery."

Sally hugged the old man and he left giving orders to the nurse.

"Did he say you shot the man?" asked Jack.

"Yes dear. Just relax."

The End

Now that you've muddled through my ramblings, please feel free to send your comments/questions to
wrziegler_author@yahoo.com.
All comments, good or not so good, are greatly appreciated.
Thanks for Reading
W.R Ziegler

Made in United States
North Haven, CT
07 January 2026